Honour's Rest

Judith Crow

First Published in 2021
Crowvus, Stempster House, Westfield, KW14 7QW
ISBN: 978-1-913182-31-1

For comments and questions about
"Honour's Rest"
contact the publisher directly at
the_team@crowvus.com

www.crowvus.com
www.crowvuschoughs.co.uk

www.judithcrow.co.uk

This book* is dedicated to Mum, Ginny and Clem, who believed in Pen from the beginning - much more than he believed in himself!

And to Alex, who changed his last name.

*apart from Napier, who I will keep for myself.

Chapter One

Who Pushed Justin?

Usually no one could have picked the fourteen-year-old out of a crowd. Aside from looking slightly older than his years, there was nothing unusual about him. He could play the guitar pretty well and was just beginning to enjoy the attention it gained him from the girls in his class. But those who knew him would say that his name was almost certainly the thing which made him unusual or, to some extent, interesting.

It was definitely weird. Many of his teachers just attributed it to his mother having spent time in a hippy colony before marrying his father. Pendragon Devon, as he reluctantly admitted to being called, had long ago realised that his mother had not considered the impact on her son when she had assigned him such a ridiculous name. About nine years ago, he had decided that he hated it and had started to ask friends and teachers to call him 'Pen'. Understanding the boy's hatred of his full name, they soon all called him by his chosen abbreviation. 'Pen' wasn't such a ridiculous name and, in fact, he had come to quite like it.

But the letter he clutched in his hand was addressed to "Dr and Mrs J. Devon, parents of Pendragon Devon, Year 9", and that was enough to betray the serious issue contained within the envelope. In fact, it was the reason why he was walking down the main street in the middle of the school day.

This usually-ordinary boy had, one hour ago, been standing outside the headteacher's office silently as two paramedics had helped a much larger boy into an ambulance car and driven away, without lights or siren but at a speed which had alarmed Pen. He had never felt so penitent nor so confused as he did at that moment, standing outside the office and reading the School Charter over and over again, until the words danced before his brown eyes.

Then Mr Carling came out of his office. An elderly and thickset man, his gaze had fallen on the boy before him as he shook his head slowly. There was something of surprise, even hurt, in the faded blue gaze which followed the boy into the office, and Pen knew why. In three years, he had never so much as missed a homework deadline. Just two months ago, he had even received a 'Services to the School' award for helping to arrange an extra induction day for the Year Sixes who would be starting in September.

"So, Pen."

"Yes, sir?"

The headmaster sat down and gestured across the desk for the boy to do the same. Pen did not want to look at Mr Carling so, instead, he stared again at the School Charter, this time the one which lay open on the desk in front of him. There was silence for a while, which the boy knew would only be broken when he looked up to accept his punishment, but he wanted to put it off for as long as possible. The headmaster seemed to feel the same way and did nothing to break the silence or demand his attention. At last, Pen felt he couldn't take it any longer.

"I don't know what happened, sir."

"I don't want excuses or denials, Pendragon," Mr Carling said. "Seven children, four of whom had nothing to do with Justin, saw you."

Pen's eyes burned. He didn't usually cry, but he was frightened that, in his anger, he had done something truly dangerous. Something which had nearly caused the death of a fellow pupil. He hadn't understood what was happening when he was dragged from the library to answer for having pushed Justin Murchison into the school pond.

"Justin's parents are furious," Mr Carling said, bringing Pen back down to Earth. "I'm not saying they don't know what he's like. I'm pretty sure they understood that one day someone would stand up against him. But he could have drowned. He's already having to go to hospital, given how much water got into his lungs. And, of course, the pond will have to be filled in. These are serious issues, Pen, and you're going to have to help me understand why you did it."

Pen wanted to scream out that he had no idea, but instead he just shrugged his shoulders. Speaking would just cause the tears in his eyes to start falling.

"I need to know why you did it."

Still silence from Pen.

"Pendragon Devon!" Mr Carling shouted, banging his hand down onto the table and making Pen jump so much that the teardrops jolted out of his eyes and ran down his cheeks. The headmaster's face softened, and he handed Pen a box of tissues from where they had been balancing precariously on the printer.

"I don't know," Pen sobbed, using the tissue to cover his face rather than dry his eyes. "I was in the library reading some stuff for Mrs Morse's R.E. class. Didn't anyone see me?"

"Had you fallen out with Justin earlier in the day?"

At this, Pen looked up, slightly bemused. "Sir," he replied, "you know I was always falling out with Justin. And whatever has happened today, you know why." He wasn't sure what gave him the courage to say the words but was relieved to see Mr Carling nod slowly.

"Yes, you've always stuck up for everyone against Justin, so I suppose that was a silly question. But standing up for people by reasoning with – or even shouting down – the bully is one thing. Pushing him into a two-metre-deep pond is another. I need you to tell me what happened."

"But, sir," Pen pleaded, "I don't know. I'm not lying, I swear. I was just reading about Mormons and then Ross came in and said that you were furious with me for pushing Justin into the pond. Then Mrs Wilson dragged me off here."

"You don't remember what happened between those things?" Mr Carling's voice sounded very gentle and almost uncertain, and Pen suddenly felt a wave of fear wash over him as he thought of possible answers for why he had behaved so uncharacteristically.

"No, sir."

"Well, Pen," Mr Carling said, his voice still gentle but now more resigned than uncertain. "I will suggest to your parents that they arrange for you to see a doctor. If you did indeed behave in that way during a period of semiconsciousness, then I'm certain it's something which will need looking at by someone with a different expertise from my own."

The headmaster typed something into the computer and the printer spat out a formal-looking letter, which Mr Carling picked up and signed with a flourish before putting into an envelope.

"I'm sorry, Pen," he said slowly, as the boy looked at him with newly-dry eyes. "I can only order a period of exclusion. It was a serious offence. I've called your parents. You will be free to come back to school after ten days. Do you need to collect anything from class?"

Pen shook his head and gestured down to his schoolbag.

"You and your parents will be invited into school next week to talk through what happened."

Now, Pen was walking down the High Street, clutching the letter. A part of him wanted to run away, hide somewhere, and reappear when his parents would be so worried that they would forgive him anything. His mum was a gentle person, who would never condone any form of violence. It had been from her that Pen had inherited his desire to help people through the power of the written and spoken word which, until today, had been the only weapons he had deployed.

His father was maybe more realistic, but Pen was equally

certain of his disappointment. He was a paediatrician in a popular private practice and would probably want to quiz him about the same thing which had made Mr Carling seem so uncomfortable. Was it a psychiatric problem, Pen wondered, which could make a person black out before a period of uncharacteristic violence? Or was it a more frightening medical problem? His mind swarmed with ideas about tumours and brain haemorrhages.

But surely there would have been other signs, he told himself as he began to feel sick. Suddenly he didn't want to run away so his parents would forgive him, but so he could spare them from being subjected to concern and fear.

Pen stood for a moment at the end of the road. He could see his parents' nice, suburban bungalow with the extremely wild garden. They had endured complaints from the neighbours about that, as his mother refused to kill any of the plants.

She's going to be furious with me, Pen thought miserably, walking towards the house with a kind of fear which dwarfed the emotions he had felt outside the headmaster's office. He leant heavily on the door handle and wandered into the kitchen.

"Hi," he called.

There was no answer.

Perhaps, he thought as he opened the fridge door for no apparent reason as his appetite was dead, *they aren't home*. He dangled the letter over the bin for a moment, tempted to leave the evidence of his exclusion somewhere his parents would never look.

"What in heaven's name are you doing, Pendragon?" It was his mother's voice which brought him back to his senses. Pen turned around to look at her but found he couldn't hold her gaze.

"I–"

"There's no point in telling any lies, Pendragon Devon," his mother snapped. "Sit down. Mr Carling rang. Your father has been called at work and he'll be home in a moment. What were you thinking?"

The telephone rang just as Pen was about to offer an explanation, and he sighed at the thought of being saved by the bell. However, as he heard his mother talking in hushed tones to whoever was on the other end of the line, he realised the phone call seemed to be making things worse. His mother was agreeing a lot and then apologising. When at last she put the telephone down, the icy stare she gave her only son coincided with the front door opening and Pen's father hurrying into the house.

"What's going on?" he demanded, breathless and clearly having run from work. He disapproved of taking the car on journeys shorter than two miles. Throwing his briefcase down on the breakfast bar, he ran over to his son, who already stood half a head taller than him. As his father pulled him into a tight hug, Pen saw his mother's eyebrows contract.

"Don't, Jarvis," she snapped, pulling her husband away. "He's in trouble. Don't give him your sympathy. He pushed a boy in the school pond."

"I know," Pen's father said, and this time it was his son's turn to express surprise. "I got a call at work."

"So, you know that Pendragon has been excluded from school for ten days? Yet you rush in here and treat him like you're somehow proud of him? Or worried about him?"

"I *am* worried," Pen's father replied. "Mr Carling said you blacked out?"

"I don't remember blacking out," Pen said. "But I don't remember pushing Justin in the pond either. I must have just been so angry."

His parents exchanged looks with each other, and Pen became aware of something unsaid passing between them. He glanced from one to the other nervously, wondering what had brought about the sudden change in his mother's attitude towards him. She reached out suddenly and took his hand, gripping his wrist in her thin fingers.

"Tell me exactly what happened," she whispered. She looked unnaturally pale, and Pen found himself guiding her through to the living room and helping her sit down on the sofa. His father followed, still breathing heavily and now clutching a bottle of whisky in his hand. He poured a glass for himself and one for his wife, then hesitated before pouring one for his son as well.

"Drink it up, Pen," his father said. His wife didn't even challenge his use of her son's nickname, but just drank from her glass as quickly as she could and then stared down at it, moving the remaining drops from side to side. "Drink it up," his father repeated as Pen looked from one parent to the other. "It's not strictly speaking medicinal, but it will go some way to calming your nerves."

Pen hadn't realised until his father had said the words just how nervous he was. Now he knew, he couldn't stop his hands from shaking as they raised the glass towards his lips and poured the peaty-tasting liquid into his mouth. He didn't like it but trusted his father too much to turn it down. Finally, once he had finished the glass of whisky, he handed over the letter and listened as it was read aloud.

"Dear Doctor and Mrs Devon. It is my regret to inform you that Pendragon has been excluded from school for a period of ten days, in compliance with School and Council procedures. This is due to him having used excessive force and endangering the safety of a fellow pupil by pushing him into the school pond. You will have the right to appeal this decision at a meeting which will be held within the next five working days and, in the meantime, work will be sent via email for Pendragon to complete." Pen's father paused for a second and looked at his wife before he continued reading. "This behaviour is entirely out of character with everything we have known of Pendragon and so I am inclined to believe he was not fully *compos mentis* when the incident took place. I'm sure you will agree that this requires medical attention, and, in the meantime, I trust you appreciate my decision to authorise an exclusion. Yours sincerely, Gerard Carling."

A strange silence fell around the room, and Pen became aware that his mother was crying silently, wiping tears away from her face as quickly as they were falling but unable to hide them from her son, who crouched down beside her and put his head on her knee. She leant down and pressed her lips against his hair, and he felt some of her tears run into his scalp.

"How would you describe the blackout, Pendragon?" Dr Devon asked, adopting an almost formal tone as he spoke to his son. "Did you have a sensation of waking up at any point? Have you had any flashbacks you haven't been able to account for?"

Pen shook his head. "No. I was awake the whole time,

reading in the library. I don't even know how I managed to get to the school pond, push Justin in, and then get back in time to be found in the library again. All during break."

"Stand up," his father said, and Pen did as he was told, although his mother kept hold of his hand for a moment, unwilling to let go. "Close your eyes. Now, touch your nose with your right hand." Pen did as he was told, feeling foolish as his fingers found his nose easily. Perhaps this would prove he had not blacked out, that he was responsible for the crime he had committed, but he honestly couldn't remember being anywhere near the pond. "Now, open your eyes."

Pen did not find out whether Jarvis had any other tests for him, as the telephone rang and his father went away to answer it, instructing his son to go to his room. Pen did as he was told. His room had always been his sanctuary from anything which was upsetting him, but now he couldn't find any comfort there, even in plucking tunes from the guitar strings. He could hear his father on the phone, sounding almost like he was pleading, and he wondered if it was Mr Carling on the other end of the line. When at last he heard his father saying goodbye, he began to listen again, but his parents were talking in such low voices that he couldn't make out what was being said. Finally, his mother called his name and he wandered through the hall and back to the living room.

"We're going to withdraw you from school, Pendragon, sweetheart," his mother said, her eyes swimming with tears. Pen looked at her. He was sure no other parents would take such drastic measures. Anyway, there were no other semi-decent schools nearby.

"So where am I going to finish school?" he asked, thinking it might be wiser to play along rather than openly challenge his parents.

"You're going to be home tutored," his father replied.

"Home tutored?" Pen laughed. "You must be joking. I don't mean this in a horrible way, but I don't see either of you as teachers."

"No, I agree," Jarvis said with a slight nod, and Pen realised that there was no hint of a smile on his father's face. "You're going to live with your Uncle Napier."

Chapter Two

Uncle Napier Devon

Pen did not know much about his Uncle Napier, other than that he was a devout bachelor who lived alone in a big house in Scotland. They had never been to the house, but Napier Devon had, on occasion, visited his younger brother's family in England. However, they had not seen him since six years ago, when there had been an almighty row about something Pen had never quite understood. Napier had accused his younger brother of burying his head in the sand and pretending he had a life quite different from the one which had been assigned to him. In his mind's eye, Pen could see Napier turning around suddenly and staring hard at the boy who was eavesdropping behind the door. After that, his memories became patchy, but he remembered his uncle marching out of the house later that day, pausing only to stare at the young boy with eyes which were both threatening and appealing.

Given that this was the last close contact Jarvis had shared with his older brother, Pen couldn't have been more surprised by his father's announcement that he was to move to Scotland and begin an education with his uncle as sole tutor. He spent the next day visiting his friends and attempting awkwardly to explain his parents' reaction to what had happened.

Two days later, Pen was sitting on his bed, looking around his room, when his mother knocked on the door and walked in. She was twisting a sodden handkerchief round and round in her thin hands and staring at her son, opening her mouth to speak but without saying anything.

"I'll miss you, Pendragon," she whispered at last and, even though her voice was quiet, it shook as she spoke.

"Then why are you sending me away?" Pen demanded, unable to keep his temper. "I didn't mean to push Justin. For God's sake, I don't even remember pushing him! I don't know why you feel the need to punish me more than I'm being punished already."

"Oh, sweetheart!" his mother gasped, throwing her arms around him. "Please don't think that we're punishing you! I promise you we're not. Your uncle is the person who can sort this out."

"You don't even like him."

"No, you're wrong there, Pendragon. Your uncle and I don't have a lot in common, apart from the fact that we both love your father. But he is a remarkable man, and he will certainly be able to help you make sense of whatever is going on. Much better than your father or I could. He's a good man, Pendragon, and I think you'll like him if you approach this by being openminded."

"Does he work?" Pen asked, hoping to change the subject without ignoring what was about to happen.

"Well..." His mother frowned. "I suppose you could say he does. Yes, I think so. But he should have time enough to commit to you, so don't worry about that for a second, sweetheart."

"I wasn't worried," Pen replied. He let his mother embrace him again and then picked up his things. His parents were going to take him to Manchester, where he would get the plane alone to Edinburgh.

The car journey was slow and stuffy in the spring sun, and Pen found his mind wandering. He tried to recall what his uncle looked like, but all he could remember were the dark brown eyes, not unlike his own and so dissimilar from his father's.

When they arrived at the airport, his father helped him check in and then they stood for a while by the doors, desperately trying to communicate without saying a word. It was Jarvis who spoke first.

"Well, I hope you have a nice flight. It looks like you've got the weather for it."

His words were so non-committal that Pen felt his eyebrows raise in disbelief. Here they were, facing the biggest division their family had ever known, and his father could only talk about the weather. How British. Pen sniffed, more out of frustration than sadness, and reminded himself that there was one question to which he desperately needed to know the answer.

"What do you believe happened to Justin?"

"I believe you," his father said at last. "And so does your mother. But trust me, your Uncle Napier will be able to make a lot more sense of it for you. If we started to try and address things now, I think we might make it worse. Your uncle did say–"Jarvis stopped talking, as though he had just realised he was giving away too many details. Pen's questions were halted by the boarding call, and his mother jumped.

"Oh, Pendragon, run! You'll never make it otherwise." She kissed her son quickly and then, after his father had embraced him, they pushed Pen towards Departures.

He stumbled away from them and, as he turned around, it was to see his sobbing mother being led away by her husband, whose hunched shoulders suggested he was feeling the same way. But they didn't look back as their son raised a nervous hand and waved to them, still believing he was being sent away as a punishment for the terrible thing everyone told him he had done.

Departures was difficult as each person reminded him that he would have to run to reach the plane before boarding closed. He only just reached the gate to the sound of a final call for him and a Mrs Pauline McIntyre. Pen sat down on the small plane and looked around. It was quite empty, with less than half the seats taken, and he wondered if any of the people questioned the fact he was alone. The hostess came up to him with a forced smile before take-off.

"You're going to Aviemore after this, is that right?"

"Yes."

"There will be a taxi to meet you at the airport. Just make sure you don't go wandering off anywhere. Alright?" She sounded almost bored, like it was more than she was being paid for to babysit fourteen-year-old boys, and Pen felt a slight annoyance towards her. In fact, and he was ashamed to admit it, he couldn't help but think of karma when she trapped her finger in the seatbelt during the safety demonstration.

The flight itself was unremarkable, with a smooth take-off and landing, and not even a hint of turbulence. Pen was slightly disappointed. He had been told that planes going to Scotland often had to make daring landings in strong winds. The air hostess nodded to each of the passengers as they disembarked and reminded Pen to look out for the taxi driver who would take him on to the station. He couldn't really have missed him as, when they walked into the main body of the airport, he was there with a whiteboard in his hands, on which he had scrawled 'Mr Pendragon'.

"I'm Pen," he said, shuffling his luggage so he could wave to the driver, but the man just nodded and walked away, beckoning for his young passenger to follow.

"Hang on!" Pen called, "I still have stuff to collect!" He waited for his twenty kilograms of home to come towards him on the conveyor belt and then followed the taxi driver into the black cab.

"Going far?" the driver asked as Pen looked across at the Forth bridges.

"I'm getting the train to Aviemore," he replied. "Is that far?"

"A couple of hours on the train," the driver replied. "Going skiing?"

Pen just shook his head. He had no idea what he should say to people who inquired about what he was going to do, as he was unsure himself. Instead, he took out his phone and began to scroll up and down his contacts list, pretending he was too busy to talk. Whether or not the driver realised what he was doing, he seemed to take the hint and didn't speak again until they were entering Edinburgh.

"We're running a bit late, so I'll drop you at Haymarket."

"Ok, thanks," Pen said. He didn't know Edinburgh at all, never having set foot in Scotland, but trusted that the driver wouldn't leave him anywhere inappropriate. Haymarket turned out to be a small, clinical train station with friendly staff, who helped him with his suitcase after the driver had dropped him off at the door and headed back into the city. Pen collected his ticket to Aviemore, via a town called Perth, which he could have sworn was in Australia, and bought a sandwich.

Unlike the aeroplane, the train was quite full, and he ended up sitting next to an old man who slept most of the way. When he wasn't sleeping, he would regale Pen with stories about how he had climbed to the top of Ben Nevis every year since he was fifteen.

"And how old are you, young man?" he said brightly, his faded eyes twinkling beneath creased lids.

"Fourteen," Pen replied.

"Ah, still time then. Still time." Then he drifted off to sleep again, leaving Pen to wonder whether their strange conversations were simply a figment of his imagination.

The change at Perth led him onto an even busier train, so this time he found himself standing by a luggage rack which was too full to hold his own suitcases. He seemed to be one of a few people who were going to Aviemore and, after the train had taken them through some remarkable scenery, including late snow, he found himself on the platform, along with twenty or so other people. They all ignored him, and Pen couldn't see any sign of his uncle, so he sat down on his suitcase and waited. Other trains came and went and, just when Pen thought he might be about to die of hypothermia, a middle-aged man appeared, wearing a smart suit, complete with a black trilby and lambskin gloves.

"Pendragon?"

Pen looked up at him and was surprised to find that, for a second, he could have believed he was staring into his own eyes. But nothing else was familiar.

"Yes, sir?" Pen said, as he had done in the headmaster's office just two days before. It could have been an entire lifetime ago.

"My name is Napier Devon. You may not remember me. You are to live with me until such time that you are ready to leave, or you are called away. Do you understand?"

Pen tried to raise his eyebrows at the man's words, but something about his tone was too frightening to allow such an unimpressed response. Whether or not he liked the introduction, he had to admit that his Uncle Napier was an authoritative figure, even if he did sound quite rude.

"Pendragon—"

"You can call me Pen."

"But that is not your name," Uncle Napier said, picking up Pen's suitcases and beginning to carry them away towards a small carpark. "Pendragon is a noble name. Carry it with pride."

"All due respect," said Pen, annoyance inflecting his words, "but it's not your name. If you were called Pendragon, then you wouldn't be so keen."

"Ah yes," his uncle said. "Being called Napier, I would have no idea what life can be like when plagued by an unusual name which can be the object of ridicule."

Pen was silent. It was clear that his uncle was as different from his father in looks and temperament as it was possible to be, and he once again found himself wondering why he was all the way up here with this stranger.

"Are you a teacher?" he asked at last, after they had clambered into Napier's beautiful, vintage racing-car and set off at an eye-opening speed.

"By God, no!" Uncle Napier said, with no laughter to his tone, just an air of indignation. "No, I don't have the patience."

"Then," Pen said, hoping the man would fully understand the significance of his words, "why did my parents send me up here to finish my education with you?"

"I'm sure you'll find that out in due course. Ah," he said, and Pen lifted his head to see that they were now far out of Aviemore and driving along a remote loch-side. "Here we are."

A causeway, partially covered by loch water, was stretching out before them and Pen couldn't stop the gasp of amazement which left his lungs as he looked at a magnificent castle on an islet in the middle of the loch.

"You live here?"

"And so will you. At least for the next few months," Napier said, driving carefully along the causeway. "It is called Honour's Rest, but I would hope you will refer to it as home."

Honour's Rest? Pen would never have believed any house could have such a strange name, although given its storybook location in the middle of an expanse of water, he thought he shouldn't be surprised.

"Did you name it?" he asked at last, as the car came to a stop in the driveway.

"No, no," Uncle Napier said, getting out and lifting Pen's suitcases from the car with surprising ease. "It is, I suppose, a company house. The name came with it."

"So, you don't own it?"

"I do own it. I will own it for as long as I live," Napier explained, "but I cannot bequeath it to anyone outside the Company. It is a highly effective set-up for avoiding disrepair."

"Are you rich then?" Pen asked, looking at the castle.

"I cannot answer that question." Instead, he led Pen into the entrance hall and put the suitcases down by an old umbrella stand which housed cobweb-streaked parasols and walking sticks and, Pen was surprised to see, an old hockey stick as well. "Your rooms are in the turret," Napier said, pointing towards a small door which led directly onto a spiral staircase. "There are two. One which will be your study – yes, I intend for you to do a lot of self-guided study – and the other is your bedroom, which has a small toilet for your convenience. It is a miserably cold house to wander through at night."

"I suppose there are ghosts, are there?" Pen asked, surprising himself by how calm he was at the idea.

"I have never seen any ghosts," Uncle Napier replied. "You must not go looking for trouble in this house though, as you will almost certainly find it. Also, for as long as you reside beneath my roof, there are three rules I expect you to obey. The first is that you never question a demand I make. Feel free to challenge any comments or opinions, but I trust it will be clear when I am making a demand. The second is that you may explore, but do not yet wander outside without me. The loch water looks beautiful and peaceful, but it can turn treacherous without even a moment's notice, and I would prefer not to have to explain to your parents why their only child drowned whilst staying at my house. Finally, you must come to accept, if not love, your name. Therefore, you will be Pendragon for as long as you live here. Should you wish to think of or refer to yourself as Pen, you may do so. But you are Pendragon."

Pen found himself nodding and then, without saying a word, began to wander up the steep spiral staircase. He couldn't believe he would be sleeping in a turret and stopped at one of the narrow windows on the stairs to admire the beautiful view of the shining blue loch water which surrounded the building. His study was quite small but kitted out with everything he could need apart from a computer. In its place was an old typewriter. His bedroom was even more incredible. At the very top of the building, he had a view which stretched out for miles and couldn't be described in words. And, to make it even better, there was his own guitar on the four-poster bed, with a note from his parents explaining that they had arranged for it to arrive separately.

Pen knew he would never forget the first night he spent in the strange house. The very walls seemed to shine in the moonlight and, with the curtains drawn back, Pen was able to watch as the large silver moon hit the loch and shattered into flickering shards of light. It was one of the most beautiful things he had ever seen.

He fell asleep admiring its beauty and so did not see the solitary figure walking through the courtyard that night, silver sickle in hand.

The following day, he was awoken by his uncle knocking hard on the door.

"What?" Pen demanded, a little more rudely than he had intended. Even despite the beauty of his room and the feeling of waking up into an ancient castle, Pen had never been good at being woken up by anything other than his own alarm.

"If you don't get up now," Napier called, "you will have to forego breakfast."

Over breakfast, which was a delicious fry-up of bacon, eggs, sausages, tomatoes, mushrooms and black pudding, Napier pointed his fork at Pen, almost accusatively.

"You can look around the place today. I don't see the point in beginning any kind of education until you fully understand the significance of where you are. Your father told me you pushed a boy in a pond. Was he a friend of yours?"

"No," Pen replied. "He was a bully. Probably the worst person in the school. I'd stood up to him over and over again, trying to talk him into some better manners. I even wrote something in the school paper."

"But you decided that none of that was working, so you pushed him into the pond?"

"Not that I remember." Pen shrugged. He was so fed up with people challenging his story that he wished he *had* made it up, if only so he could know the truth himself.

"Did anyone see you in the library at the time that the boy was pushed into the pond?"

"No," Pen spoke slowly, his annoyance starting to show in his voice. "People saw me push him. I don't think I could have been in two places at once."

"Anyway," Uncle Napier said, looking around and suddenly very interested in the breakfast room. "I am going out to work today but will be home in time for dinner. In the meantime, Honour's Rest is all yours to explore. Providing, of course, you obey my rules."

Despite how exciting Napier made it sound, Pen couldn't find the many corridors of Honour's Rest interesting. Early that morning, as he had watched his uncle driving across the causeway, he had found himself desperate to know what Napier did for a living. Particularly why, when he clearly disliked the idea of teaching, he had been assigned as his nephew's tutor. To make things worse, although Honour's Rest was full of many winding staircases and dark corridors, and appeared to be several centuries old, Pen couldn't help but be disappointed by how dead the place seemed. A creaking floorboard or a window shuddering open would have excited his senses, but there seemed to be even less chance that Honour's Rest was haunted than his parents' bungalow. So, as his feet continued to pace the ancient corridors, his mind wandered back to considering what his uncle did for a living.

He returned to the entrance hall to discover someone had left a piece of cake for him, covered by a silver dish which made him think of the period dramas his mother loved. He ate it in complete silence and, for the first time, he began to think that the quietness of the building wasn't boring, but rather unnerving. Someone had cleaned away the breakfast pots and left this cake out for him, yet there was nothing to suggest any other person was occupying the house. He decided to retreat to his room, where he waited for his uncle to return, building up a host of questions which he couldn't keep to himself once he and Napier had eaten lunch.

"What is your work?" Pen asked. "Where did you go today?"

"What is your name?" His uncle's reply was almost instantaneous.

"Pen. Sorry," Pen said sarcastically as his uncle's eyebrows raised. "*Pendragon.* Now, won't you answer my questions?"

"No. What were you doing while that boy fell in the pond?"

"I told you – pushing him in the pond. I just don't remember."

"No." Uncle Napier sounded desperate and yet there was no hint of a plea in his voice. "What do you remember doing while that boy fell into the pond?"

"Reading. Reading about Mormons."

"And?"

"And what? What do you usually do when you're reading? Maybe I was biting my fingernails? Scratching my face?" Pen's voice was raised but, when his uncle spoke, the volume in the room dropped down again.

"And?"

Then, just as Pen was about to shout at his uncle and make the swords which hung on the walls rattle with the power of his anger and annoyance, he remembered something. "And I was thinking about Justin Murchison, and how I'd seen him pushing a Year Seven down the stairs that morning."

"Ah." Napier's eyes seemed to shine with excitement. "And?"

"And I was thinking that someone ought to do

something about him."

"And then, lo and behold, the boy falls into the pond. Pushed, it would seem, by you." Uncle Napier had shuffled forwards on his seat and was twisting an invisible skein around his fingers. "Seven people saw you, yes?"

"Yes," Pen replied. "So I must have done it."

"My excellent nephew!" Napier's voice had changed, and he suddenly sounded like he was about to burst into happy tears. "Of course you did it."

"Then why can't I remember it?"

"Because you sat in the library reading and thinking as it was going on. Have your parents never mentioned the Rite?"

"What's that?"

"The Rite is the ability to harness the unknown and mould it into something that only you, and certain others, can comprehend. We are all surrounded by the unknown, but not all of us are able to use it."

"So, it's – what – like *magic*?"

"Magic?" Napier sounded disgusted, all the enthusiasm and excitement had gone from his voice as quickly as they had appeared. "Magic is for children's parties. Magic consists of a man in a colourful costume or a black cloak waving his arms to distract the unsuspecting into believing that the coin they have just slipped down their sleeve is really travelling, at that moment, through their own ears. The Rite is not magic. It is…" His voice trailed off and he shook his head. "Well, perhaps you would understand it best if I were to say 'Yes, it is magic'."

"So – what – I'm magic?"

"No, Pendragon," Napier said, clicking his tongue irritably. "You have the Rite. Now, go to your study and work out the difference between a conjurer and a thaumaturge. You will find the relevant texts are there, awaiting your consideration."

Chapter Three

The Rite

A thaumaturge is not, despite the common misconception, a wizard. Wizards belong to a world which is not real and therefore unknown. As such, a thaumaturge can harness a wizard's power, creating what might crudely be described as 'magic' through the power known as the Rite. Although many people have the ability to wield the Rite, it is now commonly confused with luck, fate or karma in the modern world, where people simultaneously know less and do not accept anything as being unknown.

For the young thaumaturge, the appearance of the Rite is often at a period of pressure, whether through positive or negative experience. It is believed there are more male thaumaturges than female, but this remains a hotly-contested claim.

Pen put the book down. He couldn't believe what he

was seeing, that there really was such a thing as magic, whatever name they chose to hide it behind. He tried to remember when anything magical had happened to him, but he couldn't think of anything earlier than pushing Justin in the pond. And his Uncle Napier had the Rite, but not his father. Why was that? When had his uncle realised that he was a wizard – no wait, what was that word? A *thaumaturge*.

"Pendragon!" Uncle Napier's voice brought him quickly back to his senses and, closing the book, Pen hurried downstairs.

"Yes?"

"What did you find out?"

"You like to call yourselves thaumaturges instead of wizards? Apparently, because wizards don't exist, you can harness their power. Although I have no idea how that's supposed to work."

"You only read the first page, didn't you?" Napier's voice was cold. Pen could understand why, given that he had been alone in the study for the past hour. He fell silent, just as he had in the headmaster's office. After a moment he looked up, running his fingernails across his thumb as he often did when he was nervous.

"So, do I need to get a wand now?"

Napier just stared at him for a moment before he began to talk in a quiet and slightly disgusted voice. "A wand? Do you believe that we are nothing more than conjurers? That we can wave a piece of wood and announce *Abracadabra*, and everything will be sorted?"

Pen was silent, not wanting to admit that yes, that was exactly what he imagined. When he did not say anything for a whole minute, his uncle continued talking.

"The Rite comes through you. Through your soul and heart and is only occasionally verbalised. You may wish to hold out your hand when channelling it, as some believe it improves your aim or focus, but there is normally no real requirement to do so. As for wands... pah!"

Pen guessed that he had said something offensive, as the man in front of him looked even angrier than before. He tried to remember what he had read about wizards, but then had to remind himself again that 'wizards belong to a world which is not real' and that he and his uncle were both thaumaturges.

"So, there are no such things as spells?"

"I wish you had made more of an effort to read the book, Pendragon," Uncle Napier sighed, steepling his fingers and looking hard at his nephew. "There are words you can say, but all they do is focus the mind. Once you have fully learnt and mastered the Rite, there will be no need for words. The Rite is beyond words. This is something every thaumaturge must understand."

"Can you show me some, er, Rite, please?" Pen asked, but his uncle's eyebrows rose.

"The first thing you must learn, Pendragon, is that we are not wizards, nor magicians, nor conjurers. The Rite is not for demonstrating at parties, nor for showing off to your friends. The second thing you must learn is that it is all around you. Had you not been feeling so sorry for yourself this morning while I was away – yes, I know that you were – you would have noticed its presence. I do not cook or clean for myself, my needs are taken care of by the Rite. Look around you; have you not noticed that these swords, tapestries, and paintings do not hang from any bracket? They are held up by the Rite, by generations of thaumaturges who made this building into a place that lives and breathes along with those who wield the Rite."

Pen looked uncertain. He had not noticed before, but now he could see that the swords and other decorations were indeed suspended some six inches away from the wall.

"I suppose," he said, "that I didn't see it because I didn't expect to."

"And that is what will keep you safe, Pendragon. There is no parallel world we live in. Those around us who do not have the Rite can see us, can even see us do the unexpected. They put it down to strange things. Like an illness, in the case of your teacher. Surely there is something wrong with the boy who claims to have been reading in the library while seven of his classmates clearly saw him pushing the school bully in the pond!" Napier laughed but Pen just scowled. "Should someone without the Rite see this house then they would be most welcome to cross the causeway and come to look. But they do not, because they imagine that the person who lives here does not wish to be bothered by intruders. In that way, we British are far luckier than many thaumaturges, who are not coincidentally guarded by cultural practice. Now, go and sit in the dining room for dinner."

Dinner was served by the time they got in, and Pen wondered if it would taste any different now that he knew it had been created by magic. However, as he chewed his way through roast beef, Yorkshire puddings, broccoli, and gravy, he became certain that the Rite was the only way to prepare food. It was all cooked to perfection, and he was relieved.

"So," he said as he finished his elderflower juice, "who's

in charge of the Rite?"

"In charge? Each thaumaturge controls their own use of the Rite, and they are trusted to do so wisely. But perhaps you mean that there ought to be someone who oversees the use of the Rite in extreme cases? There is a man – in Britain so far, it has always been a man and not a woman – called the Rendelf, whose sole job is to ensure that balance is kept. You see, perhaps the strangest thing about the Rite is that it can be used for two different purposes, but not both by the same person."

Pen look confused, unsure which particular part of his uncle's words were the best to challenge.

"At the age of fifteen, a thaumaturge must choose his or her path. There are two interpretations of the Rite. The first is Just. Most thaumaturges choose to follow this path, and they are gifted with knowledge of things like healing, as well as more frivolous abilities such as attraction and fortune-telling. In extremely rare cases it is believed they can even change the definition of time, which allows for what might be considered time-travel."

"And the others?"

"The others follow the Knave's Rite. They have the ability to attack, to cause pain and to kill. There have even been some cases of Knave's Thaumaturges being able to tamper with mortality so that death cannot reach them, but they can reach through death." Napier shook his head, but Pen couldn't tell whether it was sadness or anger which flickered in his uncle's eyes. It certainly didn't seem to be fear.

"So, how does the Rendell work then?" he asked, trying to remember everything he had heard but knowing that he couldn't take it in until he had fully accepted that this strange world was real.

"The Rendelf, Pendragon, is essentially the person tasked with stopping the Knave's Thaumaturges from killing the Just Thaumaturges."

"But why don't they all just choose to be Just when they're fifteen? I'd definitely choose the Just ones," he added, nodding to himself and sparing a glance across at his uncle.

"Your first definite use of the Rite saw you pushing a boy in the school pond. Would you give up the ability to stand up for yourself or, more importantly, others? Do not oversimplify the Rite into Good and Evil. If you wish to fight to protect others, then the Knave's Rite is the only way to achieve that."

Pen scowled again. "So, what are you saying? That I should choose to be one of the bad ones?"

"Perhaps the first thing you must learn, Pendragon, is not to oversimplify the Rite into 'good' and 'bad'."

"So, I'm supposed to be one of the *Knave's* ones. Is that what you are?"

"No," Napier replied. "I am the Rendelf for the United Kingdom and, presently, Ireland. I will, however, lose jurisdiction there next spring when they appoint the first Irish Rendelf."

"And me?"

"The Rendelf must choose a successor, Pendragon. Sometimes he chooses a son, sometimes he chooses a stranger. I have selected you."

Even if his life had depended on it, Pen couldn't have disguised the surprise he felt. The idea that such responsibility would fall to him was almost overwhelming, and his mind began to spin with the mere thought. Napier simply sat still and watched him curiously, his dark eyes scanning the boy.

"So," Pen whispered, finding he had very little voice, "I'm basically going to inherit all this? And learn... what?"

"Yes, you will inherit. Most Rendelfs are apprenticed from the age of thirteen, so we are only a little late, and they can claim the title any time from their sixteenth birthday. However, it is hoped I will live some time beyond that and, as with most of your predecessors, it is my belief that you will begin the task in your mid-thirties, by which time your control of the Rite will be well-developed. Do you have any further questions?"

Pen had fifty different questions but, as his uncle spoke, he realised he couldn't remember any of them. Instead, he just shook his head and stayed silent.

"The role of Rendelf is essentially a peacekeeping one and, perhaps unsurprisingly, it is linked to the UN, who provide much of the funding. This house, technically, is the property of the United Nations. It is also a useful thing to tell anyone you know. 'I work for the United Nations' sounds far better than 'I am a peacekeeping thaumaturge'. Do you understand?"

Pen nodded.

"Also," Napier went on, "as a Rendelf you study all aspects of the Rite. This is the greatest responsibility I can imagine any human being having. You will have the power to kill and to heal; to attack and to shield; to master time and even raise those who have gone before. Do you understand?"

Pen nodded again, a pulse in the back of his neck making his head throb. He suddenly couldn't stand the thought of all the responsibility. "And," he said, his voice slightly choked, "will I ever be expected to kill? Or to raise the dead?"

"I would say that the former is, unfortunately, highly likely. There are occasions when Knave's Thaumaturges threaten the lives of many, and the Rendelf is the only person allowed and able to act. It is a painful responsibility we have to bear."

"And the other thing?"

"Far less likely," Napier replied. "I have never been forced to do so, and I see no reason why anyone would. However, it is more important to understand that you will have this power. It does not matter whether or not you intend to use it."

Pen did not stay sitting down for much longer. The words his uncle had spoken had left him feeling as though he was sitting with something heavy draped across his shoulders. Somehow the action of getting up and walking around the large house seemed to relieve him of that feeling, and he gradually found himself calming down. He couldn't decide whether he was still excited to have found out that he was so unusual, unusual even for those who could use this strange Rite, or whether he was angry with his parents for sending him away to a place where he couldn't escape the strangeness.

He already missed his mother and the way she always encouraged him never to hurt anyone, for any reason. What would she make of the conversation that he had just endured, when his uncle had told him that, one day, he would need to kill someone? She would have been horrified beyond words, Pen was sure. She was a pacifist through and through, had marched against wars and, on one terrifying occasion, thrown herself between two men who were fighting. She had tried to pass that on to her son but, as Napier had pointed out, Pen had already used the Rite to cause damage to someone and so clearly didn't share her commitment to pacifism.

He missed his father too, a feeling made worse by the few mannerisms Napier shared with his younger brother. The idea of responsibility was one which Pen's father would often quote to him, reminding him that, as a popular young man, he had a responsibility to be seen working hard and behaving well.

Why did his father not have the Rite? Pen tried to remember any occasion when his dad had done something unusual or unbelievable.

"Often," a voice said behind him, and Pen jumped as he turned around to face his uncle, "the Rite manifests itself differently in younger siblings. Whilst I have its conventional use, your father has a magnificent and, I think somewhat unlikely, intelligence."

"How did you know what I was thinking?"

"I can feel your thoughts in my hands and, believe me, they are easy to mould. After you have learnt to use the Rite, you will need to address this issue. Otherwise, it will cause you all sorts of problems."

"What do you mean you can feel my thoughts?" Pen kept backing away as he spoke, as though the extra ten inches between him and his uncle would protect him.

"The Rite attaches itself to your senses," Napier replied calmly, but Pen kept moving away. "Some people see it, like patterns or notes across a landscape, or like speech bubbles in a crowd of people. There are people who claim that they taste it, although I cannot begin to imagine what it could smell or taste like. Others hear it, like music coming in on the wind from a great distance. Occasionally, there are people who simply know it."

"And what about you?"

Uncle Napier sighed, a slight smile dancing around his lips. "I can hold it. I can feel in my hands what it is I want to do and can mould it to do my bidding."

Pen couldn't help but feel interested. "What about me?"

"What about you?" Napier replied, a little more harshly than perhaps he had intended, for Pen's face fell and he shook his head. "I cannot tell you how you experience the Rite. It is between you and the power you have within you."

"I don't see anything unusual," Pen said, using his fingers to count the list that his uncle had given him, "and I don't think I can taste or smell magic. I love music, but I don't think I ever hear anything I can't explain, so it's not that either. And I don't ever feel something in my hands that's not there. You know," he said, unsure whether it was excitement or disappointment which was blooming within him, "perhaps Mum and Dad have got it wrong."

"You missed one," his uncle whispered.

"What? Just *knowing* it? I don't think that's me. Honestly. I'm not clever enough."

"You should not underestimate yourself, Pendragon. That is for others to do."

As Pen went to bed, he kept thinking about the idea that he could just *know* how to wield unlimited power. He imagined the Rite dancing round in his head and, as though he was just counting sheep, he drifted off.

In his dreams, he was walking over a narrow bridge, like a tiny copy of the Forth Road Bridge, in a green valley filled with low-lying trees and tall flowers. Everything seemed beyond beautiful, as though he was being granted a glimpse of the Garden of Eden. Then, as he came to the end of the bridge, he turned around at the sound of footsteps behind him and found himself looking at a beautiful woman. In some ways, she resembled his mother, with her slender frame and delicate features, but this woman had shining grey hair drawn up in a bun which poured out silver ringlets from the top of her head. Despite her hair, she did not look old, almost like silver hair had been the price of eternal youth. She noticed Pen and her smile faded, twisting into a look of sheer rage.

"So, you are here, Pendragon," she hissed, and Pen was surprised to see that her hair had suddenly turned a rich shade of chestnut while her face, perhaps through sheer contortion, had aged decades. "So seek me. So find me. So end what should never have begun."

Pen woke up as the moon came out from behind a thick bank of cloud and pierced his bedroom window, casting long shadows across the circular room. He was both surprised and alarmed to find that he was drenched in sweat, as though he had just sprinted a mile. The woman's face and voice were still clear in his mind, but the setting was beginning to fade. There had been a bridge, he said to himself as he began to fall asleep again, a bridge going across a wide, rushing stream leading down to an old farmhouse.

Chapter Four

Orkney

In the morning, Pen's dream had faded into a strange sort of memory. The bridge, valley and farmhouse had been swallowed by a second dream where he was running through the corridors of his old school, banging on each of the classroom doors to try and get in. However, as he showered and then dressed slowly, it was the woman from his first dream who occupied his mind, her face and voice as clear as they had been in his sleep. He decided to mention it to Napier who, although not easy to talk to, seemed to know a great deal about this strange world and would surely be able to tell his nephew whether there was any reason for him to dream about this woman.

They were sitting down to a continental breakfast of croissants, cheese, and cold meat when Pen finally had the chance to start talking. It wasn't unusual in his family to start going into depth about dreams: his mother made it her hobby to try and decipher any hidden meanings, or at least say why she thought her husband or son were being troubled by particular night-time thoughts.

"I had a weird dream last night," he mumbled towards his plate of ham and cheddar.

"Yes?"

"Yeah. I dreamt I was walking through this place – I can't quite remember where it was – and there was this woman. She had grey hair but looked really young. Then her hair went a kind of reddish-brown and her face got really old, and she-" Pen stopped as his uncle put down his teacup with a heavy porcelain *clunk* and reached out at his nephew, clutching his arm with white-knuckled fingers.

"What did she say to you?" he demanded, and Pen suddenly regretted saying anything about her.

"She said 'you are here, Pendragon. So seek me, so find me, so end what should never have begun.' It's a lot of rubbish. I just thought it was a weird dream."

Napier sighed and his grip loosened.

"You fool," he muttered, but Pen didn't know whether to be offended or not, as he couldn't really tell whether his uncle was just talking to himself. "If she knows that I have selected you as my apprentice I doubt this will be the last time she tries to make a connection with you."

"Who is she?"

"Reddish-brown hair which turns silver as her features grow younger? You have been contacted through your dreams by a Knave's Thaumaturge named Isolde. She harbours an overwhelming hatred towards me. Years before you were born, I was chosen as the next Rendelf, a position she wished to fill herself. She is a powerful thaumaturge, who has harnessed the Knave's Rite better than most of her generation, but for years she has been lying low in the very north of the Scottish mainland."

"And what can I do about her?" Pen asked, although he could guess what the answer was going to be.

"You cannot do anything until you have fully mastered the Rite. To begin that, we will need to travel. Have you unpacked since you arrived?"

Pen shook his head. "Not properly."

"Good. We will be leaving later today."

Pen went back up to his room after breakfast and threw what little stuff he had unpacked back into his suitcase. He couldn't believe the panic he had caused just by sharing his dreams, but there was something unnerving about the idea that this strange woman had managed to reach him in a place of safety. He also began to imagine that the woman had appeared before in his dreams, and racked his brains trying to remember if she had ever said anything to him.

After a short and early lunch eaten in silence, Napier and Pen climbed into the old sports car and began to speed through the countryside.

"Do you not have a way to use the Rite to travel somewhere quicker than this?" Pen asked, slightly disappointed at the long drive ahead of them so soon after spending a full day travelling.

"There is a way, but it is considered vulgar to use the Rite to travel except under extraordinary circumstances. If someone were dying and you had to be at their side immediately or else miss the opportunity to speak final words with them, *then* you could use the Rite. But not simply to dash off across the country for the sake of it."

Pen was slightly irritated, especially as he had been led to believe they had no choice but to travel to this unknown location for him to begin his training in how to use the Rite. He was uncertain about his uncle and, since he had detailed the woman in his dream, Napier had become even less friendly than usual, his mouth set in a constant frown and his dark eyes darting from side to side as though expecting the woman to jump out in front of them. This just made Pen feel more nervous and he found that each bend in the road seemed to threaten something terrifying beyond.

Their three-hour drive took them through magnificent countryside, with snow-capped mountains gradually giving way to moorland and rolling hills. When at last they reached a small village on the coast, his uncle braked suddenly.

"Pendragon, run and buy us two passenger tickets and one for the car." He pointed to an office a short distance from where they were parked and handed Pen a small wad of cash. "We're going to take the ferry across to Orkney."

The ferry crossing wasn't one that Pen would have wanted to repeat. Strong westerly winds had whipped the grey sea into a fury, and the journey was full of moments where the boat would rear up on the water and pause for a second before crashing back down in a cloud of saltwater which covered the windows. He had been on a boat before but nothing this rough, and he was grateful when they came smoothly into Stromness, the waves dying away into soft blue ripples which stroked the harbour walls of the small town.

They disembarked and sat for a while in the car park,

eating fish and chips. Napier still seemed on edge, but Pen's fear had given way once the sea journey was over. Somehow, the threat of Isolde the Knave's Thaumaturge did not seem as terrifying now he had faced the churning Pentland Firth and was settled comfortably on the other side.

They spent the night in a hotel in the town and left early the next morning, although not until Napier had quizzed his nephew about whether he had dreamt of Isolde during the night. Pen had been able to honestly say that he had not, but he was quite sure that, even if his dreams had been plagued by visions of the woman, he would have lied to prevent any more crazy responses from his uncle.

Orkney seemed full of wonderful places which Pen had to rush past in the car. Ancient tombs and standing stones loomed on the pale blue horizon, but Napier did not stop until they had been travelling for what seemed to be the full length of the island. Here, he pulled into a small car park where a path led out onto dramatic cliffs, which were being hammered repeatedly by the sea. Every so often, a single spectral voice could be heard crying from the bottom, but Pen was too nervous to ask what it was and too frightened to look for himself. It wasn't the fear of seeing a ghost which affected him, but his secret hatred of heights. For some reason, aeroplanes weren't too bad, but he could not stand feeling exposed at height, and the cliffs reminded him of everything which made him afraid.

Napier walked closer to the edge, once again running the invisible skein around his fingers, which Pen guessed was him working the Rite. He hardly spoke to his nephew, so Pen was left to walk the boggy path alone with his thoughts, dwelling on how much, at that moment in time, he was missing his mother and father.

Then the path seemed to lead them towards a set of stairs which went down to a cove and Pen wandered down, still ignoring the eerie cries from nearby.

"They're seals," Napier said, and Pen was surprised to hear his uncle's voice. He had been so lost in thoughts of his parents that the fact Napier wasn't his father seemed almost painful. Still, he smiled politely and nodded, grateful for his uncle's explanation of the strange noise which had haunted them during the walk. "Up you go then."

"What?" Pen asked, unable to hide his annoyance. "I've only just come down."

"Not up there," Uncle Napier replied, gesturing to the stairs they had just descended. "Up there." His arm swung round so that his finger was pointing at some stone steps which seemed to have been cut into the edge of a cliff, leading up to a tiny island.

"No, you're ok, thanks," Pen replied, turning to leave the cove. As he did, he felt Napier grip his arm tightly.

"*Now*, Pendragon."

As Pen took his first step onto the cliff-edge, his anger at his uncle's insensitivity was matched only by anger at himself for not being firmer in his refusal. An old chain hung by his left-hand side, but it was his right which faced the sheer drop down the cliff. At first, he felt fine, walking with his hand squeezed around the cold metal, but then the chain became so low that he was practically having to scramble on his hands and knees. A quick glimpse down reminded him that he had a long way to fall, and Pen was unsure whether it was faintness or sickness which swept over him.

"Uncle Napier! I can't go any further!"

"Let go of the chain," Napier called up, his voice calm. "You can't walk properly while you're clinging onto it like that."

For a few moments, indignation that his uncle could be so unfeeling outweighed his fear, and Pen was able to push himself up the remaining steps. Once he reached the top, he threw himself onto the island and, on his hands and knees, swallowed back the sickness and tears which were welling up within him. He didn't call down to his uncle again but decided to explore. He found the ruins of a small chapel and, although he wasn't completely sure whether or not he believed in God, he placed a twenty pence coin down at the front of the chapel, as a way of thanking Something for helping him reach the top in one piece.

It did not occur to him until he had looked around the rest of the island that the only way back down was to brave the cliff-side steps. It was even more terrifying going that way. The chain was so low that he thought he would overbalance if he leant forward to grasp it, so all he could do was hold on to the side of the cliff. A sudden gust of wind threatened to push him down onto the rocks below, and he found he was crying salty tears of fear. He wanted to give in, to just sit and stay there until someone came with some safer way of getting down, but he could only shuffle along the cliff edge, hating his uncle as much as he missed his parents.

Anything, he thought with an angry sob that he had enough pride to stifle, *anything but heights*. Why had his uncle chosen this task? Then Pen remembered how Napier was excellent at going into his thoughts, so he must have known that his nephew harboured that one secret and terrible fear. He looked up and realised that, in his anger he had reached the bottom. Using every part of his self-control not to strike out at his uncle, he just stormed past and headed for the safety of the other stairs, rubbing his face fiercely to get rid of the remaining tears.

"Pendragon," Napier said quietly, and Pen swung around to face him, hoping he looked angry enough to hide his tears.

"What?"

"Go back up. And, this time, please do not use the chain."

"Are you–?"

"Do it. Now."

The conversation was over, just as it had been half an hour previously. Once again, Pen found himself crawling up the stairs, his heart pounding, and his sweaty hands desperate to clutch the chain. His anger was building up until, suddenly, his ankle twisted and gave way, and he almost slipped off the steps. As he hauled himself up the remaining stairs, his whole body drenched in sweat, he collapsed again on all fours but, this time, he couldn't hold back the sickness. He wished for his mother, he wished this was all a strange dream and, at that terrible point, he even wished that he *had* just been going crazy when he had denied responsibility for Justin ending up in the pond. Anything to make it so that he wouldn't have to face those terrifying steps again.

He returned to the chapel and placed another twenty pence at the front, before turning around and walking back. As he stood at the top, trying to stop himself from swaying, Napier called up to him.

"Pendragon. There is now a barrier between you and the drop, but it is formed of the Rite so you cannot see it."

Pen's heart gave a cheerful leap, and he hurried down the steps, more sure-footed than he knew he could be. His uncle smiled as he reached the bottom.

"When I said that, there was no barrier," he said, "but I would not have let you fall. But I saw the barrier you created just by using the unknown. You have the ability to harness the Rite, Pendragon, but you must believe in that ability."

Pen nodded. He still felt a burning anger towards his uncle but couldn't deny that the man had made an effective point. He turned on his heel to walk up the terrifying steps. As his palms began to moisten with the familiar sweat, he paused.

"But what are you getting so wound up about, Pen?" he whispered. "There is a barrier there. Can't you see it?" There was indeed a barrier, a tall metal fence which impaired his view slightly but made him feel far safer. He began to run up and down the steps, each time leaving a small offering in the chapel to thank that same Something for keeping him safe. At last, Napier called him down.

"I'm getting a bit tired of watching you enjoy yourself," he muttered. "It was more entertaining when you were scrambling up on your hands and knees."

Pen scowled across and marched away over the moorland, not as concerned about keeping a safe distance from the cliff edges, as he knew that the same safety barrier would appear there as soon as he needed it. The rest of the walk took them through more bogs and along more cliffs, until they reached a small settlement of two low stone cottages, as different from Honour's Rest as it was possible to be. A middle-aged woman was lounging in the garden, an open book resting on her round stomach. She was dead to the world and, for a moment, Pen felt a bit voyeuristic just standing and watching her dozing in the chilly sunshine. Napier, however, marched up and rapped his car keys on her shoulder. She did not move.

"Mrs Shipperbottom," he said with a broad smile, "there is no point in pretending you haven't realised we're here. Come on, I've brought a friend for Marley."

"I suppose I shouldn't pretend to be ungrateful that you've picked an apprentice, Napier," Mrs Shipperbottom muttered, and she opened an eye to look at Pen. "And what is the unfortunate's name?"

"He's my nephew. Pendragon Devon."

"Of course." Mrs Shipperbottom rose to her feet and held out her hand to Pen, who shook it warmly. "It is lovely to meet you, Pendragon."

"Just call me Pen."

"No," Napier said, "don't. I have enough of a challenge to make him acknowledge his full name."

"Oh, Napier," Mrs Shipperbottom sighed. "I'm sure it can't make too much difference." She did not allow the Rendelf to speak, walking away from him briskly and beckoning for them both to follow. "Come on, *Pen*. I'm sure Marley will be very pleased to meet you."

She led them into the cottage, and Pen smiled as he looked around. It was like his parents' house, both homely and smart, and the waves of homesickness which had been rippling within him during the day now struck his heart as hard as the sea against the cliffs. He kicked off his shoes so he wouldn't walk the sticky mud into the house. Mrs Shipperbottom smiled across at him.

"It's nice to see he's been brought up well, Napier," she said, and Pen smiled. "Marley!"

There was a crash from one of the attic rooms followed by a rush of footsteps, and a boy about Pen's age burst into the room.

"What?" he asked, sounding slightly panicked.

"Have you been practising?" his mother demanded, and Marley shrugged. "Anyway, it doesn't matter for now. This is Pen–"

"Pendragon," Napier cut in.

"Pen. Devon."

"Hi, Pen," Marley said with a smile, holding out his hand.

Chapter Five

The Shipperbottoms

By the time Pen sat down at the dinner table, first taking the opportunity to clean himself after his adventures on the cliffs, he already knew he liked the Shipperbottoms. Mr Shipperbottom, who came in just after Marley, was a tall, very heavy-built man who looked like he could have been a bouncer or personal security guard. But his voice was gentle and lilting, almost like he was singing every word he spoke, which successfully challenged Pen's first opinions of him. He seemed keen to talk to Pen about everything which had happened since Justin Murchison had been pushed in the pond, and he nodded his head as Pen mumbled his way apologetically through the story of how he had travelled to Honour's Rest and discovered the existence of the Rite. After he had skated over the story of Isolde appearing in his dream, Pen thought it would be safe to change the subject.

"So," he said, "when did you find out that you have the Rite?"

"Well, I suppose I always knew. But then, I was the eldest son of an eldest son and so genetically more likely to become a thaumaturge. When I was thirteen, I was selected to be an apprentice Rendelf."

"What? I thought each country only had one Rendelf."

"You thought right," Mr Shipperbottom said with a smile. "But a long time ago – well before any of our times – a Rendelf was killed by a Knave's Thaumaturge when his apprentice was only fourteen. Well, it's no job for a child, but there was no one else to take over. After that, it became expected that all apprentice Rendelfs would select between one and three deputies. At the end of their training, they choose one of those fellow apprentices to stay on as their deputy." He paused to look at his hands. "Your uncle chose me."

"So, if he died, you would take over?"

"Yes," Mr Shipperbottom said, with an obvious shudder. "Which has been a very good reason to keep him alive all these years."

Mrs Shipperbottom was quite different from her husband, although she too was quite large and slightly threatening to look at. She was less softly spoken and had an established love-hate relationship with Napier, which Pen found fascinating. She wasn't in the slightest bit afraid of him and ensured that he heard her calling his nephew 'Pen' as many times as possible, just to wind him up. She spoke to Pen frequently but, despite this, he didn't feel she was ever giving away anything of her character, as she would quickly deflect any questions about herself.

She was motherly in a way, but Pen noticed that Marley never pushed anything with her more than once.

"What do you think to Orkney so far then, Pen?" she asked at one point.

"I've only spent a day here," Pen replied, slightly stumped for an answer. "But it seems like a nice place."

"Orkney is a Rite-rich area," Mrs Shipperbottom said. "It's believed to be a result of the close connection its people have with the land."

"But you're not from Orkney originally?"

"No. My husband is, and he's always loved the place. We moved up here and, well, had Marley. As you can see."

"Are you an only child?" Pen asked the boy, whose eyes widened at the question. Pendragon wasn't sure whether or not his uncle did it on purpose, but Napier suddenly suggested that anyone wanting a breath of fresh air could join him on an evening walk.

"I'll stay," Marley said, as his parents began to put on their coats. "Do you want to stay too, Pen?"

Despite the fact he felt he had mastered them earlier in the day, Pen did not need a second invitation to avoid the cliffs, so he accepted Marley's offer and they went upstairs to the small attic room where Marley's things littered the floor and the three-seater sofa. There was no bed.

"Is this your room?" Pen asked, looking around and reaching for a guitar which had been discarded on the floor by the door.

"It's my *study*," Marley replied. "Mum and Dad don't think that I'm advancing in the Rite as well as they would hope, so they gave me this space to practise."

"It's clearly a thing," Pen muttered. "I've got a study

at Honour's Rest too." There was silence for a moment before curiosity got the better of him. "What do you mean you're 'not advancing in the Rite as well as they'd hoped'? Isn't it a have-it-or-you-don't type thing?"

"Well, I definitely have it. I just have a slight issue when it comes to harnessing it. It's all about sound with me, but at the moment I can't hear it without some music to channel it through. Mum's furious and Dad's disappointed, so it's not great." The words were clearly out of his mouth before he had chance to stop them, and Pen got the feeling that Marley had been waiting a long time to discuss this.

"Show me?" Pen asked, picking up the guitar.

"Just random notes don't work," Marley warned him. "I've tried that. It has to be actual music."

Pen smiled. That was one thing he was not worried about in the slightest. Perching on the arm of the sofa, he began to play a medley of quick folk tunes.

Marley grinned. "Ok, you're not bad!"

As Pen watched, a winding green vine began to twist its way around the room, and from it burst a colourful variety of flowers and birds, which began to dance around Pen's head as the music became faster. Marley's foot was tapping in time but, apart from that, he was still. Behind him, the curtains folded themselves into long crinoline dresses and, breaking free from the rings, they glided over to Pendragon and shuffled up to him. It suddenly seemed too strange for the boy who, just one week ago, had been in his normal school hundreds of miles away. He stopped playing and put the guitar down on the floor, and the curtains fell limply to the ground, surrounded by a flurry of petals and feathers as the vine and its occupants disappeared.

"What did you do that for?" Marley demanded. He looked as though someone had just awoken him from a wonderful dream.

"Because it was weird. Napier's always saying that the Rite isn't about party tricks, but that's all you were doing."

"I know he's your uncle," Marley sniped, "but Napier Devon is the most boring man ever to have walked the planet. Just because he says something, it doesn't necessarily make it right. Or perhaps I should be calling you Pen*dragon* all the time?"

Marley's outburst was so passionate that Pen couldn't help but smile. He could understand what his companion was saying but didn't want to admit how unnerved he had been by the curtains cosying up to him, and the not-quite-real birds flying around his head. It seemed a lot less odd that his uncle could read his thoughts, or that every object in Honour's Rest was held up by magic alone.

"I'm sorry," he said at last. "Do you want to go again?"

Marley nodded and, as Pen began to play, the curtains once again became headless crinoline ladies who sashayed their way back to the window and used their handless arms to reattach themselves to the curtain rings. The vine did not reappear but, as Pen began to play a louder, darker piece in a minor key, he realised that the light was beginning to disappear from the room. Marley seemed to be growing taller and, although he knew something wasn't right about his companion, Pen couldn't resist the temptation to keep playing.

The music became louder still, and now he was strumming almost at the same time as plucking the notes. He thought he had never played so well, his fingers moving so fast across the fretboard that he couldn't even work out the chords he was playing. The room was very dark now, almost pitch black, even though Pen knew the sun was still out there, just beyond them. His fingers quickened, and he realised that a thick black smoke was beginning to swirl around the room, with hideous faces enveloped in its darkness. Marley's foot was tapping furiously in time with the music, but his face had a glassy expression, and the smile lingering around his mouth wasn't touching his eyes.

And now Pendragon wanted to stop playing, but his fingers were refusing to do his bidding, preferring to work faster and faster until he was surrounded by black smoke and music which went faster than anything he had ever heard before. He tried to slow it down, to enter a major key and encourage Marley to mess around with the party tricks he had complained about a few minutes earlier. The guitar wouldn't listen, and Pen began to wonder whether it was him or someone else who was controlling it now. Perhaps it was the Rite, but he hadn't yet mastered enough to make it do his bidding and not just use him as a channel for something darker.

You can do this, he thought to himself. *Don't think it, know it. I know I can do this.*

He couldn't drop the guitar, but he could hear beyond the thick black smoke that there were hurried footsteps rushing into the room. He couldn't see, but he heard the door open and felt someone pull the guitar from his grasp as another person began to shout words he couldn't understand. He felt sick, faint, and allowed himself to be dragged from the room, away from the smoke which, he only just realised, was beginning to suffocate him.

"What on earth were you doing, Pendragon?" he heard his uncle say, and Pen felt the cold Orcadian wind against his face. He was sure he had never lost consciousness, but he was now sitting on a bench outside, and the black smoke was diminishing into the distance through the open window.

"I don't know," Pen replied. "I swear I don't know. One minute Marley was making curtains into crinoline ladies, the next there was all this black smoke." He coughed and clutched his burning chest.

"Let's go for a drive," Napier said. "It will do you good to get some proper fresh air. I'll just tell the others where we're going."

"Is Marley ok?" Pen asked and Napier nodded his head.

"He is. He was in control, remember? You were just a channel. It was you who got hurt."

A few minutes later, Napier and Pen were driving down one of the twisting Orkney roads, until they reached a small beach beside an abandoned farmhouse. Here, Napier parked the car and turned to look at his nephew.

"Well, what do you think happened?"

"I have no idea," Pen admitted. "But I'm sure you're wrong about me having the Rite. I tried to stop him, I tried to stop playing that awful tune on the guitar, but I couldn't. Even when I told myself that I *knew* I could do it, I still couldn't."

"The Rite is something you will master, Pendragon," Napier said, his voice uncharacteristically gentle. "You cannot hope to always be able to do the exact thing you wish, especially when you are only just discovering its range and power. Your ability stretched to calling me. I was walking along the cliffs and I heard you call. In here," he tapped his temples. "You did well, better than I could have hoped at such an early stage. It would seem I've chosen a good apprentice."

"Is Marley a Knave's Thaumaturge then?" Pen asked.

"No more than you. He still has another seven months before he chooses his path." Napier paused for a second. "But he is more susceptible to that aspect of the Rite, because of his mother."

"His mother?"

"Yes, Mrs Shipperbottom is a Knave's Thaumaturge. She chose the path after she was left alone for her teenage years. Her mother was an alcoholic who could wield, but not harness, the Rite. Her father was a Knave's Thaumaturge. She chose to follow in his footsteps to escape her mother's world. Then she met Erlend."

"And she became a Just Thaumaturge?"

"Once you've chosen your path, Pendragon, it is nearly impossible to change it. There is one option: the Commitment. It allows a person to return to what is called the Natural Rite. From there, they may be able to develop some understanding of a different Rite. A little like becoming a teenager again." Napier glanced down at his hands for a second before looking straight into his nephew's eyes. "But it demands a very high price."

"What price?"

"You can choose. The life of your husband or wife, or parent if unmarried, or the life of your firstborn child. The Commitment is made at the expense of one of these lives and, should the thaumaturge concerned return to their old Rite, they risk the lives of their remaining family."

Pen was silent. He tried to imagine the jovial Mrs Shipperbottom trying to make such a choice.

"So, Marley's going to die?" he asked after a time. Napier looked at him, his eyes slightly narrowed and a sad smile on his lips.

"No," he replied. "Marley was not their firstborn. Their first child was a girl called Amanda. She fell off one of the cliffs when she was three. Marley was born just after the accident. A good thing, as the loss nearly drove his parents out of their minds."

There was more silence. If the idea that Mrs Shipperbottom was a Knave's Thaumaturge was shocking, then this was something going beyond that: something unspeakable. He remembered his father's embrace when Jarvis thought his son had blacked out, the panic and worry he had displayed, and then imagined it multiplied by hundreds or thousands. He found himself wondering whether Mr or Mrs Shipperbottom had seen Amanda fall, or whether they had heard her cries, or just wondered where she had gone when they noticed she was missing.

"Stop," Napier said. "You must not dwell upon these things. Just do not mention any of it to Mr or Mrs Shipperbottom. They have learnt to live with it through deciding not to discuss Amanda with anyone, and you must respect that. As Rendelf, you will come across other tragic stories, and dwelling on every detail will destroy you. Now, cough."

Pen obliged and was relieved to find that only the slightest pain remained. He smiled at his uncle, whose mouth twitched for a moment before he put his seatbelt back on and turned on the ignition.

"Each one of us must live to pay the price for our

decisions and actions, Pendragon," he said as he pulled back onto the main road. "You must always remember that."

They returned to the house in silence to find the Shipperbottoms were in the garden waiting for them.

"No harm done," Napier said as they got out of the car and Marley hurried up to Pen.

"I'm so sorry," he said. "I didn't mean to do that. You see what I mean about not being able to master it now?"

Pen chuckled and the two boys went into the house and voluntarily began to clean the attic room. Pen was saddened to see that the guitar was damaged, with scorch marks across the fretboard. He glanced down at his fingers, but there was no mark on them.

"What a day," he muttered, folding up a green shirt which had been thrown over the sofa.

Marley was more careful about the Rite after their misadventures of the first day, and only used it when his parents or Napier were present. His mother encouraged him to keep trying, but his father kept joking about what had happened and Pen could see that, although it wasn't meant to be horrible, his constant teasing was undermining Marley's confidence. By the end of the week, Marley needed to be listening to something by Beethoven or Mozart to be able to produce anything with the Rite.

"I know he doesn't mean it to do any damage," Marley grumbled as he and Pen sat together in his study, "but he doesn't realise that each time he challenges me, I lose a bit of interest in the whole thing. I'm really worried that I'll only ever be able to master the Knave's Rite, and I already know I don't want that. But you saw, didn't you, Pen? It's the only thing I'm any good at."

"I saw you having a lot of fun before," Pen reassured him, putting his feet on the guitar, which they had upcycled into a footstool. "You can do again." He stopped and a broad smile crossed his face as something dawned on him which he hadn't considered before. "What are your plans for the future, Marley?"

"I don't know. Dad works at the school when he's not helping your uncle. Mum's a self-employed artist. No one thinks anything of it because Orkney's full of them. She sells paintings and postcards. That sort of thing. How about you?"

Pen barked a laugh. "I think that's all set out for me already. I will be 'working for the United Nations'." He wiggled his fingers as speech marks as he quoted his uncle's words.

"Oh, of course. I forgot."

"I was wondering actually, Marley," Pen said, taking a deep breath and trying to swallow back the sudden fear of rejection. "Would you like to train to be a Deputy Rendelf, like your dad?"

Chapter Six

A Deputy Apprentice

The fact that Marley Shipperbottom accepted Pen's offer eagerly did not make his parents any less horrified by the news. Marley had warned Pen that they wouldn't be keen, but when they announced it at the dinner table that night, the chaos was unbelievable. Napier wasn't surprised, but then he seemed to spend half of his time reading his nephew's mind so had almost certainly seen this coming. But, rather than offer them any support, he sat back in his chair and watched the situation unfold with an almost macabre interest. He was only brought into the conversation when the other adults at the table began to petition him to speak some sense to the two boys.

"What do you think, Napier?" Mr Shipperbottom asked, his face scarlet.

"You won't like what I think, Erlend," Napier replied, drumming his fingers slowly on the table. "I can only quote the law to you. *An apprentice Rendelf may appoint up to three deputies at any time that he sees fit. Nothing apart from ill-health may prevent them from fulfilling their duties once such an appointment has been made.*"

"You're right, we don't like what you think," Mrs Shipperbottom spat, and now her motherly nature seemed to have transformed her into a lioness. "This is ridiculous. Marley has his whole life ahead of him." As she spoke, both Pen and Marley opened their mouths to reply, but it was Napier's calm voice which got there first.

"Oh, come on, Bernadette. He hasn't been given a death sentence. His whole life is still as ahead of him as it ever was, and he will now have more chance of escaping being a Knave's Thaumaturge."

"Which, of course, would be my fault," Mrs Shipperbottom cried. "My fault. Like everything our family has ever been through. Like *Amanda*."

"Get out, both of you," Napier said, addressing the two boys who were sitting silently at the dinner table, still clutching their knives and forks. "Now."

Without question or comment, Marley and Pen leapt up and hurried out of the room, going up to the attic study where earlier they had made plans. Pen didn't know how much Marley knew about his dead sister, and didn't want to broach the subject, but it meant they couldn't find anything to talk about. There was still a heated argument going on downstairs and now it sounded like crockery was breaking against the floor or the walls. Pen wondered nervously what it was like when three people with the Rite began fighting. It had been unsettling enough if his mother and father rowed, but this was potentially far more dangerous.

"I don't want to change my mind, you know?" Marley said at last, drowning out the crashes and shouts from downstairs. "I think it's not very fair of my dad to be against me doing this. He's been a Deputy Rendelf for decades. He wouldn't even have met mum if he hadn't been working with Napier. And then for her to say that about, well, you know?"

"I don't want you to change your mind, Marley," Pen replied, fidgeting with the burnt fretboard on the guitar-footstool. "But maybe we should have spoken about it with your parents or my uncle first."

"Your uncle, maybe," Marley said. "But my parents' reaction would have been just the same. Except they'd have been able to forbid me if I hadn't already committed to the role. I don't really want to upset them, you know, but this is an amazing opportunity."

Silence descended again, and now Pen could hear Mrs Shipperbottom crying and her husband trying to console her. He had preferred the shouting.

"Don't worry," Marley said. "Whenever she even hears the name Amanda, she starts crying. I think it's a spiteful rule that you have to pay such a high price for wanting to do something good with your life. Just because you made a mistake when you were fifteen."

Pen just nodded. He agreed with Marley but knew he didn't understand their strange world well enough yet to pass comment. *Perhaps*, he kept telling himself, *there was a perfectly logical reason why people who wanted to switch from Knave's to Just Thaumaturge had to endure such a catastrophic loss.*

"I'm not saying you can't take him," he heard Mr Shipperbottom's voice say. "But you've got to understand. I haven't forgotten what happened to Ramin. And you shouldn't either."

"I haven't forgotten, Erlend," Pen heard Napier say, his voice shaking slightly. "How could I ever forget what happened to him? Or her?" Pen wanted to hear more, but Marley broke their silence.

"Who are they talking about?"

"Someone called Ramin," Pen replied with a slight shrug of his shoulders. "I don't know who he is."

"I've never heard my dad mention the name. Maybe he was Napier's Deputy Rendelf before Dad?"

"No," Pen said, shaking his head. "Your dad said he was apprenticed when he was thirteen. Unless Ramin was the Deputy Rendelf for the previous guy. *Not* my grandfather, by the way, he was a bank manager."

By the time they had stopped talking, the only sounds coming from downstairs were gentle sobs and the lilting voice of Erlend Shipperbottom speaking inaudible but soothing words to his wife.

Marley was in the bathroom when Napier went to speak to his nephew, so they had the study to themselves. Sitting down on the sofa, his uncle explained that they would have to leave Orkney tomorrow morning.

"Mr and Mrs Shipperbottom have been through worse," he said, with a hint of a smile. "But I do not think it is fair to intrude on their hospitality after giving them such an unpleasant shock."

"You think I did the wrong thing, don't you?"

"It is up to you, and nothing to do with me. However, had you discussed it with me before announcing your plans to Marley's parents, perhaps I could have given you some advice on how to handle telling them. You are, in that way, more like your mother than your father."

"What do you mean?" Pen snapped, angry at the thought that his uncle was making some unfair judgement about his mother.

"Nothing. Only that, perhaps because we grew up with the Rite, your father and I are often more guarded and cautious. Perhaps that is why he and your mother have enjoyed such an unusually successful marriage. Because opposites really do attract."

He left the room without another word, and Pen began to wonder whether his comment about opposites attracting was really about his parents, or whether Napier had been making a reference to Mr and Mrs Shipperbottom. When Marley came back, Pen feigned tiredness and wandered to bed, thinking of all the things which had changed during the past fortnight. His old life seemed so far away now, and he missed it more than anyone could know. Napier's few words about his parents had just made him more homesick, and he hoped he would soon be able to start seeing Honour's Rest as home.

After all, he thought with a slight tinge of bitterness, *it will be your home now until you die.*

Pen pretended to be asleep when Marley came into the room. He didn't want to ask after Mr and Mrs Shipperbottom, who had cornered Marley as he came out of the shower to try to persuade him to change his mind. Pen felt guilty about his own actions and angry about the Shipperbottoms', and he knew from everything his mother had instilled in him that he could only make matters worse by trying to persuade anyone that he had acted for the best. Thinking of his mother was painful, and the homesickness welled up within him again.

Pen didn't remember falling asleep that night, but he knew he stayed awake until the early hours of the morning. He could hear Marley's quiet snores and the conversations going on in the rooms downstairs. Once again, Mr Shipperbottom was reminding Napier about the person called Ramin, who seemed to be his choice of ammunition against Pen and his uncle taking Marley away with them. The conversations were quieter now, apart from Mrs Shipperbottom's occasional sobs, and Pen couldn't make out everything which was being said. It must have been the concentration which lulled him to sleep as, the next time he heard his uncle's voice, Napier was standing in the doorway to the bedroom.

"Get up, boys," he said, rubbing his hands together as though incredibly excited. Pen glanced out the window and saw the pink streaks of dawn decorating the sky. When he sat up fully, he could see that they were reflected in the sea. Marley was pulling on his clothes without even seeming to be awake, so Pen thought he ought to do the same. Napier, who had left the room after ensuring he had succeeded in getting the two boys up, could be heard downstairs, scratching butter across a piece of toast. The sound made Pen hungry and reminded him that he had been sent away from the dinner table last night before he had eaten anything.

He was just finishing his own breakfast when Marley shuffled downstairs, rubbing his eyes.

"When are we going?" he asked with a dramatic yawn. Napier looked at him, unimpressed.

"As soon as your parents are up. We can't wait here

any longer, it is unfair on them and unhelpful for us." He gave no room for discussion and, when Mr and Mrs Shipperbottom came into the room a few moments later, he encouraged Pen to thank them for their hospitality and leave.

Napier's sports car was attached gracelessly to a tow truck, and he gestured for Pen to clamber into the cab and take the middle seat.

"The car is too small," Napier explained, "and I think this looks less strange than having three of us apparently crammed into an open top car which scarcely has room for two."

Pen did not mind. As much as he loved the sports car, it was a different experience to sit in the truck and admire the excellent view that such a vantage point afforded them. They sat in silence for a while, Napier running that invisible skein through his hands once again.

"Have you dreamt about her again, Pendragon?" he asked at last. Pen was puzzled for a moment before he recalled the reason they had left Honour's Rest.

"No, not at all," he replied, with what was intended to be impressive nonchalance. "I don't think it's all that important if she's forgotten me."

"Pendragon," Napier's voice was clipped. "Assume that nothing is harmless when it comes to Isolde. She is truly dangerous. The most dangerous thaumaturge I have ever met."

Pen felt a slight shiver run down his back and he tried to change the subject to avoid having to think any more about this person who frightened his powerful uncle. "Who is Ramin?"

"I knew you would be listening," Napier said with a

smile. "That was why I was guarded in what I said. Don't worry, I'm not cross. A Rendelf must be willing to discover the truth through any means, so listening at keyholes is hardly an offence."

Pen was relieved by his uncle's understanding, so relieved in fact that it was only once Marley had joined them and they were driving down the bumpy track that he realised Napier had deliberately avoided answering his question. He was still no closer to knowing who Ramin was, whether he was alive or dead, and how Erlend Shipperbottom and Napier Devon came to know him. He did not, however, think that it was wise to push the issue while Marley was in the truck, and he was certain Napier was relying on this.

The boat journey was uneventful, apart from Pen having to drag Marley away from an elderly couple who were listening to Moonlight Sonata very loudly on a mobile phone. Throughout the last week, it had been the music which could best focus Marley on the Rite, and the lights began to flicker when he heard it. Pen didn't need the apologetic announcement from the captain to realise it was time to remove Marley from the area and prevent any potential damage.

The drive down to Honour's Rest seemed to pass quickly as Pen and Marley attempted to better one another at using the Rite. It somehow seemed far more interesting now that he had someone his own age to learn and practise with and, for the time being, Napier kept his eyes on the road and made no comment about their behaviour.

The loch which surrounded Honour's Rest looked particularly deep, and Pen was surprised at how the water moved away from the small lorry as it powered across the causeway. He heard Marley gasp as he caught sight of the magnificent house and was pleased he had been able to call it home before bringing his first friend in this strange world to admire it. For a moment he thought of his other friends, back in the 'normal' world, but it seemed too odd to imagine them when standing outside a castle in the middle of a Highland loch.

"This place is amazing!" Marley gasped, running his hands along the wall as though he couldn't experience the building fully enough. Napier just smiled across.

"Your rooms are in the other turret. I am sure Pendragon will show you the way." Then he disappeared with the tow truck and Pen was left to invite Marley into the house.

Pen didn't know for certain where the other turret was but, by process of elimination, he was able to work it out. There was a study set out for Marley which was much the same as his own, but the books were more concerned with *Avoiding the Knave's Rite* rather than Pen's *Introduction to the Role of Thaumaturge*. Marley just looked at them and let out a nervous laugh.

"My mum can't help being who she is," he said. "She had a really difficult decision, you know?"

"I know," Pen replied. He didn't want to talk about how much he knew of Marley's history, but didn't want his new friend to feel awkward about it either. He suggested they explore the rest of the house, which was far more enjoyable now he had a companion to laugh and mess around with.

"This place is enormous," Marley grinned.

"My uncle says that if we look for trouble then trouble will find us. I don't know how that works, but I suppose there's something in the warning."

As a result, the boys didn't go looking too far into anything and, after dinner, Napier told them to retire to individual study and then bed. Marley was initially reluctant, but Pen already knew his uncle well enough to realise that the suggestion was not up for discussion. He headed to his study and continued to read from where he had left off the week before.

In a very dry tone, the author was detailing the process of decision-making which faced each thaumaturge, and the benefits and challenges of selecting either path.

Many thaumaturges believe that their problems will be solved if they are selected as a Rendelf. There are, however, two major challenges presented by this. The first is that only one Rendelf is selected per country and so the likelihood of being chosen is extremely low. Even selected Deputy Rendelfs must make their Choice between Just and Knave's Rite on their fifteenth birthday.

The second challenge is that the position of Rendelf brings with it a susceptibility towards the Knave's Rite, without having had the training offered to Knave's Thaumaturges to help them master the Rite correctly. This has brought about the death of five previous known Rendelfs during the past one hundred years and remains a high job-related risk.

The book was as dry as its yellowing pages, and Pen found his thoughts drifting as his eyes began to close and the words danced in front of them. He hauled himself out of the chair and walked up the spiral stairs to his bedroom where, after taking off his shoes, he dropped down, fully clothed, on the bed and was asleep before he could remember anything else.

He was standing on the tiny suspension bridge again, but this time the woman was behind him. He knew because he could see her shadow to the side, but something made him scared of turning around to look at her.

"Are you nervous, Pendragon Devon?" she cooed, and he tried to force himself to turn around, but to no avail. "A great Rendelf *you* will make." Now she was laughing openly. "Afraid of a shadow! Still, fear runs in the family, doesn't it?"

"No!" Pen shouted, spinning around. Her hair was once again a silvery-grey, and her face was young and beautiful. She stared at him innocently, her large eyes widening.

"No? Then perhaps you'll come and find me. Here, in the far north. Find the bridge and you will certainly find me." She laughed slightly and the dream began to crash down as daylight poured over Pen's face. He awoke to find that the night had passed and he was still lying on the bed, fully clothed.

He changed and shuffled down the stairs to meet his uncle and Marley, who were already eating breakfast. Sitting down beside them, Pen helped himself to a croissant and began to pick at it.

"Whereabouts did you say Isolde lived?" he asked as casually as he could, but he couldn't hide the purpose of his words from his uncle.

"Why on earth would you need to know that, Pendragon?" Napier demanded. "I have told you she is more dangerous than anyone else I know. Please God, do not tell me that you intend to go looking for her."

"I dreamt about her again last night."

"Because she knows you are here!" Napier's voice was

raised, and Pen wished he had never brought up the subject. "I absolutely and categorically forbid you from going off on a ridiculous journey to find a woman who will happily torture and kill you just to cause herself pleasure and me pain."

The room fell silent for the rest of the meal, but Pen couldn't help but wonder if his uncle was just displaying the very cowardice that the beautiful, ageless Knave's Thaumaturge had spoken of in his dream.

Chapter Seven

The Kelpie and the Sword

Napier wouldn't speak to Pen about Isolde any more, whether that was discussing where she lived or even acknowledging his nephew was aware of her existence. He had clearly decided that Pen would give up on his dangerous interest if he was left to dwell on his thoughts alone, so Pen found that Marley was the only person available he could speak to about the strange woman who continued to contact him in his dreams.

"Sometimes she looks really young," he explained one day as they sat outside, their feet cooling in the loch. Summer had arrived at Honour's Rest now and the loch water was a sparkling blue. Every so often, a car would go past, and the two boys would wave, keeping a tally of how many people waved back. It was always fun to see the look of surprise on people's faces as they realised that the strange old building was still inhabited. "But she's got this mane of silver hair. Then she'll turn around and, the next time I see her face, she's all wrinkly and looks like she's about ninety. But her hair is this fabulous red-brown. I don't know if people can shapeshift using the Rite but, if they can, then I bet she turns into a fox. Like an Arctic Fox, which can change its colours in winter."

"What are you two talking about?" Napier called from the doorway and the boys got to their feet. Pen had been developing a strong dislike of his uncle after he had refused to listen to what Isolde was said to Pen in his dreams. For his part, Napier didn't seem to care about what his nephew thought, but just set him more and more reading. Pen now fully understood the role of a thaumaturge and how the Rite was able to be harnessed, but he hadn't yet backed it up with practical work.

One of the things Napier was pushing now, probably because the boys would be turning fifteen in the coming months, was the importance of making the correct Choice for yourself. A Knave's Thaumaturge, he made them repeat, was not predestined to do only works of evil. He gave them countless examples of Knave's Thaumaturges who had simply kept themselves to themselves and used the Rite to create rain or to influence the course of a sporting fixture. There were others who became conjurers, in high demand at parties because of their fascinating abilities.

Now though, Napier was staring at the two boys who stood in front of him. Pen scowled at his uncle as he walked past and, for a second, he thought that Napier was about to catch his arm, but he was wrong. He walked back into Honour's Rest and found that the entrance hall had been cleared of all furniture, so the tapestries, paintings, and swords which hung from the wall looked even more impressive in the sparseness of the room itself.

"Time to put all that reading into practice," Napier said, sitting down on one of the steps which led into the main body of the building. "You first, Marley."

Somewhere in the large house, a solitary violin began to play something quiet, beautiful and, to Pen's ears, sad. The sound was so distant that he could almost believe he was imagining it, or that it was a ghost making the eerie music. Clearly, Marley had heard it, and he glanced across at Napier for some further instructions.

"Do whatever you feel comes naturally to you," Pen heard his uncle say above the sound of the violin, which was now joined by the spectral sound of a piano without a player. He watched as Marley's face hardened in concentration and he began to move his hands slightly, as though playing the violin himself. Pen listened, transfixed, as other instruments began to join the violin and piano, until the hall was full of the sound of an orchestra. He couldn't help the smile which spread across his face as he saw how proud Marley was.

"Now make it darker," Napier instructed, wrapping the invisible skein around his fingers. "Come on, Marley, don't be worried. I swear I will not let you do anything beyond my capability to fix."

The music became faster and darker almost instantly, and Pen was reminded of that sunny evening in Orkney when the sky had been blacked out and his fingers had burnt scorch marks across the fretboard of a guitar in order for Marley to wield the Knave's Rite. Marley's smile was becoming wider, more like a grin, but his eyes were cold and steely, and his foot was tapping frantically in time to the music. Pen heard a loud noise behind him and spun around at the heavy beating against the door, as though someone was spraying a water cannon in their direction.

Through the window he could see that, where the loch had been shining blue water just a few minutes before, it was now churning grey. Pen's curiosity got the better of him, and he ran closer to the window to see what had reached the door of the house.

A great horse was there, so tall that its watery head reached the window of his study, and its hoof was beating against the door. It had no hair or skin, but the water forming it had twisted into the shape of muscle and sinew, so it looked like an anatomical drawing in some terrifying biology textbook. Pen glanced across at Napier, knowing that he couldn't hide the panic he was experiencing, but his uncle seemed very calm.

"That beast does not belong out of the loch, Marley," Napier said, addressing him as though nothing unusual was going on. "It cannot survive for long without doing your bidding. You must commit him back to the water where he can rest."

Marley's face contorted with concentration. The orchestra began to sound discordant, as though its invisible players were arguing about what piece they ought to be playing. Pen thought the piano was beginning to play Moonlight Sonata.

"Concentrate, Marley," Napier said. "I can help you, but you are the person who summoned the kelpie, and you are the only one who can send it back where it belongs."

The sound of the orchestra was now so terrible that Pen moved his shoulders up to try and block his ears, as his hands seemed stuck to the window ledge. The piano music was becoming louder and clearer though and, as he watched, the gigantic horse threw back its watery head and plunged into the loch with a splash that soaked the house and made it difficult for Pen to see anything else out of the window. The orchestra stopped playing and Pen turned back to the room to see Marley staggering onto the step which had previously been occupied by Napier.

"Bravo!" Pen's uncle exclaimed. "You have a lot of talent, Marley." Despite the fervour in Napier's voice, Marley did not seem convinced but gave a faint smile.

"What was that?" Pen whispered. His voice seemed to have dived into the loch along with the enormous beast.

"A kelpie," Napier replied. "Also called a water-horse. They live in many of these lochs and can be called by a Knave's Thaumaturge."

"You mean Marley–"

"As you should understand by now, Pendragon, at fourteen a thaumaturge is neither Just nor Knave. It is a decision that is imminent, however, and so it is important you both experience the Knave's Rite as well as the Just." He turned away from his nephew and back to Marley. "A kelpie will only obey the person who summons it from the water. However, you must be careful as they are far keener to appear than to do any other bidding you may have. It takes a great deal of control to master a kelpie, but you managed it."

"With your help," Marley said, still slightly breathless.

"I swear to you; all I did was ensure that Moonlight Sonata came through that terrible cacophony. You can be a powerful thaumaturge, Marley Shipperbottom, but you must learn to control the Rite without any help from

Beethoven." After he had finished speaking, he walked down to the door and opened it to look out on the loch. The same blue blanket of water spread around the house and, looking beyond his uncle, Pen couldn't believe that such a terrifying creature had appeared from its depths just minutes before.

"You next, Pendragon," Napier said, spinning around on his heel so his piercing brown eyes stared straight into those of his nephew. Pen walked into the middle of the hall and stood for a moment. There was no music for him, which was understandable as he did not have the same requirements as Marley, but it made him feel a bit ridiculous. He could hear Marley behind him, still trying to catch his breath after the effort he had made in banishing the kelpie. "Go on," Napier said, marching up to his nephew and standing so close to him that Pen could hear him breathing. "Whatever comes naturally."

Pen knew that Marley had been studying from different books, books that had highlighted the role of how to interpret and use the Rite, whilst he had only been reading about the importance of the thaumaturge and the history of different Rendelfs who had lived and died in Honour's Rest. Nothing would come naturally to him, he was sure, but he thought of what he would most like to do and was both shocked and pleased when he heard a cry of impressed surprise from Marley. He turned around and saw that, just as he had intended, Marley was being harassed by a curtain which had taken the form of a lady in crinoline, just as those in Orkney had done. However, the curtains in Honour's Rest were far larger, so Pen couldn't help but laugh as the curtain-ladies almost enveloped his friend in their voluptuous folds.

"Now something darker, I think," he heard Napier's voice say, but Pen tried to close his mind to his uncle's words and focus only on the laughter of his friend. He would not be tricked into using the Knave's Rite, he told himself. For the first time, he found himself breathing the Rite. He could feel it flowing through him, permeating every sense he possessed and filling his mind with the knowledge and freedom it offered.

Suddenly, he felt a sharp stinging sensation against his cheek and his left eye began to water. He heard Marley's laughter stop and turned around to face his uncle, in time to duck as Napier flicked an elastic band straight at his face.

"Stop it!" Pen shouted, desperate not to lose the Rite he was only just beginning to find. Napier paid him no attention but just flicked another band into his face. It hit the lid of his watering left eye and Pen felt the pain mixing with the Rite which was coursing through his body. It no longer felt like a freeing experience, but he and it were wrapped around one another to take revenge on the man who was causing him pain. Another elastic band whipped against his ear and he turned back to face his uncle, his eyes burning with anger.

"Stop that!" he screamed again, and he felt the force of his anger leave him for a second and strike Napier. He thought his uncle would fall, but Napier seemed to catch Pen's anger in his hands and, after moulding it slightly for a moment, he threw it back at his nephew.

Pen felt himself growing angrier. He could almost visualise the Knave's Rite weaving its way around his body, his blood coloured by it and his watering eyes glowing as furiously red as they felt. He could see his uncle winding that invisible skein around his fingers, and Pen wanted to snatch it away and leave Napier helpless to whatever revenge he chose to take against the man who had so painfully dragged him from the happiest state he had ever known.

He glanced up at one of the enormous swords which was hanging on the wall and imagined himself severing the Rite which kept it there. His own was more powerful, as it lived and breathed along with him. Pen could see his uncle still winding the ridiculous invisible skein around his fingers and felt a sudden superiority. He did not need music or ridiculous hand gestures to wield the Rite. He could do whatever he wished just by thinking, breathing, knowing…

"That's enough," he heard Napier say, but that only made him angrier.

It was fine then, he thought bitterly, *for his uncle to make him experience the Rite like a performing monkey and then shock him out of the experience through pain.*

The sword began to shuffle away from its moorings, causing a cascade of dust and spiders' webs to fall the twenty feet. He heard Marley calling his name, but he didn't care. At that moment, he just wanted to show his uncle that he had the power, ability and focus to punish him for his actions.

"Stop that!" Napier shouted, just as his nephew had done seconds before. But Pen was no less stubborn than his uncle, and the sword continued to move across the room. "Stop that now!"

The hint of panic in Napier's voice gave Pen a sense of satisfaction. He had achieved what Marley had not. He could see Napier's fingers working frantically as he wound the Rite around them. The sword was now above his head, the pointed tip of the blade only six feet above him. With an angry cry, Pen sent it crashing down, commanding it to reach its target no matter whether or not Napier stepped out of the way.

There was a loud crash of metal as the sword fell on the floor, and the noise seemed to bring Pen back to his senses. The anger was gone, but it had been replaced with a sickening feeling of remorse and guilt which was already feasting on his insides.

"I'm so sorry," he said.

His uncle's face was almost as white as his right index finger, around which he had pulled the Rite tightly to prevent the sword from hitting him. Napier looked at him in silence for a few moments before shaking his head.

"It can't be helped," he said, his voice as calm as ever. "I should have known you had it in you. And every Rendelf must face the darker side of his apprentice sooner or later. I should be grateful it happened before you have full control of the Rite. I'll tidy this place up. You two go and enjoy what's left of the sunshine."

Without another word, Pen and a very pale Marley went outside and returned to where they had been sitting earlier in the day. For a while, neither of them spoke. Then Pen turned to Marley and gave him a forced smile.

"At least all you did was bring a giant horse to the door," he muttered. "I think I really wanted to kill Uncle Napier. I told the sword to fall on his head, even if he moved."

"He was winding you up to get a reaction," Marley shrugged. "You looked really in tune with the Rite before he did that though. Much better than me. I don't know why I don't just give it all up now and accept that I'm going to end up as a Knave's Thaumaturge."

There was another silence, during which Pen wondered if Marley knew just how dark the thoughts were that had gone through his head. Yes, he had been in tune with the Rite, but nothing good had come of that. He had used it to perform the very party tricks his uncle had repeatedly warned him against and then, when challenge presented itself, he had allowed the Rite to control him and give him some kind of bloodlust.

"I sometimes spoke to my mum about the Knave's Rite," Marley said, and Pen glanced across at him, although he was struggling to keep eye contact. "She said she chose it because it seemed easier and more natural. I think I'm the same."

"Me too," Pen shrugged. "Perhaps Napier needs to find a new apprentice and we can merrily go off and become Knave's Thaumaturges." He hadn't meant it to sound funny but, with the relief at escaping the day without causing any serious damage, he found himself laughing along with Marley.

Later that day, however, he excused himself for an early night. The sun was still shining through his bedroom window and so Pen lay awake for some time, thinking about the events of the day. He could still imagine the Knave's Rite stirring in him, and he tried to focus on something which would calm his thoughts.

He was walking through an overgrown valley, beside a stream which was pouring down from the green hills. There were birds singing and, despite never being any good at identifying birds, Pen simply knew they were skylarks. Then he heard another noise: a child was crying.

He couldn't tell whether it was in his imagination or if, somewhere in Honour's Rest, beyond the valley and his dreams, someone was sobbing.

He sat up, suddenly awake, and thought for a moment he caught sight of a silver blade a long way below his window. By the time he had the energy to get to his feet and look out, all he could see was the surrounding darkness of the loch, which pulsed gently in the moonlight as though a horse was cantering its way across the bottom.

Chapter Eight

In the Loch

Napier didn't talk about the events of that afternoon again but directed both Marley and Pen to return to the theoretical side of the Rite, overseeing them sitting alone in their studies reading books he selected. Marley was given a new text entitled *Nature versus Nurture in the Rite,* which he seemed to be enjoying as it reassured him that he wasn't predestined to become a Knave's Thaumaturge just because of his mother.

Pen, on the other hand, had been given a book which focused on anger management, which he guessed was his uncle's way of punishing him. He couldn't help but be annoyed with Napier, although he agreed that there had been cause for concern in his behaviour. It made him think of Mr Carling's horror at the discovery that Pendragon Devon, of all people, had a darker side. Pen wondered what his school friends were doing in their long summer holiday, and whether they were wondering what had happened to him.

He received handwritten letters from his mother, which were little more than notes on what she and his father had been doing. During a period of annual leave, they had gone abroad to Slovenia and his mother mentioned that they had met with 'someone who works with your uncle', who Pen assumed was the Slovenian Rendelf. His mum never made any attempt to understand her son's new world, but her little letters went a long way to reassuring him that his parents remained interested in what he was doing. He hadn't the heart to tell them that, during an angry outburst, he had almost sent a claymore crashing down upon his father's brother's head. *But then,* he thought with a smile, *maybe they would understand.*

He tried to turn his thoughts back to the book in front of him, reading about how dangerous a bad temper could be for someone with access to the Rite. There were graphic examples of Knave's Thaumaturges who had burnt entire settlements to the ground and killed hundreds of people because they had been barred from the local pubs. There were even three examples of Rendelfs who had been executed between 1487 and 1793 for letting a bad temper make them cause destruction which ruined the lives of several innocent thaumaturges.

Pen put the book down, feeling that Napier had made his point. He wondered if he would have such a bad temper if he had been encouraged to let out his emotions more, and he felt a little resentment towards the mother who had always tried to ensure that her son was a 'good person'. They should all have known just how bad he was when his first act with the Rite was to push Justin in the pond.

Pen could hear the breakfast gong but did not want to go downstairs. That had been the story of his life for the past week, and he was beginning to enjoy being a recluse. He had no opportunity nor inclination to hurt anyone while he was in his room and, as his dreams about Isolde were becoming more frequent and detailed, he had started to pour his thoughts about her into a notebook. He didn't care if his uncle found his ramblings, he thought as he glanced across at the leather-bound book, as it might encourage him to take his nephew's concerns more seriously.

The breakfast gong rang again, and this time it was accompanied by an impatient call from Napier, whose voice reminded Pen that his uncle was a force to be reckoned with, however annoyed he may be feeling. He certainly didn't have any intention of making him angry, so went down the spiral stairs as fast as he could and joined Napier and Marley at the breakfast table. They were already eating cereal and talking about the books that Marley had been reading. It just made Pen feel more isolated, as though he was contaminated by what had happened last week.

"Good morning, Pendragon," his uncle said at last, and Pen raised his hand in a greeting but couldn't bring himself to say anything. "You're sullen again this morning."

Pen felt his teeth clamp together, but then reminded himself that he was supposed to be keeping his temper and that his uncle was probably testing whether he had successfully learnt to do so. "Sorry," he whispered. "I'm just a bit tired." He knew that his uncle was able to read his mind and see that he was lying, but it didn't stop Napier from nodding at his nephew.

"Well, boys," he said, pushing his chair back and relaxing with his hands behind his head. "I have a meeting with the First Minister in Edinburgh today, and it isn't something which can be postponed. What I want to know is whether or not I am safe leaving you here? I can't easily let you loose in Edinburgh, I'll probably never find you again, but I don't really want to leave you in the car outside Holyrood either."

"We can be trusted to stay here, can't we, Pen?" Marley said cheerfully, but his face fell as Napier looked at him.

"Marley, unless you would like to be known as 'Ma' for the remainder of your time at Honour's Rest, I would recommend that you refer to Pendragon by his correct name."

Pen glanced across at Marley and felt a smile spread across his face. "Yes," he said, before anything else could be decided. "I'm sure we won't cause too much chaos."

"Well," Napier began, sounding very unconvinced, "it is a lovely day. I would suggest you take the boat out and do some fishing on the loch. Just remember not to go in the water."

As the two boys stood in the doorway, waving to Napier as he drove across the causeway, Pen was surprised at just how excited he was at the idea of fishing, of doing something ordinary and non-Rite-related. Marley seemed equally keen and, an hour later, they were nervously directing the boat out onto the loch. However, if there were any fish, they seemed to be deliberately avoiding the line and the most exciting thing they caught all morning was a large clump of something Marley called 'Poison

Parsnip', which Pen threw back in the water.

They went back to discussing their favourite topic of how they were doomed to become Knave's Thaumaturges. Pen found it therapeutic to get his concerns out in the open. Today, he shared how he had started blaming his mother for always forcing him to be good and suffocating the darker side of him, meaning it had become like an angry, caged animal.

"Funny how we both blame our mothers," Marley said, casting the line out again. "Definitely nothing Oedipal going on there. Freud would be disappointed."

Pen laughed slightly. "I don't *want* to blame my mum," he whispered. "I just don't like the fact that I've got this bad temper and no explanation for it. I mean, every time I try to wield the Rite, something seems to go wrong."

"What are you talking about?" Marley laughed. "You're going to be a brilliant thaumaturge – and Rendelf – one day! Look, I'll tell you something that I've never said to anyone else, so you have to promise you won't repeat it."

Pen nodded, suddenly hungry to hear what Marley was going to tell him.

"I'm not proud of this. In fact, I'm really ashamed of it. I was walking along the cliffs one day, a couple of years ago, and I was thinking about Amanda. You know, my sister who died."

Pen nodded but said nothing. He had a horrible, sickening feeling that he might be able to guess what his friend's confession was going to be.

"My mum and dad have always been so cagey about her. I knew that she died on the cliffs, but I didn't know how and, for some reason, that's all I wanted to find out. So, I put myself in the 'zone'," he wiggled his fingers to form speech marks as he spoke, "and imagined the sounds that might have been there that day. It was easy. I could hear the seals singing and the sound of birds anyway. And I could hear the waves beating against the foot of the cliffs like a heartbeat. *Put-toom, put-toom.*" He was telling the story so well that Pen could imagine a slightly younger Marley there, about to do something which would haunt him for the rest of his life. "And I saw her. She was a fast three-year-old! My mum was running after her, but she tripped up on a stone. Amanda just looked back for a second and then–"

A car horn blared as it shot past Honour's Rest and Pen spun around, his heart thumping from being brought out of the terrible world that Marley had been creating. He saw a black Land Rover speeding down the road, and a deer leaping through the undergrowth opposite. It had clearly been the target of the warning sound. Pen turned back to hear the rest of the story, but Marley's face had hardened, and that familiar cold smile was playing around his lips.

"It's fine," Pen said quickly, but there was nothing he could do. For the first time since he had known him, Pen saw Marley channelling the Rite without listening to music. He raised his hands and shouted something Pen couldn't make out, and the great beast, who a week ago had been banished to the loch, rose out of the water.

"Follow them," Marley said, in a voice which sent a shiver running down Pen's spine. The kelpie let out a terrible whinny, which sounded like the desperate screams of every person who had ever drowned, and threw itself back, rearing up and soaking the two boys in the tiny boat.

"Are you insane?" Pen shouted, desperately trying not

to fall into the water. He felt his own abilities surging within him as they had done on that afternoon when he had tried to kill his uncle, but this time the Knave's Rite did not manifest itself. He was filled with a kind of courage he had never experienced, as though all the times he had stood up to Justin Murchison and the other bullies had been building up to this moment. He leapt up, higher than he knew was possible, and grasped hold of the kelpie's watery head.

"Pen! No!" Marley screamed, but Pendragon didn't listen to his terrified cries. He couldn't allow the beast to be set loose on someone whose only crime was to interrupt a conversation they could never have known was going on.

"Take me instead," Pen hissed into the horse's enormous ear. The next thing he knew, the kelpie plummeted into the cold water of the loch and Pen was being forced down to the bottom.

He wasn't sure whether it was that the loch was very deep, or whether the kelpie was shrinking, but the surface seemed a long way above them as he rode the water-horse along the bottom. He had never ridden a horse so could make no comparison, but it seemed surprisingly easy, and he was suddenly aware that he felt as conscious as he had above the water. Bubbles left his mouth, but he couldn't imagine where his oxygen was coming from as he had no opportunity to breathe. After a while, Marley's screams were left behind them and the kelpie galloped on, leaving Pen to realise that he was quite enjoying himself, although it confused him to admit it.

However, just as he allowed a smile to creep across his features, he was thrown headfirst from the horse and, as he put his hands out to break his fall, he felt his left palm strike something sharp. Blood began to pour from his hand and, in the water, it looked like red clouds. He was bleeding more than he had ever done before, but his curiosity was still piqued and, at the moment, he couldn't feel any pain. He seemed to have cut himself on a silver sickle, which he could identify through his school project on the history of agriculture. *What on earth was a silver sickle doing at the bottom of the loch?* he asked himself. There seemed to be letters on the blade, but he couldn't make them out as blood clouded his blurring vision.

He would have sworn but he couldn't make any noise so, instead, he took some comfort from flicking his middle finger up in the direction where the kelpie had disappeared and then again wherever he thought Marley might be. He still didn't feel as though he was drowning, but the sight of his own blood swirling in front of him was making him lightheaded. Suddenly, he felt something catch the back of his collar, and he was being pulled slowly upwards and was faced by a light brighter than anything he had ever experienced. Now, Pen felt as though he was drowning, and he gasped for air, not only through that strange sensation of suffocation, but also because his hand was burning with pain.

"Next time, Pendragon," he heard his uncle say, "you will stay in the car at Holyrood."

Pen did not know anything else until he awoke some time later and found himself lying on a chaise longue in what appeared to be his uncle's study. His injured hand was strapped to the top of the couch so that it had a strange sensation of numbness. Napier was sitting at a desk with his back to his nephew, apparently far more interested in his books.

"Is Marley alright?" Pen asked. His uncle didn't turn around.

"Always your first question. Marley is fine. Why wouldn't he be? He didn't try to sacrifice himself to the kelpie." Napier turned around to face his nephew, and Pen couldn't tell what expression, if any, coloured his uncle's features.

"He didn't mean to do it," Pen persisted. "He was telling me something that had happened, something that had frightened him. These idiots just—" He stopped. He knew they hadn't been idiots, and he could hear his mother's voice in his head reminding him not to tell lies. They had only been interested in staying safe on a dangerous road and, as he had identified at the time, didn't deserve to be hunted down by the kelpie for having frightened a deer away from their path.

"He's not in trouble, Pendragon. If you put two young people together with access to the Rite, then there are bound to be some casualties. Today, it was you. Tomorrow, it may be someone else."

"What do you mean?" Pen asked, his curiosity once again getting the better of him.

"There are dangerous things in the world, and the Rite is a certain way to invite danger, especially when it is wielded by people who have not yet learnt how to control it. The kelpie was waiting for Marley to call it again and so he did not need to try hard to catch its attention. You are fortunate that kelpies' chief experience of human beings is from a time when honour and valour were valued above anything else. The kelpie accepted your self-sacrifice and so transferred its allegiance to you and did not hunt down its quarry."

"How could I breathe underwater?" Pen asked. He felt feverish and his mind jumped from one question to another as he attempted to take everything in.

"It is not unusual," Napier said. "If you had read the books I set you then you would know that many thaumaturges are believed to have some selkie blood in them. From the Neolithic period, when the two species cohabited and interbred. However, if a thaumaturge stays underwater for any length of time then they will have to stay there, as they will be unable to breathe above the water. You were lucky I caught you just in time." He paused and looked smug for a moment. "If you can call it luck."

Pen stayed silent for a while as his uncle loosed his hand. There was a long line of what looked like dried leaves stretching down his palm.

"Dried yarrow," Napier explained. "It will help it heal. Healing has never been a strong suit of mine. I know enough, but where a modern or herbal remedy is available, I will take that. I wondered whether to take you to get it stitched, but we'll see if this works. If not, you can always go to the hospital tomorrow."

Pen nodded and got to his feet. He still felt slightly light-headed, but it didn't feel right to stay in his uncle's study any longer than necessary.

"Pendragon?" he heard his uncle say and turned around to find that he was being stared at very hard.

"Yes?"

"How did your hand get cut?"

"I can't remember," Pen lied. He was quite certain that Napier would be entering his mind and finding out the truth, but he couldn't bring himself to admit that he had found something so strange at the bottom of the loch. Keeping his

injured hand across his chest, he walked out of the room and wandered through Honour's Rest to share the whole story of his experience with Marley.

Chapter Nine

Hitchhiking

Pen's hand was still bleeding the following day, so his uncle insisted on taking him to the Minor Injuries unit of the local hospital for stitches. The nurse there wanted to know how the injury had happened and, before Pen could think of a response which wouldn't sound crazy, Napier explained that his nephew had cut himself by leaving a knife in the washing up bowl.

"I told him," he sighed, in a concerned voice. "I told him that he should be more careful about that sort of thing. But, you know, sometimes you just need to learn from your own accidents, don't you?"

Pen had a horrible feeling that his uncle was speaking more truth than he was comfortable with. He had certainly dived in with both feet without considering the consequences. For the first time since he had caught hold of the kelpie, he realised that he should have drowned at the bottom of the loch. The nurse simply smiled and shook her head.

"At least you do the washing-up though, ah, Pendragon? Crumbs! Is that what they call you at school? I don't think I've ever met anyone with that name."

"No, you can call me Pen." Pendragon couldn't help the sense of satisfaction he got at his uncle's disapproving look, compounded by the fact that he couldn't appear too overbearing in front of the nurse.

"Well, Pen, it looks like you'll need a couple of stitches. Nothing too dreadful. I'll get the doctor to come and do them as soon as she's free."

Pen glanced up at Napier for reassurance but received none. He wished that Marley had come along but, at the same time, he was pleased to be able to hide his dislike of needles from his friend. He wasn't terrified but wished it hadn't come to this. His mother hated needles, which had always been a long-running joke in the family as his father, a doctor, was very used to them. Pen wished that either of his parents were with him, instead of his cold uncle who simply looked around the room as though he expected something terrible to jump out.

"Here we go," said the nurse cheerfully, pulling back the curtains and introducing the doctor. She did not seem a lot older than Pen was himself, and he felt himself relax slightly.

"Ok. Pen, is it?"

He nodded.

"I'm going to give you an injection of some local anaesthetic and then I think it will take about five stitches to close this up. The injection will just be like a scratch."

Pen nodded again, but his hand gave an involuntary twitch away from the doctor as she reached out to take it. Napier spun around and stared at him.

"It won't hurt," he said. "You *know* it won't hurt."

The doctor and nurse remained oblivious to the hidden meaning behind Napier Devon's words, but they both commented on how brave Pen was when he didn't even blink as the needle pierced his skin.

"I don't think this is your first rodeo," the doctor said with a smile, which Pen could only return mutely. There was no way he could possibly explain his behaviour without telling lies or revealing the fact that it was the Rite which had numbed any pain.

"Does that always work?" he asked his uncle as they walked across the car park. "Can you always use the Rite to get rid of pain?"

"Physical pain, yes. But if the mind is affected then the ability to control the Rite is impaired and so it becomes a lot harder."

They had taken the racing car to the hospital, with Marley left alone at Honour's Rest and under strict instructions not to attempt any use of the Rite. It meant their journey along the country roads was particularly enjoyable in the summer sunshine. Pen looked down at his bandaged hand and thought again of the silver sickle. If his uncle had looked into his mind and seen how the cut had happened, then he hadn't mentioned it or asked any questions. *Perhaps*, Pen thought, *he knew that the sickle was in the loch and so that's why he wasn't surprised by what had happened.*

They knew that something wasn't right as soon as they turned onto the causeway. There was another car in the drive: a little run-around which had been parked quickly, leaving long skid marks in the gravel. The front door to Honour's Rest hung open on the hinges and, as both Napier and his nephew leapt out of the car and hurried in, Pen was terrified of what they might find.

However, he could hear Marley's voice as soon as they walked into the entrance hall. He was in the living room and was trying to offer some comfort to a man who was crying hysterically.

"Thank you, Marley," Napier said, stepping into the room and pulling off his driving gloves. "If you and Pendragon could go and park the car, I would be extremely grateful. I think there is rain coming."

The two boys left the room and Marley tried to fill Pen in on what had happened. Apparently, the man, who Marley only knew as Patrick, had come to ask for Napier's help in finding someone who had gone missing.

"I think he said it was his daughter but, honestly, he was all over the place and I couldn't very easily follow where he was going with stuff." He paused. "It didn't sound very good, whatever it is, and I think he wants Napier to pull some strings and find whoever it is."

They parked the car carefully in the garage and then returned to the building, just as Patrick was leaving in his own small vehicle. Napier, who had followed him out, walked over to the two boys and spoke to them in a quiet and quick voice, which was very unlike his usual tone.

"Mr O'Hare has lost his daughter," he explained. "She is a little younger than you boys and had just started exhibiting definite signs of channelling the Rite. I cannot know for certain who has taken her, but I will need to go away for a time to see every effort is made to ensure her safety. Do you understand? That means I will have to leave you alone at Honour's Rest."

The two boys nodded, unsure if there was anything they could or should say to such startling news.

"I will not be able to hurry back at a moment's notice like last time. This is a serious issue and deserves my full attention. Please do not summon me back unless it truly would make the difference between life and death."

Pen and Marley nodded again.

"Pen," Napier continued, "as you are the Apprentice Rendelf, Honour's Rest will obey your command during my absence. However, I would advise you to continue following the rule of avoiding looking for any trouble. Marley, kindly ensure that my nephew keeps his temper and, for heaven's sake, please do not summon the kelpie again. It is only a matter of time before it does real damage." For a second his eyes flickered down to Pen's bandaged hand, but then he stared at the two boys in front of him. "I will not be taking the car. This calls for something more. If I am not back in a week then I will send news of my whereabouts and, Marley, perhaps ask your father to come and look after you both. Take care. Don't burn anything down. This house has stood for over nine hundred years, and I would hate to return to find it in ashes." He smiled drily at them both. There was a loud crash behind them and, when they turned back to Napier, it was to find that he had disappeared.

Pen and Marley wandered back into the house together, unsure exactly of how they could fill their time during the next few days without Napier there to marshal them. Without knowing how the meals were made, the two boys had to make their own food, which consisted mostly of canned soup, and bread that they found in the freezer and defrosted in the oven. Pen had never paid attention to his parents when they were cooking, and he had never found any interest in it at all. Marley seemed to have the same background and so, by the end of the evening, they were both hungry and miserable.

Pen excused himself and went to bed before ten o'clock, and Marley seemed relieved to do the same. Despite his hunger and tiredness, Pen stayed up for a while reading the books which lay open on his study table, hoping to find something to give him the sense of place he was searching for. It eluded him and he soon found himself drifting off to sleep, his head resting against the pile of books.

After a while of sleeping dreamlessly, he once again found himself standing on the tiny bridge and looking out across the valley which had become so familiar to him. Never having been able to make his way across, he decided to set out now, while the strange woman was nowhere near him. He had only just stepped off the bridge when he felt a surprisingly heavy hand upon his shoulder and turned around to find the green eyes of the Knave's Thaumaturge, Isolde.

"Where is your uncle, Pen?" she sang. "Searching for something that belongs to me, I believe. You can find her if you find me." She turned from him and, beckoning, began to walk away. Pen tried to follow, but something was pulling him away, out of the valley and back into Honour's Rest. He fought against it, trying to focus on the green valley and the silver hair of the woman who was gradually disappearing into the distance.

"You idiot, Pen," he heard Marley say. "I bet you're

really achy if you've spent all night here."

Pen blinked his eyes open and saw that morning had arrived while he had been lost in his dreams. It took him a moment to work out where he was, and he gave Marley a tired smile, which his friend returned.

"So, what do you want to do then?" Marley asked, rubbing his hands together to mimic Napier. "We've got the whole place to ourselves."

"I know where Patrick O'Hare's daughter is," Pen replied, the dream coming back to him as he was reminded that his uncle was no longer at home.

"How?"

"There's this Knave's Thaumaturge. The one I was telling you about."

"Isolde?"

"That's her. I think she's using the girl as bait for my uncle, but she doesn't realise that he hasn't worked it out yet. I think we should go and find her."

"I don't think that Napier wanted us to leave Honour's Rest," Marley said, sounding less sure.

"He won't mind, especially not once we've got the girl back." Pen clenched his teeth slightly as he realised that Marley still wasn't convinced. "Don't come then, but I think I've got a decent chance of getting this girl back to her father so I'm going to head off this morning."

"We can't drive."

"Then we'll hitchhike." Pen refused to be defeated and, at last, Marley nodded.

There was definitely something adventurous about the idea of hitchhiking their way through northern Scotland but, as they wandered along the road without seeing anyone, Pen began to question the wisdom of his selected mode of transport. He didn't share these concerns with Marley, who would probably have taken it as the perfect excuse to return to the comfort of Honour's Rest and read his books.

At last, Pen almost threw himself in front of a lorry with his thumb waving frantically in the air, and the vehicle slowed to a standstill. He knew that his age wouldn't be questioned, he had always looked older than his years, and he did the talking and pretended that Marley was his younger cousin.

"I'm only going to Inverness," the lorry driver said with a slight smile as his two young passengers told him they were heading north. "I'll make sure I drop you somewhere you'll get a lift."

He didn't speak much after that, which was useful as it gave Pen chance to try and outline his plan. He tried to speak in a kind of code, but he gave up after a while and stopped talking about the 'enemy' and the 'quarry', which was a bit disappointing, but Marley hadn't been able to understand what he was talking about.

The lorry driver dropped them off on a busy road just outside Inverness.

"I hope you find Isolde," he called as they thanked him and slammed the door. They could hear him laughing to himself and Pen wasn't sure whether he was grateful or annoyed that the stranger hadn't realised just how serious the issue was.

They soon found another lift, this time with a man who was heading back to a village called Halkirk after a family wedding. Unlike the lorry driver, he had clearly picked the boys up with the intention of having someone to talk to, and it was Pen who ended up in the front seat having to try to hold a conversation.

"I didn't really want to go," the man said, after introducing himself to Pen as Luke. "It's just that she's my only sister, you know?"

"Yeah," Pen said sympathetically, wishing the man would just be quiet and drive.

"And she's been left at the altar once before."

The conversation continued until Pen could have recited Luke's family history, including the fact that his parents had died when he was four and he had been raised by his grandparents, who had also died during the past few years. He had been married but his wife had left him because she found him depressing, and his former brother-in-law had just gone off the rails because his only child had run away from home.

Pendragon felt as though the will to live was gradually leaving him and he wondered why they had chosen to hitchhike instead of taking the bus or train. Surely he would have been able to find money somewhere in Honour's Rest?

"Where's Halkirk?" he asked, suddenly nervous that the man's journey would take them miles off-course.

"It's just near Thurso," Luke replied. "Where's it you're going again?"

"I've – ah– I've forgotten the name," Pen lied, hoping that the man wouldn't be able to pick up on the change in tone. "It's a valley. There's loads of trees, and a river with a little suspension bridge..."

"That sounds like Dunbeath Strath," Luke said. "It's along this road. I'll be able to drop you off on the way. There's no one lives there any more though. Just an empty farmhouse."

"Oh, no, we're not going to see anyone like that," Pen replied, trying to think on his feet. "It's more of a gathering, really."

"Oh, right," Luke said and, for a blissful moment, there was silence in the car. "What kind of gathering did you say it was?"

Oh, won't you please shut up? Pen wanted to scream, but he just smiled and said, "Young writers." The pun was too much for Marley, who gave a loud snort from the backseat, which Luke took to be a sign that he was feeling car sick.

"I always find that music helps," Luke said, and put the radio on. He didn't seem to want to talk over the top of the music, so Pen was able to enjoy the scenery for the first time while they listened to *Sunshine Hits of the 80s*. He recognised snatches of the scenery from travelling to Orkney with his uncle, but most of it felt new to him until they reached the hairpin bends on one of the hills. Unlike Napier, Luke slowed right down and took them so cautiously that Pen was slightly afraid they might just roll back down.

About ten minutes later, Luke pulled over in a wooded area beside what seemed to be a recycling centre. "Well," he said with a sigh, "this is where you go to the Strath." He pointed to a road leading down to a pounding river. "Thanks for the company."

Having disposed of his passengers, Luke pulled away and disappeared. Pen couldn't contain his laughter any longer and, for a while, he and Marley tried to improve on each other's impressions of Luke's miserable drawl and the list of gloomy facts he had given them about his family.

"And then," Marley choked, laughing so hard that he was bent double, "when you said 'young writers', I thought I would actually die. Thank God he turned the radio on so that he couldn't hear me!"

Pen knew it was cruel to laugh at the man's misfortunes, but he couldn't help himself. It was as though the reality of what he had done in running away from Honour's Rest had finally dawned on him and laughter was the only thing which could hold fear at bay.

At last, however, they began to wander down the Strath. It was a hot, humid day and, in the damp stickiness, midges had descended in swarms, so the two boys were separated by a biting grey cloud swirling around their heads. Pen could hardly look up for fear of the insects getting in his eyes, mouth or up his nose. He wondered if it would be possible to use the Rite to create a breeze but was nervous about using it in case he did it wrong and ended up bringing a hurricane down on Dunbeath. Instead, he waved his arms in front of him and sacrificed them to the midges so his head was spared.

Everything was green and lush but, for the first while, they saw no sign of a suspension bridge and Pen began to wonder if he had described it correctly. He would have a terrible job explaining the adventure to Napier if they had just gone to some random place in the middle of the North Highlands. Once he caught sight of the bridge, however, he wasn't as relieved as he thought he would be. The reality of the task ahead struck him like a heavy blow to the stomach.

The bridge was quite frightening to walk across, and Pen insisted that he go ahead of Marley, who had been dragged into the adventure against his will. As soon as they stepped foot on it, it started to sway dangerously, and Pen's nerves were not helped by the sign stating that the original bridge had been washed away during a storm. The only way he could keep going was to stare straight ahead and remind himself of their noble purpose.

As soon as he was at the opposite side, Pen felt a hand on his shoulder just like in his dream, only this time he knew it was Marley. He turned around to smile at his friend but found himself staring straight into the hooded green eyes of Isolde, whose chestnut hair seemed to be blocking out the light. She looked older than anyone he had ever seen and the nails on her outstretched hand were long and twisted.

For all the world, Pen thought for a hysterical second, *she looks like a fairy-tale witch who could have already snatched Marley away to a gingerbread house in the woods.*

Marley had disappeared.

Pen's eyes widened as he tried frantically to channel the Rite, but the heel of Isolde's hand struck his chin and he found himself falling backwards into the river. But the river never came. Instead, there was a thick, strong-smelling darkness which reeked of rotting vegetables and animal waste. He couldn't see if Marley was there but, somewhere in the encumbering shadows, something began to move towards him.

Chapter Ten

Imprisoned

The Thing in the darkness was still moving towards him, sometimes slithering and, at other times, scurrying like an enormous rat against the straw-covered floor. As certain as he was that there was something in the prison with him, Pen knew he was the only human being there. Whatever it was, it didn't seem to be coming any closer but, every so often, Pen would catch a glimpse of a flash of red, as though the Thing's eyes were flaring. Then, just when the room went silent, he would see some remnant of light reflecting in long, sharp teeth, while the sound came from the other side of the space.

Pen tried to push himself into the corner but, even as he crawled backwards, it suddenly occurred to him that he was somewhere extremely high up. He imagined shuffling backwards, away from the Thing but, instead of finding the comfort of anything solid, simply falling a great distance. He tried to envisage a barrier, as he had done on the cliffs in Orkney, but found that attempting to access the Rite just made him feel even weaker, as he couldn't do anything. His left hand was wet and sticky, and Pen realised that some of the stitches had burst.

The Thing moved again, but this time it sounded heavier: a giant predator pacing the floor in anticipation of helpless prey. Pen tried to remember how he had laughed with Marley about the man in the car. He couldn't even remember his name now. Was it O'Hare? His thoughts seemed to be burning through his mind as though they were being scratched across his brain by a sparkler, which fizzled desperately before abandoning him to the darkness.

His eyes felt stretched and dry but, even though he couldn't see anything with them open, closing them would make him more vulnerable. Those occasional glimpses at least confirmed that he wasn't just imagining there was something there. He rubbed his eyes to try and wake himself up, as though it was simply tiredness which was making him imagine things, but his left hand left a smear of blood across his face and some went into his mouth. As he swallowed, he retched as the thick, metallic-tasting liquid slipped unwillingly down his throat. Pen thought of the silver sickle and began to wish he had something that he could use as a weapon. What on earth would his mother think to that?

For a moment, he thought he heard the Thing speaking with his mother's voice, but he told himself that he was imagining it. Or was he imagining all these things? Once again, the thoughts sped through his mind, and now Pen tried to cover up his ears to avoid them. He didn't want to hear the panic in his mind which reminded him how he had led Marley into danger, or hear Napier's voice, sounding more disappointed than angry or upset. He remembered him saying that he should only be summoned if it was a matter of life or death but, although Pen was fairly sure this qualified, he couldn't remember if he had ever known how to summon someone using the Rite. He began to will his uncle to hear him and come looking for him, but the sound of the Thing sliding across the floor towards him stopped him in his tracks.

The darkness seemed to be thickening. Now, Pen was having to take heaving gasps of air, but the smell of rotting vegetables was making him feel sick. He found himself considering that this should have been how he felt at the bottom of the loch when he had ridden the kelpie down to the watery depths. He couldn't see, or speak, or breathe. The acceptance that he was going to suffocate made him start thinking about the emptiness of death. He wished he had paid more attention to people who had tried to encourage him in spiritual thoughts, but he wondered if those people had ever found themselves locked in a dark prison with only the threat of something terrifying to keep them company. Well, maybe some of them, but none of the people he had ever met. Somewhere in the back of his mind was the story of a priest singing hymns in a Nazi death camp, but his voice wouldn't come so he couldn't vocalise so much as a nursery rhyme.

He reached out behind him to where he believed the great drop would be but could not feel anything. However, as his hands rested on the floor, he felt something that seemed like a cold face, still and hard in the darkness.

He became convinced that the smell surrounding him was a dead body, and he felt tears prickling his dry eyes. How did he end up in this situation? He couldn't find his voice to sob, but hot tears rolled down his cheeks in patterns dictated by drying blood and dirt. The Thing shuffled towards him, now sounding all the world like a person stumbling blindly, with no sight or thought but one determined purpose.

Pen could feel his fear getting the better of him, and his heart was beating so loudly that he was certain the Thing was being attracted by the noise, and so fast that it was making him feel light-headed. In his fourteen years, he had never passed out until he had gone to live with Napier and now he wondered if it would happen again. He had always been so unshakable, it had been commented on by all his teachers since he had started primary school, but now he felt as though he was losing his mind, as though it was dissipating into the darkness around him and only strengthening the Thing.

Perhaps, he thought with a slight new lease of life, it was all a test to see if he could regain his self-control under such challenging circumstances. He cleared his throat and the sound nearly made him jump out of his skin. He had not realised how silent the room had been, as though all the noise from the Thing had been happening at a great distance, or only in his mind.

"Marley?" he whispered. As he spoke, he felt himself being pulled upwards, flying through the air until he landed once again on the grassy bank beside the bridge. Isolde, now a beautiful young woman with a mane of silver hair, looked at him with a smile dancing around her red lips.

"Impressive, Pendragon Devon," she said, nodding her head slightly. Pen just glared at her, hoping he could make his feelings known without speaking and allowing his fear to show. "There are few people your age who would have been able to break through that."

Pen wanted to ask what she meant, what strange prison he had been trapped in, but he didn't dare speak in case it was the buried sobs which escaped before any words. He looked around for Marley but could see no trace of his friend.

"Oh dear," Isolde said, her voice as silver as her hair. "You are going to have to make this a little harder for me. I think you would be better at hiding your fear if you spoke the words instead of just thinking them. Napier still has a great deal to teach you."

"How do you know my uncle?"

Isolde tilted her head and looked at him, her smile dropping but her gaze as firm as it had been. "I know him from long ago. From before you were born. He killed the man I was in love with."

Pen sat silently on the bank, staring at the woman before him. For a moment, he found himself feeling sorry for her, but then he remembered what his uncle had said about killing Knave's Thaumaturges who threatened the safety of others. That must have been what happened.

"Oh, what misplaced confidence," Isolde scoffed, and Pen looked up at her. "You see; this was when we were all your age. Napier, being who he is, had chosen three deputy apprentices. I notice you have only selected one thus far."

"Yes," Pen replied. His voice was hoarse, but it seemed to distract the Knave's Thaumaturge from looking into his thoughts and seeing his fear and uncertainty.

"Oh, very good," Isolde laughed. "You do have a voice." She sat down on the bank beside him and began to pluck blades of grass from the ground and slice them into narrow strips with her fingernails. "Well, there was Napier, who had been selected very young; me; Erlend, who I have no doubt you have already met, given you have appointed his son; and Ramin."

"Ramin?" Pen repeated, a memory stirring in his mind of when he had heard the name before.

"Yes. Ramin was by far the most talented of any of us. He ought to have been chosen," Isolde spat the words out and threw aside the handful of grass. "But no, it was Napier. And, for the most part, we enjoyed growing up together. Napier played everything by the rules, Erlend was funny, I was beautiful, and Ramin was brave."

"You *were* beautiful," Pen snapped, trying to hurt the woman before him, but she just laughed.

"You think that I care about my appearance? No. Why should I? Youth was the price I paid to meet again with the man I loved."

"After he was dead?"

"After your uncle killed him, yes. But he was never dead to me. Or in this place, where we had been happiest. He died one week after his fifteenth birthday. That is what your uncle did. I had to choose the path of the Knave's Rite to make sure I could see him again."

"That's barbaric," Pen snapped, and for a moment he thought his uncle had spoken through him. He had never used the word 'barbaric' in his life.

"It doesn't matter to me what you think," Isolde replied. "I have faced worse condemnation than from a fourteen-year-old boy. I live now for one purpose only: to cause pain to the man who condemned me to this life. Your uncle."

"You're just a twisted old bat," Pen snarled, jumping to his feet. He could hear Erlend warning Napier against 'forgetting what happened to Ramin' and it made him wonder if the woman was speaking the truth, but he didn't dare reveal the thoughts which were spinning through his head.

"Oh, darling!" Isolde was laughing so hard that tears were forming in her beautiful green eyes. "You speak like a little child. It's really endearing."

"How did my uncle kill Ramin?" Pen demanded. Isolde stopped laughing and looked at him curiously for a moment before replying.

"He poisoned him."

"I don't know why you think I would believe you," Pen shouted, although everything pointed to the fact that Isolde was telling the truth. Most of all, it explained why Erlend had been so desperate for his son to avoid the role of deputy apprentice because of what had happened to the mysterious Ramin.

"Well, you don't have to," Isolde said. She looked bored now, and Pen regretted losing his temper. Without the ability to channel the Rite because of whatever had happened during the past few hours, his arguments were limited to screaming and shouting.

Pen took a deep breath to calm himself. "You're just jealous, aren't you? What a sad existence. So jealous of the power Napier can wield that you've lost sight of everything. I don't know the truth about Ramin or how he died, but I'm willing to bet he wouldn't be impressed if he could see you now."

His instinct had been right, Isolde was far more annoyed by his calm and well thought out argument than she had been at his screaming and shouting. He remembered standing up to Justin Murchison in the corridor on that fateful morning at school and telling him that he would end up in prison if he kept going. As he faced Isolde, the feeling of terrified courage was multiplied.

"How dare you?" she hissed, and Pen just grinned. When Isolde spoke again, anger was clearly getting the better of her. "Perhaps it would have been better if the Kashkaan had silenced you properly."

"The what?" Pen did not need Isolde's explanation to know that she was referring to the Thing in the prison.

"The Kashkaan is darkness," Isolde said, getting to her feet. She began to walk slowly around Pen, who could feel her sickly breath against his neck as she kept speaking. "It doesn't live, so it can't die. It exists only to subject its enemies to so much fear that the Rite leaves them, and they are defenceless. No one sees the Kashkaan. It is darkness. But it will take the form of anything it thinks will cause you terror." Each time she spoke a hard consonant, Pen felt spit hitting his skin. The closeness made him balk. "It feeds from the Rite, from what makes you different from any other silly... little... boy." She raised her hand and, once again, Pen found himself crashing through the earth and into the darkness.

The prison smelt different this time but no less suffocating. There was something else different too, and Pen became certain he wasn't the only person there.

"Hello?" he whispered, relieved to find his voice still working. "Hello? Who's there?"

"Me."

He heard Marley's voice, but the word was little more than a sob. Pen got onto his hands and knees and began to fumble around in the dark, trying to find the quickest way to his friend and certain he would fall over if he tried to walk.

"Say something again, Marley," he hissed. "And stay still so I can find you."

"Where are we?" Marley sobbed again.

Pen didn't answer, but he did manage to pinpoint where his companion's voice was coming from and, a few seconds later, his bloody left hand met with Marley's shoe. He could feel him shaking. For a while they sat together, and Pen let Marley cry onto his shoulder. He didn't know what to say, whether to admit that all Mr Shipperbottom's concerns for his son had been justified, or whether to tell him what the strange sounds in the room were. But Pen could imagine his mother reminding him that he shouldn't say or do anything just because he could, so he kept the terrifying knowledge to himself.

"What happened to you?" he asked after a while, and he felt Marley tense slightly.

"This," he replied, and Pen felt Marley take his hand. He pulled away as he realised that the third finger on Marley's left hand was missing.

"Oh God, Marley," Pen sobbed. He felt sickeningly responsible, remembering how he had persuaded his friend to leave the safety of Honour's Rest. He let go of Marley's hand and, despite the pitch darkness, Pen covered his face so that his tears were hidden.

"Don't feel guilty," Marley said, swallowing his own sobs as he attempted to comfort Pen. "I knew what I was letting myself in for when I agreed to be your deputy. My dad's always made it very clear what a dangerous job it is, so it's not like I went into it blind."

"Why did she do it?"

"I wouldn't let her inside my head," Marley replied. "She wanted to know why Napier hadn't come looking for her, and who had alerted him to the fact that the girl was missing."

"How did you stop her?"

"Something my mum taught me." Pen thought his friend had shrugged his shoulders as he had spoken. Marley just wouldn't be able to credit his mother too fully while he continued to hold her responsible for his inclination towards the Knave's Rite. "I suppose the easiest way to explain it is that you just imagine something really terrifying for the other person."

"But how did you know what would frighten Isolde?" Pen asked. Although he still felt guilty, he couldn't help but be impressed by his friend's control of the Rite.

"She was shouting and screaming at me, trying to find out about Napier. Clearly the best way to frighten her was for her to look into my mind and see Napier defeating her. It worked. She was fuming." Marley's voice was starting to shake again, and Pen was sure that he was crying. "She held my finger over a candle flame and asked me to answer her. It was awful. I don't know if she had made the flame hotter or more powerful by the Rite, but it felt like it was burning straight through me."

"It was burnt off?" Pen whispered.

"No. She got tired of torturing me. I think that she could tell it wasn't getting anywhere, so she told me I had to pay a blood forfeit for my dad's actions. She cut it straight off with a curved knife." Pen felt Marley trembling beside him. "She's insane, Pen. I don't know why, but she's totally insane."

After Marley's explanation, they sat in silence for a while. In his mind, Pen thought he could hear movement above them, but he was certain they were buried deep in the earth, so it must just have been in his imagination. He wondered whether he should warn Marley about the Kashkaan or explain what had happened to Ramin. *No, he reminded himself, you're not going to worry Marley anymore.* Hadn't he already suffered enough because Pen had been so certain they would be able to waltz into this place and rescue the girl, like dated heroes in an old film?

As he was thinking, Pen thought he saw a light some way in the distance coming slowly towards them. Marley seemed to have passed out and, in the darkness, Pen had no way of knowing what the time was. The light was definitely moving closer, and he got to his feet, being careful not to wake Marley. He was certain this was something he wanted to meet standing up and, although his initial thought was of the Kashkaan, he realised that his overriding emotion was curiosity, not fear.

As the light came closer, it seemed to diminish, and Pen realised that he was looking at the form of a girl who was probably a couple of years younger than he was. She held a wavering candle in her hand and her almost luminously pale skin was reflecting the candlelight. As she moved up to him, Pen noticed that a bandage was tied around her eyes and she was having to feel her way across the room.

"Hello," she whispered. "Are you Pendragon Devon?"

"Yes," Pen replied, taking the girl's hand and guiding

her safely across the rest of the room. "Who are you? Where did you get the candle?"

"Niamh O'Hare. I always have the candle."

"Are you dead?" Pen felt the words slip from his mouth before he had chance to realise how ridiculous they were.

"No."

"Why do you have a candle if you're blind?" *Another stupid question,* Pen thought to himself, but Niamh didn't seem to think anything of it.

"I wasn't always blind," she whispered. "When Isolde realised I could harness the Rite visually, she blinded me."

"Why would she take you?"

Niamh shrugged her shoulders.

"Come and sit down," he said, but the girl shook her head.

"If Isolde finds me here, I think she'll do worse than take the Rite away from me. I just knew I needed to speak to someone from outside. It feels like I've been in this prison for so long."

The candlelight caught in Niamh's smile before she turned on her heel and began to walk away, to wherever she had come from. Pen watched as she disappeared into the shadows. The light faded along with her, leaving him in the thick, cloying darkness once again.

Chapter Eleven

The Truth About Ramin

For a long time after Niamh disappeared, Pen kept his eyes fixed on that patch of darkness, willing her to return. He swung from being concerned about her to being annoyed that she hadn't offered them the candle. She couldn't really benefit from it, and he and Marley were both still enveloped in darkness. Marley wasn't stirring, and Pen didn't know whether it was time to sleep, but something in his instincts kept him as awake and alert as possible.

His hand found Marley's wrist and he tried to feel a pulse to reassure him that his friend was going to be alright. It was something he had always been bad at and, for a sickening moment, he couldn't find any beat, before he realised that his fingers had been too far up Marley's arm. The rhythm made him feel better and, as Marley slept on, Pen was reassured to know he wasn't the only living thing buried however far beneath the earth. He could hear nothing else and was beginning to wonder whether this was the same prison as before, as the Kashkaan had not made any reappearance since his conversation with Isolde.

After a while, Pen became positive he could hear voices talking a long way above him. He couldn't make out any words, but the fact that there was life, human life, within earshot went some way to making him feel better.

Pen began to consider what he had learnt that day already. It seemed so long since he had awoken with his head on the desk in his study and enthusiastically persuaded Marley to hitchhike their way up to northern Scotland. He wondered what the lorry driver was doing now. He must have finished his shift, and perhaps he had returned home to a busy family. Pen smiled as he imagined a hoard of tattooed children, all as warm-faced and silent as their father, and perhaps a wife who, in Pen's mind, looked like a madam out of an old Clint Eastwood film. He wasn't sure why that would be.

Then the other man, who they had laughed at so much for his depressing outlook on life and his eagerness to share his tragic stories with the two total strangers. He wondered if Luke had questioned why the two boys had wanted to be dropped off in such a remote corner of the country, when there was clearly no convention going on. But maybe he wasn't the sort of person who would worry about anyone else's problems but his own. He was probably sitting in his living room, alone and drinking wine straight from the bottle. Pen smiled a little bitterly as he thought of the two drivers who had been so instrumental in getting them to the place they desperately wished to reach, only so they could be imprisoned and tortured.

But the person who flickered in and out of his thoughts the most was Ramin, the boy just a few weeks older than him who had been killed such a long time ago, and whose death had sent his three friends into a pattern of sadness, insanity and anger which had damaged them all in different ways. Pen wished he had pushed his uncle to tell him more, instead of just letting the subject go when it became clear that Napier didn't want to discuss it. He should have sought the answers and made his uncle tell him what had become of the boy, who must have been closer to him than his own brother.

Pen's father must have had a strange upbringing, knowing there was something odd about him, but even odder about his big brother. For the first time, Pen wondered why his father and his uncle had been given surnames as their Christian names. Napier and Jarvis. They must have been picked on when they were at school. Or perhaps Napier hadn't gone to school?

The voices above him were becoming more animated, and sometimes the shouts gave way to angry screaming. A man and a woman were having a raging argument, and Pen knew that they must be putting a lot of energy into it for him to hear it all the way down in the bowels of the earth. Then, when the voices went quiet for a while, the silence was filled by the sound of something crashing which, as it continued, began to make dirt fall in flurries from the ceiling of the dungeon. Marley stayed asleep throughout and, every so often, Pen would look again for reassurance from the steady pulse in his friend's wrist.

The crashes were becoming louder and Pen shouted up in the hope of attracting attention but no response came. Perhaps it was workmen, using heavy machinery to dig into the ground. Pen shook his head. He couldn't bear to believe they were anything other than rescuers, who would pull them out of the strange darkness and bring them once again into the sunlight he had never fully appreciated. He made a silent vow to be thankful for feeling the sun or wind on his face, and never forget the stifling darkness of the prison. That was somewhat reliant on him getting out alive and, as the voices and crashes faded away, Pen began to wonder whether that was just too remote a possibility.

Just as he closed his eyes with a strangely relaxed acceptance of his fate, a louder crash struck the earth above them, and Pen leapt to his feet as a slither of daylight appeared. Very awkwardly, he picked Marley up in a fireman's lift and, with every fibre of his being, he imagined a ladder which could take him to the surface. He was certain someone was helping him with this, as the ladder appeared and he began to climb, with considerable difficulty but a resolve which made him believe he could achieve anything.

Once he got to the top, he felt tears prickle in his eyes. He knew he could blame it on the sudden exposure to the air, which was cold in what appeared to be dawn, but what was really responsible was the man who stood in front of him. Napier looked exhausted, as though he had just run a marathon and then been told to walk home, but he smiled at his nephew and carefully lifted Marley out of his grasp. Once Pen was free, he instinctively began to go down the ladder again.

"What on earth are you doing?" Napier demanded. "Don't tell me you liked it down there."

Pen shook his head with a slight smile. "No, but the girl you're looking for – Niamh O'Hare – she's down there."

"Leave her for now, Pendragon."

"No!" Pen couldn't believe what his uncle was asking of him. He had always been taught to stand up for people who were threatened, and this girl was living in darkness, cut off even from the Rite, the one thing to give her any hope or company. He continued to climb down the ladder, but suddenly found his feet wouldn't move any further down.

"I am sorry, Pendragon," Napier said, "but I cannot let you return down there. Marley is hurt and needs to get to a healer or a hospital. Niamh is alive, and there are things about her which you should know before you offer her friendship. Isolde will not kill her or harm her anymore."

"She's down there in the dark!"

"That darkness does not bother her, Pendragon." Pen noted the repeated use of his name and realised that Napier was trying to plead with him in the only way he knew how. "For me, this instant, my priority is to get Marley some help. And you. Your hand is worse than before."

Pen looked down at his left hand for the first time and saw, beneath the dirt and blood, that three of the stitches had burst and the wound was an angry red. He had to accept that his uncle was right but, as he climbed back to the top of the ladder and walked silently to the waiting truck, he felt he was betraying the person he was by not rescuing Niamh from the dungeon.

Marley had woken up and insisted on stumbling to the vehicle by himself, although Napier kept a firm grip on his arm to stop him from falling. He did not speak and every time he looked down at his three-fingered hand, he retched as though he was about to be sick.

"We need to get away from the Strath," Napier said, as he and Pen helped Marley into the truck and then clambered in after him. "As soon as we're safely away, we can stop and get cleaned up."

He drove away, past the hairpin bends, which he took so fast Pen had to screw up his eyes in case they were about to go flying off the edge of the cliff. Once they had driven a short way further, Napier pulled into a lay-by.

"There's a first-aid kit in the glove compartment," he said, pointing it out to Pen, who took out the green bag and looked into it. "First, clean your hand."

Pen did as he was told. It was hot and extremely painful to touch, but Napier was looking at him impatiently, so he didn't dare waste any time. As soon as the swollen wound was cleaned, Napier pulled his nephew's hand towards him and looked at it.

"That looks sore," he said, quite unsympathetically. "You're going to need to get it seen to. I can't take you both into the hospital though, I'll probably have Child Services around, so we'll take Marley to the Allans' place. Mrs Allan is a superb healer. You will just need to get that re-stitched."

Pen nodded and stayed silent as his uncle bandaged his hand with more precision than gentleness. He tried to use the Rite to stop the pain, but it only took the edge off. They had to double-back to get to the Allans' house and Pen got the impression that his uncle was thinking on his feet. When he saw the sign for the village 'Halkirk', Pen couldn't hide his surprise.

"This is where the guy who gave us our last lift lived!"

"I know," Napier replied, and Pen scowled at him.

"I wish you wouldn't read my thoughts. It made me very vulnerable against Isolde."

"Yes, that is something we have to work on," Napier agreed. "But I am not reading your thoughts now." He didn't explain his mysterious statement but, when they pulled up outside the small house and a young couple came out, Pen realised how his uncle knew.

Luke was there, looking far happier than he had in the car, and he offered his hand to Pen. "It's great to meet you properly, Pendragon," he said, with a broad smile. "Sorry, I couldn't resist winding you both up. I couldn't believe you lapped up as much of that stuff as you did! You were really challenging my resources in the imagination department! And you shouldn't look so shocked. I guessed who you were. Young *writers*!" He laughed and Pen found himself laughing too, despite the sense of overwhelming embarrassment.

"You'd have been in far worse trouble if I hadn't contacted Luke about something completely unrelated," Napier snapped. "We can talk about that later. Now though, I need to know if we can leave this boy in your care, Felicity."

Pen helped Marley out of the truck and Luke's wife looked him over for a second before nodding her head. "That's Erlend's boy, isn't it? Take him inside please, Luke."

Luke patted Pen on the shoulder and then lifted Marley up and carried him into the house with no apparent difficulty.

"Well," Felicity continued, "can you stay, Napier?"

"No, thank you," Napier replied. "Pendragon has an exciting date with some sutures." He thanked the Allans and then he and Pen went back to the truck.

They drove in silence for some time and Pen found himself drifting off into the sleep which had been missing during the night. The pain in his hand kept waking him but he was so tired he was soon able to find sleep again.

"Now," Napier said. Pen awoke to see they were just crossing the large bridge which served as the northern gate to Inverness. "You're absolutely filthy, so we'll stop at the supermarket. You can get cleaned up in the toilets and I'll buy you a new set of clothes. I really don't think it's wise for you to attract any more attention than you already are doing at the hospital."

It was the same doctor on duty, but this time she didn't seem as friendly. She was clearly annoyed that Pen had done something resulting in his stitches coming open, and stood over him while he read a leaflet called *How Should I Care for My Stitches?* She also prescribed him a course of very strong antibiotics and lectured him on the dangers of blood poisoning. Napier only reinforced what she was saying by nodding his head at various intervals, which made Pen furious. His uncle was aware that, even if they had not been sensible, his intentions had been good.

"I'm not going to call your parents," Napier said when they finally got back to Honour's Rest. "It won't do any good for them to worry about these things. Go up to my study and settle down on the chaise longue. I have a couple of things to do before I make it upstairs."

Pen did as he was told and, a few minutes later, he

was lying on the chaise longue, his thickly bandaged hand resting against his chest and his eyelids heavy with exhaustion and the effects of the medicine. However, as he watched his uncle enter, Pen tried to force himself to stay awake to ask the questions which were burning within him.

"What happened to Ramin?"

Napier sat down at his desk. "I thought it was too much to hope that she wouldn't speak to you," he sighed, and Pen realised that he had never seen his uncle look so sad. "Against the suggestions of the last Rendelf, I appointed three deputy apprentices. He thought no one should have more than two, but they were my three greatest friends. Yes, I'm afraid that did exclude your father. As you know, there is a big age difference between us and, due to the way that the Rite manifested itself, we don't have much in common."

Pen shrugged. Staying awake felt like the most strenuous exercise he had ever done, but he needed to know the answers to stop the questions from haunting him.

"About three months after I had taken the Choice to become the next Rendelf and one week after Ramin had chosen to become a Just Thaumaturge, we did something not dissimilar from what you and Marley did yesterday. We went to right some wrongs by taking on a Knave's Thaumaturge who had killed a child. It all went extremely well. Between us, we could wield the Rite very powerfully and, unlike you and Marley, we successfully overpowered the thaumaturge and, I'm afraid, it was inevitable that I should kill him."

"When you were fifteen?"

"I have told you before, Pendragon, you must be prepared to kill if you wish to become Rendelf. Anyway, we all made a move to leave the house, but the Knave's Thaumaturge had sealed the door with the Rite, so the only way we could open it was to drink poison. I believed that, if we got to a healer fast enough, any poison would be curable. Ramin and I were the two most accomplished thaumaturges of the group. We agreed that one of us would have to drink the poison and the other would have to go for help, while Isolde and Erlend made their own way out."

"Did you make Ramin drink it?"

"*Make* him?" Napier sounded incredulous. "If that is what Isolde told you then she is not only soiling my reputation, but the memory of the boy she claimed to love. It was my responsibility to get them all out of the mess I had created, so I was the one to take the poison. I was also the strongest of the four of us, so it made sense that I drink it. Ramin agreed but told me Erlend and Isolde deserved to be given the chance to have their input. I turned around to explain what was going on. The hesitation was, quite literally, fatal. Ramin took the poison and drank it. It opened the door so we could get out, but we didn't have chance to get help. Erlend is now an excellent healer but, back then, he had only just started to experiment with that aspect of the Rite."

"So Ramin died?"

"Yes," Napier whispered, staring out of the window. "He died. He wasn't angry with us though, he managed to make that... quite clear. We had to return him to Honour's Rest and explain what had happened. It was the most painful day of my life, despite anything which has happened since. Isolde took her Choice a month later and opted to follow the Knave's Rite. She was perfectly open about the fact that she held me responsible for what had happened to Ramin and, at the time, I was foolish enough to believe her. It was Erlend, the youngest of our group, who convinced me that it had been Ramin's bravery which meant he was the one to pay the ultimate price."

Pen wiped his non-bandaged hand over his face and was surprised that there were no tears there. He thought he had been crying. His mind was clouded, and it was beginning to affect his vision, meaning he could only focus on a small part of the room around him.

"Pendragon," Napier said gently, "you look absolutely shattered. Get some sleep."

Although he did not need another invitation to succumb to the tiredness which had been overcoming him for the past three hours, Pen knew there was another answer he needed before he could allow himself to drift off to sleep.

"Why wouldn't you let me go back for Niamh, when you had left to save her?"

"You saw her, didn't you?" Napier said. "What did you notice about her?"

"She was frightened. Isolde had blinded her."

"Anything else?"

"She had a candle. Even though she didn't need it."

"Her candle is very important, Pendragon. She has a very interesting parentage," Napier whispered, his voice only serving to make Pen feel more tired. "I am afraid that, twelve years ago, urgency demanded I cut corners, which means my hands are now tied."

"I thought she was the daughter of Patrick O'Hare?"

"No, she was adopted by the O'Hares as a baby. Isolde is her mother."

For a moment, Pen's mind swelled with the revelation, but then he felt his head fall back and he couldn't avoid sleep any longer. The last thing he remembered of that strange day was the sound of Napier's pen scratching across a piece of paper.

Chapter Twelve

Memories Made, Lost and Changed

The events and revelations of that strange week in August were discussed less and less as the summer gave way to autumn. By the time October arrived, and with it the promise of Pen's fifteenth birthday, it was hardly referenced at all. Marley had stayed with the Allans for three days and then returned home to Orkney for a month to stay with his parents, leading to one of the angriest rows Pen had ever witnessed. Bernadette had arrived on the doorstep of Honour's Rest one evening with the expressed intention of telling Napier exactly what she thought to the fact her son was now one finger short. Napier remained patient to a point but, after Pen had been sent to his study, he heard both parties shouting. He knew that neither of them would use the Rite as Bernadette couldn't risk the Knave's

Thaumaturge in her to jeopardise her family's safety.

Marley and Erlend had been apologetic for her behaviour when they arrived three weeks later for Marley to stay at Honour's Rest until his birthday in mid-December. Napier assured them that Bernadette was perfectly within her rights to make her feelings known, but Marley had been extremely embarrassed by his mother's behaviour. He didn't dwell on the loss of his finger, apart from the fact that it made him feel, in his own words, that he must have achieved something in making Isolde so angry.

After Pen had spent the two weeks following the adventure almost drunk on painkillers and antibiotics, he had appreciated the opportunity to have some time alone with Napier, who worked with him to ensure that people would not so easily be able to enter his mind. It was really more like lessons of the human condition, as he learnt to spot the things in people which would make them afraid. Napier used himself as an example and Pen learnt to concentrate on the story which haunted his uncle, when Ramin had died from drinking poison to set his friends free. After a while, Pen didn't need to focus so hard, as Napier became more reluctant to read his mind.

The months which had passed saw both Pen and Marley being encouraged to recognise their roles, and Pen could now command the Rite far better than when he had set off to face Isolde in summer. However, he did not feel the need to attempt it again, although Niamh O'Hare rarely strayed far from his thoughts, as though her candle flickered always in the back of his mind.

As autumn began to swallow up the summer, it became increasingly dark in the mornings and the evening light did not last long either, leaving several hours which were plunged into darkness. As a result, Pen could no longer rely on broad rays of daylight to wake him in the morning and started trusting his alarm to wake him up in time for breakfast. It did nothing to improve his temper and, on one day in early October, he was horrified to be rudely awoken when someone came and switched his light on at only five o'clock.

"Go away," he mumbled, turning away from the door and burying his head in the pillow.

"Pendragon, we're heading out in half an hour, so if you want some breakfast then I would suggest you get up now. Marley has been awake for twenty minutes already. I knew you weren't listening last night."

He sighed as he heard his uncle close the door and walk down the spiral staircase. Napier was right: he hadn't been listening. Pen had just mastered the ability to create and hold fire, and he had been showing this off to Marley with proud enthusiasm. Now, he couldn't remember what they had decided to do today, although he was impressed that Marley had managed to pay attention to both him and Napier.

Pen couldn't actually stomach any breakfast so early in the morning, so just sat down at the table drinking as much coffee as he could manage. By the time Napier came and fetched him to leave, his hands were shaking with the overload of caffeine, but he finally felt awake.

They took the truck again as there were three of them, and Pen sat between his uncle and his best friend, playing with the stereo and, when he thought Napier wouldn't notice, using the Rite to tune into his preferred radio channels. It had been during the past two months that he had managed to develop his abilities to a point where he felt confident using the Rite without worrying that something terrible would happen. He was, however, painfully aware that, whilst those dangers would disappear for most fifteen-year-old thaumaturges, he would continue to face them.

He knew that Napier wouldn't have been able to know his thoughts, but Pen still jumped when his uncle spoke. "It's not all as glamourous as having meetings with local or national governments or going to the United Nations. Most of the role of Rendelf is about ensuring that peace is maintained across the country, which is a big ask of one person. Over the next couple of weeks, we're going to go meet a couple of individuals who are on the At-Risk Register."

"There's an At-Risk Register?" Pen asked and, although Marley elbowed him sharply, it wasn't enough to stop Napier from throwing him an annoyed glance.

"You should learn to listen instead of show off, Pendragon," he snapped. "The At-Risk Register is made up of different thaumaturges who, for whatever reason, require an extra hand. They might be Just Thaumaturges who have suffered at the hands of the Knave's Rite, or something more mundane. They might be Knave's Thaumaturges who are descending into a life of crime. It gives the Rendelf – which will be you one day, so I hope you're listening – the opportunity to hear what is concerning them and let them know that their problems are not going unnoticed. And that help is available."

"So do we help them too?"

"No, no," Napier replied, waving his hand away from the steering wheel. "There are social workers who do that.

The Rendelf is responsible for keeping overall peace. But, say, if we go to someone's house and they tell us that they are having issues with a Knave's Thaumaturge, and then we visit three other people who all make the same claim. Well, that's a sure sign that we are going to need to visit that Knave's Thaumaturge."

"And are they always willing to let you in?" Marley asked, much to Pen's relief. Clearly this subject hadn't been discussed the night before.

"Not always, but they don't really have a choice about it. Most of the Rite that Knave's Thaumaturges would use to conceal themselves has been mastered by the Rendelf, so they cannot avoid a confrontation. It almost always goes better if they don't try to hide."

He pulled into the driveway of a neat little bungalow in a small village. It seemed odd to Pen that somewhere which so resembled his parents' home could house someone with the Rite. He had imagined them all to live in vast castles like Honour's Rest, or ancient sea-swept stone cottages like the Shipperbottoms'.

"This is where the Mackenzies live. They're an old couple, and they met when David – that's the husband – was evacuated during the war. The wife – Ishbel – was the daughter of the Knave's Thaumaturge he was placed with. When they eloped a few years later, he cursed them."

"You didn't tell me it's possible to curse someone!" Pen gasped.

"Not in the traditional sense of the word," Napier explained. "What Ishbel's father did was promise they would have an unhappy marriage. Until he died, he ensured his promise was kept. They had six children who all drowned on their fifth birthdays. Then he died and they had a surviving child, Charlotte."

"So, why are we here?"

"When someone is subjected to continuous abuse through the Knave's Rite, they become susceptible to it. Just like Knave's Thaumaturges who have made a Commitment find it much easier to break than those who are Just and opt-out. You have both experienced the Knave's Rite. You both know it is more penetrating than the Just."

Marley and Pen nodded silently, each remembering their own mistakes, and it was with these thoughts in mind that they clambered out the truck. Napier rapped on the door, which was opened by a very elderly man who beamed at him.

"Napier Devon," he said, shaking the Rendelf's hand.

"Hello, David. How's Ishbel?"

The old man looked sad for a second and, for one terrible moment, Pen thought that he was about to say that his wife had died. Then a second person appeared at the door, a small old lady with wispy white hair still in rollers.

"Oh, Napier," she said, as though she had never been more pleased to see anyone in her life. "You've found them."

Napier looked quizzically at her husband, who opened his mouth to explain but the old woman continued.

"Davy!" she cried, addressing Pen. "Look at you! You're all grown up! And you've come with Will too. Both looking so handsome. Oh, I wish that Charlotte was here. She didn't believe me when I said you'd come back. Come on inside, I'll get the kettle on."

As the old woman led them into the house and Pen

and Marley began to wish that they were risking their lives somewhere against a Knave's Thaumaturge, Napier turned to David.

"How long has she been like this?" he asked.

"About a year," David replied. "She's certain all the boys are coming back to her. I think it's all the struggling. That, and age. Finally catching up with her, I suppose." He sounded almost like a deflated balloon, and it dawned on Pen that Ishbel believed that her two young guests were, in fact, the children who had died. "You know she was diagnosed with Alzheimer's a couple of years ago, don't you?"

"Yes," Napier replied. He sat very still on the seat, with his hands clasped together and giving the distinct impression that there was nothing else on his mind, or even in the world, apart from David and Ishbel.

"Well, she's been having treatment from a nurse who's been coming round."

"A thaumaturge?"

"Yes. It was all going well until about a year ago, and then her memories started to go a bit, well, wrong. She's been looking out for the boys for the past twelve months. The postman had to stop coming because she was convinced he was Philip." David Mackenzie removed his glasses and brushed tears away from where they had gathered in the wrinkles around his eyes. "You know there's nothing I can do about any of this. But you could."

"It is not within my power to end her life," Napier said gently, reaching over and placing his hand on David's arm. "Until such action is legalised, it would be wrong of me to do anything. She seems happy enough."

As he was speaking, the old lady bustled in with a tea

tray, and Pen found himself surveying her with watery eyes. She took his tears to be relief at finally being home and moved over to put her arms around his shoulders.

"Oh, don't cry, Davy," she crooned. "I don't mind how long it's been, so neither should you. Your father was beginning to give up hope, but you know I didn't do that." Pen opened his mouth to speak, although he had no idea what to say, but Ishbel continued. "And don't worry, I know you're going to have to head off again, just like Philip. Just promise you'll come back."

"How are you then, Ishbel?" Napier asked, drawing her attention away from his dumbstruck nephew.

"I'm fine. Fine, David," she said, looking pointedly at her husband. "I miss the children, you know, but they keep coming back. Charlotte comes most weekends, and the boys are coming back now too." She gestured at Pen and Marley, who smiled awkwardly.

"Well," Napier said, his voice level and polite, and Pen wondered how he could betray so little emotion, "I'm glad to find you so happy, Ishbel. David, I know it's a long time past your retirement, but the truck has been making a bit of an odd noise. I wonder if you could have a quick look at it after we've had a drink?"

The old man nodded slowly.

"Oh, yes," Ishbel laughed, pouring tea for everyone there. "David won't pass on the opportunity to get his hands oily. Will you, David?"

She kept talking while they were sitting down. It became apparent to Pen that her whole world was different from theirs as she chatted about the jobs her children did. Philip was a postman, she said, John and Andrew were both teachers and Michael had joined the army. "Of course," she said, with a fond glance at the two boys, "Davy and Will are too young to be doing anything yet, but Charlotte's a nurse now with her own family." She didn't question the fact her daughter, the youngest of seven, now appeared to be the eldest.

Before Napier took David out to look at the truck, he volunteered the two boys for washing-up duties, and Pen was grateful as it meant that the old lady let them go into the kitchen alone while she walked steadily around the living room, plumping up the cushions. Neither Pen nor Marley felt much like talking as they did the job, but Pen didn't want Ishbel to take the silence to mean they were upset, so he put on the radio and found a channel which might take their minds off the surroundings.

An hour later, they left the house. Pen and Marley said nothing as Ishbel reminded them that they were always welcome and, if they could convince John and Andrew to come along too, she would be over the moon. Once they had pulled away and were driving down the open road, it was Napier who broke the silence, his voice still as calm and distant as it had been in the Mackenzies' living room.

"You might think that, being a Rendelf, the worst part of the job is when you have to play judge, jury and executioner if a Knave's Thaumaturge goes on a rampage. I think you've seen now that isn't the case."

"Why doesn't she remember her children died?" Marley asked.

"Or," Pen added, "more to the point, why does she think they grew up?"

"Memories are easy to confuse," Napier replied, his eyes fixed on the road. "If you start trying to address things like Alzheimer's Disease then you can accidentally leave someone with the memories you want them to have, rather than the ones they *actually* have. At the moment there is a lot of research going into whether constant attacks by those wielding the Knave's Rite can lead to a disproportionate vulnerability to things like dementia."

"What does that have to do with the Rendelf?" Pen whispered.

"Two things. Firstly, these are people who have suffered because, at some point, the Rendelf failed to protect them. I am sure you are aware of the saying that 'those who cannot remember the past are condemned to repeat it'? Secondly, it is the Rendelf who presents any body of work on the matter and, as neither you nor I are scientists, it helps to have some personal, emotive experience as a point of reference."

The rest of the morning was given over to visiting more people and, although nothing affected Pen and Marley as much as the visit to the Mackenzies, they both noted that the name Percy Fields was being mentioned repeatedly. At last, just when they were beginning to feel it was time to eat something other than the biscuits they accepted at every house, Napier began to look troubled.

"I think I can't, in good conscience, go back to Honour's Rest without meeting with Percy," he sighed. "I've never had a problem with him – he keeps himself to himself – but, by the sounds of things, he's making plans. You're going to have to wait in the vehicle though."

They didn't argue, still somewhat shell-shocked by the events of the day, and watched as Napier walked smartly and alone into the large farmhouse where the Knave's Thaumaturge lived. Pen saw Napier knock on the door and then, less than a second later, he had vanished. They waited for an hour, by which time they were both beginning to feel queasily hungry, before Napier reappeared and got back into the driver's seat. He said nothing, and Pen and Marley realised it would be pointless to push him for information on what had been said.

It seemed like weeks had passed since they had set out across the causeway that morning, and Pen was relieved to see Honour's Rest, feeling like a soldier returning from battle. He guessed it had not been a coincidence that his uncle had waited until the day before his fifteenth birthday to show him this aspect of the Rendelf's job, and he just wanted to sit in his study and watch the Highland mist curl in around the loch.

However, when he absentmindedly tried the doorknob whilst waiting for Napier and Marley, who were still gazing out at the landscape, Pen found the door was no longer locked. Knowing he hadn't used the Rite to open it, he felt slightly spooked as he wandered in, as quietly as he could. The entrance hall was just as it had been left but, as he turned to walk up to his room, he heard the soft sound of bare feet on the floor behind him. It reminded him of something from what seemed like another life, and he stood still, not daring to turn around in case he had misinterpreted the sound.

"Pendragon?" he heard his mother's voice say. Now he spun around, a broad smile stretching across his face. "Oh, my goodness, look at you! You are so grown up!"

She hurried over to him and, for a moment, Pen couldn't escape the thought that this was the second time today he had been greeted in that manner. But the feeling passed as he buried his head in his mother's shoulder, breathing in the smell of meadow flowers which he always associated with her. He had forgotten how short she was, or perhaps he had just grown, but everything else seemed so familiar that he could believe they had never been apart.

"Are you here for tomorrow?" he asked.

"Yes, of course. It's all been arranged for ages." She was as young and happy as ever, and Pen was glad that so little had changed. "But I wanted it to be a surprise. Your dad's in the living room. What a beautiful place to live, Pendragon!"

They all sat down together for an extremely late lunch, and Pen enjoyed just looking at his mother and father. Sometimes during the six months since he had last seen them, they had seemed so distant that he might have dreamt their existence. His father had been pleased to see him but was almost equally glad to speak to his older brother.

After the meal, Napier suggested that anyone who wanted could take the boat onto the loch and go fishing. Pen's mother declined, fishing was against her principle of never causing harm to any living creature, and Pen offered to stay with her. The others were all eager to go out and enjoy the autumn weather so, half an hour later, there was only Pen and his mother in Honour's Rest. He took her up to his study and explained everything which had happened since they had last seen each other, even the things he had already shared by letter. She kissed the scar on his hand and pretended to cover her ears as he described the prison in which he had found himself in August, but she was evidently proud of him.

"Let me see something you've learnt," she said with a broad smile.

Pen held out his right hand with the fist clenched and

then gradually uncurled his fingers. Flames danced in the palm of his hand and his mother gave a gasp of excitement at the spectacle. Pen, however, couldn't feel excited by demonstrating his ability, and just gave the smallest of smiles before letting his hand drop back down, the flames disappearing.

"There's something worrying you though, isn't there, Pendragon?" she whispered. They both turned their gaze out onto the loch where the others were clearly having a great time fishing.

"Yes," he replied, so relieved to be able to share it with her. "I don't know if I can make the Choice tomorrow that I should."

"Don't forget who you are, sweetheart," she whispered, getting to her feet so she could wrap her slender arms around him. "Pendragon Orion Devon. You have always been a champion for people who have needed you. I can remember going to your first parents' evening when you were four. You'd restore peace in the classroom by talking to each individual child and working out what was wrong and what they needed to make it right. You've been given a great gift, Pen."

"But what if I fail people? Like whichever Rendelf failed the Mackenzies."

His mother didn't ask who the Mackenzies were, but she bent her head down next to his ear and whispered, "If you do your best for people, Pendragon, just like you have always done, you can't fail anyone. You have a good teacher in Uncle Napier. He'll make sure you're ready to take over when the time comes. You have a lot to offer the world."

It was these words which lulled him to sleep that

night and made his dreams placid and gentle, rather than haunted by an old woman who had forgotten that her six eldest children couldn't return from the deaths which had been forced upon them.

He made his Choice in the small chapel in Honour's Rest, which he had not entered before. His mother, who seemed to have been sent his measurements, had bought him a beautiful suit, but insisted on his making the Choice barefoot, as she and Jarvis had been at their wedding. His parents, Napier, and Marley were there, along with a man who introduced himself as working for the United Nations, who witnessed Pen state that he would willingly become the next Rendelf and would commit himself to studying everything his uncle could teach him.

There were presents afterwards, and a card which had been signed by the Prime Minister and the First Ministers of Scotland, Wales, and Northern Ireland. It was slightly surreal to see the four signatures below 'TO PENDRAGON DEVON, HAVE A SPLENDID BIRTHDAY, WITH OUR MANY UNITED BEST WISHES'. His father was particularly excited by it.

"I wish Mr Carling could see this," Jarvis grinned. "I wouldn't have thought there are too many people who get a fifteenth birthday card quite like that."

After the present opening, Napier treated them all to a meal in a beautiful restaurant in Inverness. The UN official was invited but, having delivered the card and witnessed the brief ceremony, he declined. It was a lovely meal and Pen, sitting between his mother and father, took the opportunity to be grateful for how good life was to him.

Chapter Thirteen

Decorating the House

Although Pen knew that his fifteenth birthday would be a memory to stay with him forever, he discovered that nothing changed afterwards. His parents returned to England the following weekend, and he continued to be plagued by the knowledge that he still had to contain the Knave's Rite, without the consolation of it being inaccessible to him. Napier worked both apprentices hard and there were evenings when, through sheer exhaustion, Pen was unable to muster the Rite. He and Marley had less chance to talk now the evenings were darker, especially as Napier insisted that Honour's Rest was a perfect place for stargazing. Three evenings a week, he would make them stand outside in the freezing darkness and stare silently up at the heavens.

It was usually a lot more misery than it was worth, but one night they had been treated to an outstanding display of the Northern Lights. While Napier had droned at length about the science behind the indescribable beauty of green searchlights beaming down from heaven, Pen had felt the Rite rushing through him in a way he hadn't experienced for months. He had thrown his arms out towards the incredible spectacle and, as he did so, his sheer wonder had manifested itself in a reflection of the light, sending his own variation of the spectacle out towards the heavens.

The following day, Napier had thrown newspaper after newspaper at him, each with a headline marvelling at 'The Aurora Borealis Which Came Down to Earth', while Marley laughed almost hysterically into his cereal.

"I have to go down to explain this next week," Napier said angrily. "What were you thinking, Pendragon?"

"I wasn't thinking anything," Pen protested. "It was just so beautiful."

"You need to *learn* to think then," Napier snapped. "And I don't know what you are finding so amusing, Marley Shipperbottom."

Napier was in a foul temper for the rest of the day, so Pen and Marley stayed out of his way. With only three weeks until Christmas, they had plenty to get excited about, especially Pen, who was desperate to return south and spend time with his parents. Jarvis had invited his older brother to spend Christmas with them, but Napier hadn't had a Christmas away from Honour's Rest for years and didn't want to miss the festive season there. To ensure he wouldn't be alone, more for their own peace of mind than his needs, the Rendelf's two apprentices had written to Erlend and Bernadette to suggest they came south for Marley's fifteenth birthday, which was one week before Christmas, and stay until the new year. Napier had taken it well and seemed genuinely pleased at the opportunity to spend more time with his best friend.

"What I think would be really amazing is if we decorated the house for Christmas," Pen whispered. He and Marley were sitting together in the living room, trying to avoid Napier and his comments about how his nephew's behaviour was juvenile and proved just how far he had to go until he could present himself as a viable Rendelf. "It would look really incredible. We could order some tinsel and get a tree and–"

"And you plan to do all this without asking your uncle? Are you feeling particularly suicidal at the moment?"

Pen laughed, but there was no denying that, behind the humour, Marley was making a serious point. Napier was clearly disappointed by how Pen had allowed excitement to adversely affect his control of the Rite. After all the practising they had been doing, he ought to have been able to control himself better. Still, even though he was penitent, Pen couldn't regret the thrill he had experienced as the Rite had welled up within him at the sight of something so magnificent. He sat for a while in silence, pretending to be reflecting on his mistakes but secretly focussing his mind on that closeness to the Rite.

"We could always just risk it and ask him?" Marley suggested, breaking the silence with a suggestion which Pen thought was ridiculous.

Surely there was no way Napier would let them have so much fun when he was this angry with them? He looked across at Marley, hoping it would be clear just how unconvinced he was.

"Look," his deputy pointed out, "if he says no then it hardly matters, does it? We just won't have any Christmas decorations. If he says yes, then we can work on getting everything ready for when he gets back. He said he'd be away three days. That's loads of time."

Eventually Pen was convinced, and he wandered off to find Napier, who was in his study writing a report on the typewriter. He wasn't sure he was the best person for the job but Marley's faith in him had given him the necessary confidence. Pen knew that his uncle wouldn't want to be disturbed and, for a moment, he almost turned around and left, but then he remembered how excited he had been at the prospect of decorating the house for Christmas and summoned the courage to knock on the door.

"Yes?" Napier called.

"Can I come in?"

"If you have to."

Pen pushed open the door and shuffled into the room. "Marley and I were wondering if you ever decorate the house for Christmas?"

"No, I don't. Honour's Rest hasn't been decorated for Christmas for the past thirty years. Is that what you wanted to ask? If you could do that?"

"Just about," Pen whispered. "While you're away."

"Fine," Napier sighed. "But take care." Pen thanked him and was about to leave when his uncle stopped him. "Just since you're here, could I have a word with you, please? Close the door."

There was no opportunity for Pen to escape, so he sat down awkwardly on the chaise longue. He hadn't been in his uncle's study since being ill in summer and he was surprised to find the seat was actually very uncomfortable.

"I have no intentions of dying in the near future, Pendragon," Napier said bluntly, "but illnesses and accidents happen. I need to know that, from the moment of your sixteenth birthday, you are ready to take on the role of Rendelf. You have the intelligence, the spirit, and the dedication to others, but I do not see any discipline in you yet. I can explain away your little outburst to people who do not fully understand the Rite, but it concerns me. You cannot just give in to it. Remember, you need to make sure you do not channel it until you are confident that you are in control."

"Yes."

"It would be inadvisable to try and decorate Honour's Rest without use of the Rite, but I do not wish to come home and find the place in ruins. Therefore, I need your word that you will take care."

"I'll take care," Pen said with a smile. "And Marley seems better than me at control these days anyway, so I'm sure you don't need to worry about him."

"If you believe that then I think you need to spend more time speaking to your deputy. Anyway, you can leave now. I have to finish this report and, if you stay too long, I may be reminded that I wouldn't be having to write it if it weren't for you."

Pen ducked out of the room with a smile and a jovial nod of his head. Ignoring everything else his uncle had told him, he felt excited to be able to return to Marley and announce that they had not only got a free rein to decorate the enormous house, but also to use the Rite to do it. Marley was as excited as him, and they stayed up late discussing the different possibilities for how they could make the house as Christmassy as possible.

The following day, Napier left at six o'clock in the morning. Marley did not get up, but Pen went to the door to see his uncle off, feeling very responsible for Napier having to turn out on such a horrible morning. There had been a thick snowfall during the night and much of the loch had frozen over, leaving vast stretches of snow and very little sign of where the path stopped and the ice began. The causeway was covered with snow, but Napier simply waved his hand and it swept onto the frozen loch, creating deep drifts on either side.

"I'm sorry you're having to go," Pen said as Napier pulled up in the car, which had the roof on for the first time Pen had ever seen.

"You can stop feeling guilty now, Pendragon," Napier replied. "Just take care, and make sure everything is still in one piece when I get back."

"You take care," Pen said fervently. He stood in the snow, waving his uncle off as the car disappeared along the causeway and down the snowy road. After Napier had driven out of sight, Pen walked back into the house and had breakfast. He could now arrange his own meals without having to worry about too much hard work so, after he had eaten, he just wandered through the house, waiting for Marley to get up. It was another two hours before he was no longer on his own, by which time he was just sitting in the living room.

"Did he get off alright?" Marley asked, rubbing his eyes. Pen nodded.

After Marley had eaten breakfast, they began to make plans and, an hour or two later, they were both standing outside, pointing out possible Christmas trees. They had opted against buying one and would, instead, bring one from the hills, using their combined control of the Rite. Having finally decided on a tree, Pen watched as Marley's foot began to tap slowly and the tree they had chosen gave a sudden lurch as the trunk was cut cleanly, leaving two feet of stump. Some of the ice on the loch cracked, and Pen could imagine the great water-horse moving in the icy depths. He used his own Rite to secure the tree as it floated down into the valley and landed at their feet with a rush of finger-like needles. Marley said nothing, but it was Pen alone who transported the tree into the entrance hall and raised it up until, like the pictures and ornaments around the walls, it was left suspended by the Rite alone.

Pen and Marley spent the rest of the day creating Christmas decorations to hang on the tree. Pen, who felt he had effectively mastered fire now, used tiny glass bottles they found in one of the store cupboards and placed a minute flame into each one so it flickered yellow and orange.

It was about half past three in the afternoon and the daylight was beginning to fade when the two boys realised they had forgotten to eat lunch. Marley didn't seem as happy as Pen had been expecting, so he offered to prepare the meal. His friend, however, did not want to be left alone in the room full of the beautiful objects they had been making, each one living and breathing along with the Rite which had created it.

As they sat down to lunch, which Pen made from the things he had found in the pantry and more resembled a midnight snack than an actual meal, Marley sighed, and Pen realised he could no longer ignore whatever it was that was upsetting him. However, when asked, Marley wasn't keen to say anything until Pen assured him that whatever he said would be treated in absolute confidence.

"I noticed what happened earlier," he murmured at last.

"When?"

"When we were getting the tree. I don't know how, but you obviously realised that I'd been tempted. That power at my fingertips – I'd never even thought of being able to move something that size."

"I don't know what you mean," Pen said, trying to sound nonchalant but disappointed he had been unable to hide his concern.

"No, you were right to be worried, Pen. I did think about doing something terrible with it. Leaving it in the road for the next person who's speeding when they go past. Or something equally bad."

"But you didn't, did you?" Pen said, hoping he sounded like he wasn't as worried as he felt. "So, it doesn't really matter."

"But it's there, isn't it? The knowledge that the most powerful way for me to access the Rite is through its darkest form."

"You want to become a Knave's Thaumaturge?"

"It's not about what I *want*, is it? I want to become a thaumaturge, and I think the only thing I'm good for is the Knave's Rite."

"I wanted to be a Just Thaumaturge," Pen whispered. "The day before my birthday, I had the same crisis of confidence."

"But you *are* a Just Thaumaturge, aren't you?"

"No. I'm Apprentice Rendelf, remember? If you choose the Just Rite, you won't even be able to access the Knave's Rite anymore. Don't you see how great that will be? Yes, things may not always be that easy, but at least you won't be able to accidentally cause any damage. I know I'm always going to have to look out for the side of me which channels the Knave's Rite, because I'll never be rid of it. Then, one day, I'm going to have to use it to kill someone, or something, and that temptation will just grow."

They didn't say anything else to each other for the remainder of the meal. Marley seemed to have realised the sense Pen was talking, which was good because Pen felt naked after exposing so much of his soul. They returned to making Christmas decorations and, although they began to laugh throughout the afternoon, neither of them could forget the earlier confessions they had made to each other.

By the time they went their separate ways, Pen was so tired that he threw himself down on the bed and, covering himself in the thick winter blankets to keep out the wind blowing through the window, he fell asleep.

He slept through the sound of a car crunching its way over the snow crystals and being driven slowly into the garage, and the front door being unlocked to give way to someone who tiptoed up the stairs without seeming to even notice the Christmas decorations. However, when he awoke in the morning, it was to find that Napier had returned in the small hours but was only just admiring the tree and the many festive garlands which had transformed Honour's Rest.

"Well done," he said as Pen walked up to him. "It looks absolutely magnificent. And you even hid it from me." When Pen asked his uncle to explain the comment, Napier smiled. "Well, whether you intended to or not, I did not see any of the decorations until this morning."

"That must have been Marley. What are you doing

back, anyway? You were supposed to be gone three days."

"You seem to have made a positive impression, Pendragon," Napier said with a smile. "I didn't have to do too much explaining. All they wanted to talk about was how your fifteenth birthday celebrations had gone, and how you were progressing in your education."

Pen grinned. Despite the fact the Rendelf could be cantankerous and irritating, Honour's Rest would never seem right without Napier, however much fun he and Marley might have in his absence. His uncle seemed to know what he was thinking, and his smile broadened for a second before disappearing entirely.

"I hope you don't think your Christmas holidays will begin any earlier just because you've decorated the house."

As seemed to happen when Pen was surrounded by beautiful things, he found the Rite was much easier to channel but harder to control. Over the next ten days, Napier pushed him mercilessly and Pen had to avoid a repeat of what had happened with the sword earlier in the year. He didn't feel able to reliably control the Rite, which would suddenly manifest itself with a surge of electric excitement, only for him to have to rein it in. He wasn't ready to control the sheer joy and excitement which pulsed through his body without ever having experienced it fully, but Napier made it clear he wouldn't trust Pen with anything further until he had learnt the 'simple' lesson.

Pen went shopping in Edinburgh with his uncle for Marley's birthday present and, while Napier had opted for a star-chart which the bookseller claimed was an eighteenth-century reproduction of a lost work by Galileo, Pen had bought his best friend a magnificent camera, to which he attached a label with the words *For the recording of adventures!*

Marley was clearly nervous as he stood in the chapel and recited the words spoken by most thaumaturges for hundreds of years, committing to study and master only the Just Rite and leave the Knave's Rite behind him. His mother wiped her eyes a lot during the ceremony, and Pen was pleased to see just how proud she was of him. He wondered if Bernadette Shipperbottom would ever know how worried Marley had been that he would end up following in her footsteps of the Knave's Rite.

The day after, Napier drove Pen into Aviemore to catch the train which would take him down as far as Edinburgh, from where he would fly down to England. It felt strange to be leaving Honour's Rest for more than a day, but he was grateful for the opportunity to be returning home after a year which had left him feeling wiped out.

As the train pulsed down the tracks, Pen thought over everything which had happened since he had last sat there. He was surprised to find there was one person who lingered in his thoughts. Not Marley, nor Napier, nor even Isolde, but the strange girl with the candle, Niamh O'Hare. He wondered what she was doing this Christmas in the darkness of her blind world.

Chapter Fourteen

Home is Where...

Pen loved Christmas, and his parents always Christmassed in a way which made anyone else's pale in comparison. When he had been little, his father had spent Christmas Eves dressed in a Santa Claus outfit and would take Pen out shopping while his mother prepared Christmas Dinner. Although Jarvis was a slight man, a few well-placed pillows had been employed to provide him with the necessary padding, and Pen had taken great pride and pleasure in showing his father off to anyone they passed. One year, they had gone to a pantomime together, and Jarvis had been invited to go up on stage and wish the audience a Merry Christmas.

As he had grown older, Christmas Eve had involved less dressing up, and Pen was now allowed to celebrate the season with a festive drink with his parents, telling ghost stories.

The tradition was employed again this Christmas Eve, and his mum and dad were disappointed to hear that he hadn't seen any ghosts at Honour's Rest.

"The place must be eight hundred years old, if it's a day!" Jarvis had exclaimed, but Pen could only shrug his shoulders and apologise that there had been no ghostly activity. He didn't want to talk about the girl he had seen with the candle in Isolde's dungeons, although the first question he had asked came back to him: *are you dead?*

Christmas Day was wonderful. His mother had cooked a roast for each of them: turkey for her son, who was a traditionalist; pork for her husband; and a nut roast to match her own sensibilities. Pen tried them all and enjoyed them, but what he loved best about his own were the turkey and stuffing sandwiches which formed the basis for tea on every remaining day of the holiday.

It was New Year's Eve by the time he was able to meet up with his friends from school, but it was weird to be around them. They all thought his parents had overreacted in taking him out of school after the suspension, and he didn't want to explain what had actually happened, although they pestered him to address the various rumours surrounding his disappearance. Was it true that he was ill, or even dying? Had he really been sent to a 'special' school? Their fascination with the mundane made Pen feel very homesick for Marley, who understood the life he lived. He no longer had anything in common with these people, he realised, and he headed home well before midnight to see in the New Year with his parents, who asked no questions. Pen was beginning to understand how Napier had become so detached from the 'normal' world, buried in his mastering of the Rite and the politics which surrounded it.

"I wanted to tell them everything," he explained to his mother and father as they waited for the new year. "I can't stand all the rumours going around about me."

"But does it matter, Pendragon?" his mother whispered. "When you know just how much you've achieved during the last eight months?"

"How many of them got birthday cards from the Prime Minister and all three First Ministers?" his father added, gesturing up to the framed birthday card which had generated so much excitement in October.

Pen only smiled and nodded, unable to agree but knowing their words made sense. The silence lasted until ten seconds before midnight, when his mother turned the radio on and joined in the countdown. As soon as the clocks chimed midnight, she leapt to her feet and took the hands of the two men opposite her and, as they had done for as long as Pen could remember, they started the New Year together, singing Auld Lang Syne with gusto. This year Pen couldn't accompany them, having left his guitar in the turret at Honour's Rest. When Marley had moved in, he had thought he would never get used to being unable to play it, but Pen's determination that Marley would not lose control of the Rite had made it easier. Now, he realised, his friend was no longer in danger from that temptation, so the next year he could begin to play again.

Pen hadn't told his mother and father how much he was missing Marley. He couldn't bear for them to think he could be homesick for anywhere other than their house or for anyone other than them. He did miss Honour's Rest though. He had expected that being back at the bungalow in his parents' quiet street would feel 'right', but it didn't. He missed being able to walk around a house until he became lost, or until he found a tapestry, painting, or even doorway he had never seen before. Honour's Rest was an adventure in itself and, as he wandered to bed listening to the New Year revellers singing their way down the streets, he vowed to learn more about the place which he now realised held his heart even more than his own home.

When the seventh of January dawned, noticeably earlier than it did in Scotland, and he prepared to leave, Pen felt as though his heart was being torn violently between the two worlds. He was looking forward to being back with Marley and Napier, who both understood who he was and what he was going to become, and to Honour's Rest. On the other hand, he would miss his parents with the familiar scratching hollowness which was already beginning to tear at his insides. They were being deprived of the opportunity to watch their only child grow up, and he wanted nothing more than to share his successes and failures with them. But they weren't a part of the Honour's Rest World, and never could be.

He wasn't taking the plane this time as his father was attending a conference in Edinburgh. They drove up together, talking about how much they had enjoyed the holiday.

"So," Jarvis said as they passed the Scottish border and Pen experienced a strange sensation of combined belonging and homesickness, "how often do you think your Uncle Napier can spare you?"

"I don't know. I'm hoping I might get home at Easter. It seems like a long time away, I know."

"If you were at boarding school, you would stay that long," his father pointed out. "Just make sure it's not any longer than that. Your mother and I miss you, you know?"

Jarvis dropped Pen off at Waverley Station and stood on the platform, waving until the train had disappeared, even buying a ticket for himself so he could get through the barriers.

As the train pulled away from the station, Pen remembered the man who had told him about climbing to the top of Ben Nevis each year since he was fifteen. He wondered if he would have the opportunity during the next nine months to create any traditions of his own. No one on the train spoke to him this time, and most of them seemed to be hungover or returning home after their first day back at work. It soon became dark, but Pen sat staring at the windows, watching the reflections of his fellow passengers, who remained oblivious to being the source of so much interest for the fifteen-year-old.

He fell asleep after Pitlochry and the conductor had to shake his shoulder gently to tell him they had arrived in Aviemore. He thanked her and picked up his rucksack. As he stepped off the train and the cold air hit his face, Pen's eyes watered, and he began to think of the warm bed at Honour's Rest and imagined curling under the blankets and sleeping until the darkness and cold had slipped into daylight. However, he was brought rudely from his imaginings by a hand on his arm, and he spun around to see his uncle, who pulled him out of the floodlights and into the darkness.

"Be quiet, Pendragon," he said, before his nephew had spoken a word. "You were not the only person to have alighted here. We will have to wait until everyone else is gone before we leave."

"Look," Pen said, slightly annoyed and much louder than he had intended, "I'm tired. Can't we just–" He stopped as his uncle's grip on his arm became painfully tight.

"You are as impatient as you were when you first arrived, Pendragon," Napier hissed. "Think for a second. Much as I might appreciate it, I am not asking you to be quiet for my own amusement."

Pen suddenly remembered that he was back in the world of Just and Knave's Thaumaturges, and his thoughts leapt to Isolde.

"No," Napier said absentmindedly, "it is not her." Then he stopped and looked at his nephew, a look of horror uniting their features. "Don't let me do that! Have you forgotten everything?"

Pen didn't need Napier's anger to tell him that he should have stopped his uncle from entering his thoughts. Throughout the three-week holiday it hadn't occurred to him that he would forget anything of the Rite, but apparently the things he had started to take for granted had slipped from his mind. His uncle couldn't have been more furious with him than he was with himself, but that still didn't explain why Napier was so jumpy.

At last, the station cleared, and Pen and his uncle went silently to the car. As they drove along the country road, Pen realised there was absolutely no point in asking the Rendelf for details about what had caused such nervousness. Each shadow made Napier jumpier and, when a deer leapt out in front of the car, instead of braking, Napier waved his hand out and the creature was thrown backwards into the undergrowth. Pen's eyes widened, but he didn't say anything in case he provoked a similar response.

Honour's Rest was in darkness as they arrived and, on his uncle's instructions, he went straight into the house, where there was quiet music playing in the living room. He walked in and smiled at Marley, before throwing himself down on the sofa and looking around.

"What, in the name of everything, is going on?"

"Hello," Marley said, his mouth twitching as he fought to contain his sarcasm. "I had a lovely holiday, thanks. How was yours?"

"Sorry. It was good, but I missed this place. Why is he being so weird?"

"Do you remember that day we met all those people, and they were talking about a Knave's Thaumaturge called Percy Fields?"

Pen nodded.

"Well," Marley continued, "earlier this month, just after the New Year, this Percy Fields sent Napier a parcel. I don't know what was in it – he secreted it off to his room and would only let my dad in – but it was obviously some kind of threat."

"I'm surprised he doesn't get more things like that," Pen laughed. "Not only because of his position, but also his charming personality."

"Well," Marley said, "it wasn't just that. Percy apparently sent another letter, one which he sent copies of to people all over, stating that he was challenging Napier for the role of Rendelf and, if he didn't go public with what had happened, he would assume that Napier was resigning."

"I don't think that's how these things work," Pen said, but his sense of humour was beginning to wane.

"No," a voice behind him said, and he turned around to see that Napier had just entered the room and was in the process of removing his lambskin driving gloves. "It isn't."

"Then why are you so worried?"

"Percy is, in many ways, incapable of seeing beyond his own interests. And he is singularly narrow-minded in them. I have recommended to Marley's father that, until the issue is resolved, he should go into hiding. But it has not occurred to Percy that, should I die, the role of Rendelf will pass not to him, but to Erlend Shipperbottom."

"So where is the threat?" Pen asked. The last three weeks felt like a dream and all the homesickness for Honour's Rest had vanished from his heart, leaving only a desperate wish to return to his parents. "If he can't become Rendelf?"

"Because Erlend should not need to become Rendelf and, if it is alright with you, Pendragon, I would rather remain alive."

Pen knew he shouldn't find his uncle's tone funny, but he couldn't help the smile which stretched across his face. To disguise it, he tried to find something to say. "Why did he want you to tell everyone what had happened?"

"Because he wanted to know what the parcel contained."

"What do you mean? Marley said Percy had sent it."

"So he did," Napier replied, dropping into the large armchair and, for a moment, staring into the hypnotic orange glow of the fire. "But he sent me a Dapplegrim skin."

"What is that?"

"The Dapplegrim are a breed of giant horses in

Scandinavia. They are extremely rare but, when killed, their skin takes the form of whatever the person looking at it most dreads."

"So, you saw your worst fear?"

Napier nodded.

"Which means he would know exactly how to attack you?"

Napier nodded again.

"So, what was it?"

"I'm sorry?"

"What did you see?"

Napier looked up from the fire, his piercing eyes gazing beyond Pen's own and into his mind, his soul. Pen fought to keep his thoughts away from his uncle, but he got the feeling that Napier was looking beyond those too.

"Your head, Pendragon," his uncle said at last, his gaze sliding back into focus and watching as Pen's face fell slightly.

For a moment, fear and pride battled within him and he found that his voice had disappeared.

"My...?"

"Yes," Napier said, looking back into the fire. "Do not be too flattered. It is the natural human way to be concerned with succession. That will have come into it somewhere."

Pen noticed Marley glance across at him and shake his head slightly, but he decided it was better to say nothing else about the matter. Instead, he asked the question which had been plaguing him since he had been snatched away at the platform.

"So why all the worry now?" he whispered. "Surely there's nothing he can do while we're here. And you didn't tell him what you saw. Did you?"

"No, I did not tell him. But that only made him angrier. He sent another letter this morning stating that he would come to claim Honour's Rest at some time during the next two days. It was sensible to get you here as quickly as possible. I am certain I do not need to tell you that this is the gravest threat we have faced during your time here, so you must not leave the house. I have sealed the doors and windows with the Rite, and no Knave's Thaumaturge can break that. But you can. Do you understand?"

Pen and Marley nodded.

"Now, if you would excuse me, I have to go to my study. Perhaps the most irritating thing about this is that Percy has written to all sorts of people who should not have received letters. The First Minister will almost certainly want an explanation, and Number Ten has been in touch as well. This whole thing is ridiculous."

"Has this happened before?" Pen asked, as his uncle stood up and moved towards the door. "Have you ever been challenged like this?"

"Once or twice," Napier replied. "The difference this time is that you two make me more vulnerable. Don't protest," he said, raising his hands to silence the boys before they even started speaking. "It is not a criticism, only an observation."

He left the room and Marley and Pen looked at one another. They stayed silent for a while before Pen inquired about the holiday, and Marley explained they had enjoyed Christmas, and that Napier had been excellent company.

"He's nicer when you're not around," he said. "I'm sorry, but it's true."

"I know," Pen whispered, thinking about how strange

it was that his uncle so feared his death. He had a deputy of his own and had been training Marley almost as thoroughly as his nephew. Pen faked a yawn to excuse himself from Marley's company and then wandered up the spiral staircase to his room, where he shuffled under the blankets.

It seemed slightly odd to think that he couldn't sleep now, despite how tired he had been on the train, but nothing like as strange as it was to remember this time last night, he had been in his cluttered room at his parents' bungalow. What would they have to say if they knew Napier had been sent an impression of his severed head? Or if they knew Pen was here, in the dim light, waiting for someone to arrive who wished to kill him, Napier and Marley? He thought of Napier alone in his study, writing letters of apology to the most powerful people in Britain and assuring them he had the situation under control.

As he turned over in bed and switched out the light, plunging himself into the pitch darkness which only seemed to exist in Scotland, Pen remembered how angry he had been with his school friends for not understanding. But then, he realised with a smile, there was no one in the world without the Rite who could even begin to understand, and he found himself grateful to be living with two people who did.

Chapter Fifteen

The State Room

By the time Pen had managed to get to sleep, a snowstorm was swirling around the house. He awoke to discover the loch had once again frozen over and, using his blanket to wipe condensation from the window, he saw that everywhere he looked was smothered in smooth snow. It was so beautiful that, for a moment, Pen turned to run down the stairs and challenge Marley to a snowball fight, until he remembered they were housebound until the Knave's Thaumaturge, Percy Fields, had been dealt with.

Instead, he got ready slowly and wandered downstairs. The reassurance Pen had found in Marley's and Napier's company the evening before had died away, so he was once again wishing he was back in England where the worst thing he had to worry about was coursework and mock exams.

It seemed bizarre how preoccupied his old friends had been with their schoolwork. He wondered if any of them would ever find themselves locked in an ancient castle, without even the opportunity to get out and take a breath of fresh winter air. The thought made him feel very claustrophobic.

Marley was sitting at the breakfast table, pushing his food to the sides of his plate with a fork as though he couldn't bring himself to eat it. Napier was standing a short distance away with his back to them, staring out of one of the tall windows.

"I understand your concern," he was saying as Pen walked in and sat down beside his friend, "but you have to understand that the friendship which exists between your father and me could not survive if we did not trust one another."

"It's not about trust," Marley mumbled.

As his uncle turned around and looked at him, Pen got the distinct impression he shouldn't have stumbled into this particular conversation.

"Good morning, Pendragon," Napier said brusquely. "How long have you been there?"

"Not long."

"Good. Then you haven't heard the conversation I've been having with Marley. Essentially, I need you to start to live the Rite more. It shouldn't just be something you use because you need it, it should be something that breathes in time with you."

"Right." Pen knew that there was some more coming: his uncle had quite clearly been speaking about something which was making Marley uncomfortable.

"Today that is all you will be doing. Tomorrow, we'll

put it into practice."

"So how will I do it today without practising?" Pen asked, helping himself to scrambled eggs from a warm tureen in the middle of the table.

"I would advise you to start now." His uncle's voice was as flat and polite as ever, but Pen got the distinct impression he wasn't being given the full story of what was planned.

"So why were you talking about trust when I came in? Or do I not get to hear that bit?"

For a second after he had spoken, Pen thought that his uncle was going to hit him, and he recoiled slightly as Napier made a sudden movement towards the table. Then he realised it wasn't the table his uncle was moving towards, but the window on the corridor outside.

"Well," he sighed, "he's here. Finish your breakfast both of you. It's time we got started." With that, he marched out of the room and disappeared up the staircase which led to his study. Marley and Pen looked at one another.

"So, what *was* he saying about trust?" Pen asked, stabbing his fork with gusto into a chestnut mushroom.

"He's going to use the Knave's Rite against me. You're going to have to come to my rescue."

Pen dropped the cutlery, which clattered to the ground. "No," he whispered, "he wouldn't do that to you. For a start, wouldn't your dad kill him?"

"No," Marley replied, with a forced half-smile. "He made the point that this has been part of the role of Deputy Apprentice for as long as such a position has existed. I suppose he won't let anything too bad happen, but I'd rather you didn't let it get to the point where we have to find out."

After breakfast, the boys walked up to Napier's study,

from where they were directed to a small empty room which neither of them had ever seen before.

"This is the State Room," Napier explained when he entered behind them. "Since 1583, whenever a Rendelf has entertained any monarchs or political leaders, it has taken place in this room. Legend has it that James the Sixth stayed here after the fall of the Gowrie Regime. I'm afraid that the last person I entertained here was Tony Blair, so I think you can imagine how long ago that was. In the time it isn't being used for parties, it is generally kept empty and so is a good place to find focus. So, Pendragon, tell me how often you have missed the opportunity to use the Rite."

"What? Since when?"

"Since this morning, when I told you to start thinking about it." Napier's tone was clipped, and Pen didn't think it wise to push things too far, but he was too annoyed to say nothing.

"Well, I suppose I could have seen that Percy was outside without prancing across to the window."

"You need to stop thinking that adults care about your childish taunts, Pendragon," Napier snapped, sounding for all the world as though he definitely cared about these apparently childish taunts. "You could have used the Rite to determine the provenance of the room. You could have used it to do simple tasks such as open the door or create us all somewhere to sit." Here, Napier gestured, and three seats appeared in front of him. He sat down heavily on one of them. "You could also have used it to stop me speaking once you realised how much I was annoying you."

"I don't think you'd like that."

"No, I wouldn't. But the Rite is not always about doing

173

what you think will please people. As Rendelf, you will sometimes have to do things that you know will make people – good people – unhappy, but you must always consider what is for the best."

Pen stared, trying to work out if Napier was goading his apprentice into silencing him, and he tried to, but had no idea how to do it. Napier stood in front of him, his voice droning on in a way which made Pen become angrier and angrier. He thought of how he was caged in the strange house, locked out of the world from which he had been snatched nine months ago: a world where he had been happy and normal, and had enjoyed the company of other happy, normal people. He thought of the Knave's Thaumaturge, Percy Fields, who was outside and waiting for the people in Honour's Rest to make even the slightest slip which would grant him access, who had sent something that appeared to be Pen's head to his uncle. He thought of Isolde, ever a silent enemy who was even more notable in her absence from his dreams and who had chosen a dark path because she had been in love with someone who died to protect Napier. His thoughts quickly moved on to Niamh O'Hare, clutching her candle and blinded by the mother she had never properly known. It reminded him how Napier had stopped his nephew from rescuing her and bringing her back into the light, where she would have been reunited with the adopted family who still sought her, perhaps unaware that Napier knew exactly where their daughter was.

He threw his arms out and his uncle was thrown off his chair, only breaking his fall with the Rite at the last possible second.

"Every time you allow yourself to give in, you open

yourself up to the Knave's Rite," Napier snapped. "Try to do some good with the gift you have been given."

Pen shouted wordlessly in frustration, and the whole room began to shake with the power of his anger. He did not have long to think about it though, as he was suddenly pushed up against the wall, his uncle's forearm pinning his neck still.

"I will no longer waste my time on you, Pendragon Devon. If you wish to bring the house down around us then, please, make yourself at home. I have better things to do with my time than deal with a petulant child who shows nothing more than promise at the best of times." He moved towards the door, but Pen glanced across at the handle and, when Napier tried to turn it, he found it wouldn't move. He looked back at his nephew. "Much better," he said with a nod. "So, do you want to fight more, or talk?"

"I want to know when you're going to hurt Marley," Pen said. He was fighting to regain his temper but couldn't help but look at his uncle with the contempt he deserved.

"I am not going to hurt Marley. You have a very poor opinion of me, don't you, Pendragon? It is not really fair, as I don't think I have done anything to warrant such suspicion. I have asked Marley to help me in ensuring that you can overcome the Knave's Rite and he has, albeit reluctantly, agreed. Perhaps he would not have been so reluctant if you could demonstrate better control."

Pen stood there, staring hard at Napier and imagining what it would take for his uncle to stop talking, to stop criticising him, when suddenly Napier stopped and smiled across at his nephew, nodding his head slowly. Whatever he had done had worked, and Pen realised his uncle could no longer speak. He closed his eyes and tried to imagine what Percy Fields was thinking and what the driving force was behind his attempt to take over the role of Rendelf.

"Isolde is Percy's sister," he said, the information coming to him as clearly as if he had heard it in a news bulletin.

Napier nodded. "Yes," he said, as Pen released his voice. "Well, almost. They are half brother and sister. She was always the more controlling of the two."

"He wants to kill you. And he doesn't want to be Rendelf himself, he wants Isolde to do it. She must have put him up to all this."

"Very good," Napier said. "Keep looking."

Pen could feel Percy trying to block him from his mind and had to concentrate past the images of Napier being strangled by Isolde, or Honour's Rest burning to the ground. The Knave's Thaumaturge really didn't know him well enough to think of anything which could scare Pen away from his determined effort to know more.

"He is here until either you or he dies, and I don't think he really minds which." Pen sat down on the chair Napier had summoned earlier. Although he felt a great sense of achievement at having deciphered so much from the Knave's Thaumaturge, it had come at the cost of every bit of energy he had, and now he just needed to relax. He covered his eyes with his hand, hoping Marley and Napier would leave him to the silence which had descended since he had last spoken, but they didn't. Instead, Napier clapped his hands together and began to rock backwards on his heels, clearly excited.

"So," he said, and Pen couldn't help but look up. "Are

you ready to put this kind of control into practice?"

"What do you mean?" Pen spluttered. "That's what I was doing just then!"

"Well, yes," Napier replied with a broad smile. "But I'd still like to see you working without giving in to the temptation to produce something with the Knave's Rite."

"But I'm shattered!"

"Yes," Napier said, now nodding sagely, which just made Pen even more annoyed. "But that is something you must learn as Rendelf. You will often be required to use the most complicated Rite when you are at your most exhausted."

"This is ridiculous."

"It is not ridiculous, Pendragon," Napier snapped, the eagerness vanishing into anger. "I will not stop you from challenging what I ask you to do. Indeed, I would rather you *did* challenge it as it shows independence of thought. However, kindly never dismiss anything I ask of you as ridiculous. You may rest assured that I will never require you to do anything which is without purpose."

Pen scowled at his uncle, who seemed unbothered.

"I won't let anything terrible happen to Marley, don't worry. But the longer you take to address the Knave's Rite, the more danger you will put us all in. Do you understand?"

"Yep."

"Hide and seek then," Napier said, rubbing his hands together. "You close your eyes, Pendragon, and count to one hundred. Marley, come with me."

Pen did as he was told and, still sitting on the chair, he pressed his fingers into his eyes until he could see sparks of silver shooting towards him through the darkness.

It made him think of the candle Niamh carried. He wondered what she was doing, whether she had been set free from Isolde's prison where Napier, the man who was supposed to protect those who wielded the Rite in Britain, had left her.

He lost count as he thought about her, but Pen was quite certain when he heard one of the clocks chiming the hour that he had been waiting for at least one hundred seconds. He got to his feet and tried to find his balance. The whole room seemed to be swimming in his tiredness and shock at how bright it was after the darkness of his voluntary blindness. For a moment, he stood still and tried to pick out any sounds which would give away what direction Napier and Marley had gone in, but the whole house had been plunged into an unfamiliar silence. He had never played a game of hide and seek which had started with such a feeling of nervousness, as though everything depended on which direction he walked out the room.

As he opened the door, something occurred to him which he had not registered before. He had heard no sounds as he was counting, so of course he wouldn't be able to use his hearing to work out where his uncle and best friend were. He stepped out of the room and began walking through the corridors, listening as his shoes struck the floor in an echoing rhythm.

"Hello?" he called, pushing aside the tapestries which decorated the walls as though he expected to find his quarry behind them, like a normal game of hide and seek. The house was bigger and less familiar than it had been for months, and he realised this could be his uncle using the Knave's Rite to make it appear so. Pen tried to focus on the knowledge that it was his home, and how he knew each doorway and window, even if he had never seen them before. It seemed to work, as he managed to find his way to the Rendelf's study.

As soon as he rested his hand on the door, Pen was sure he had found what he was looking for. The faint strains of Moonlight Sonata were audible, but it sounded like it was being played on one of the pianos he remembered from Sunday School: the type which had sat for a long time in a damp village hall and had become gradually out of tune, until the notes were barely distinguishable from one another.

He pushed open the door and looked around. There was no one there. The music seemed to be coming from behind him, in the direction he had just come from. The room, he realised with a sigh, was as empty as the one he had just left. With a sickening jump which seemed to divide his body from his mind and soul for a moment, Pen felt himself jerk backwards. It was like being on a particularly violent rollercoaster, and he struggled to keep his balance as he found himself back in the State Room.

It had changed since he was there just five minutes before and was now swamped by a darkness which was simultaneously suffocating and inviting.

Pen was certain he could hear voices he knew talking to him through the darkness and, for a moment, Marley passed from his thoughts. He wanted to listen to what the strange yet familiar voices would tell him. Besides, he had his uncle's assurance that he wouldn't do anything to hurt Marley. Surely there could be no harm in waiting a moment?

He wasn't sure what made him think of it, but Pen

suddenly remembered the story of Amanda and, more precisely, the fact Marley had used the Rite to watch what had happened to her. He remembered what his friend had said about how she had paused for a moment before falling from the cliffs to the death assigned to her before she was born.

The darkness was becoming less tempting, and now the voices seemed to be more demanding, commanding him to listen to them rather than think about his friend. He shook his head, trying to silence them, and moved through the shadows.

In the centre of the room, Marley was standing silently with his hands pressed against his eyes and his hair plastered to his pale face by sweat. Pen did not need to ask what he was trying not to see; certain it was the memory which had just occurred to him. He put his hand out and caught hold of Marley's sleeve, cursing Napier for causing his friend so much pain.

"Marley?" he whispered. "Come on."

"No," Marley sobbed. "Don't make me move! If I move, it will all happen again."

"It's already happened," Pen said, as gently as he could, but he could feel his free hand clenching into a fist as the darkness swirled around him and encouraged him to seek revenge. He could feel the pulse in his wrist throbbing down into his hand, its tempo reminding him how angry he was.

"The Knave's Rite will work best with anger," he heard his uncle say. "While you want to get revenge for what I have done, you will be unable to address it."

Pen tried to relax, but it was so exhausting that he immediately despaired. He could see Napier out the corner of his eye, but he didn't want to acknowledge him or to endure any further advice or help. The sense his uncle had spoken only annoyed him more, and he tried to focus on the memory of his mother telling him to inhale patience and exhale his frustration. At last, his clenched fist relaxed and fell by his side, and he let go of Marley's arm.

"Come on," he said again, more softly this time. "I won't let it happen." He knew Marley wouldn't be troubled by the vision again and, as soon as he had reached this realisation, he saw Marley relax too and the darkness disappeared.

"Impressive," Napier said, clapping his hands. "I would rather you had not required a reminder about not giving into temptation, but I suppose it was the best we could hope for."

"At least you didn't take that long to find us," Marley said with a laugh, wiping his forehead with his sleeve. "Any lunch?"

Pen looked at his friend, utterly baffled. A moment ago, it had seemed that the torture he was enduring would break him at any second, yet now he seemed to have forgotten it. As Napier nodded and told him to go and set the table, he turned to his nephew and smiled.

"You seem to think that I am a monster, Pendragon. I can ensure he will never know what passed through his mind during those minutes, but that means you must not tell him. Do you understand? Do you understand, Pendragon?"

"Yes," Pen snapped, pulling the door open so forcefully that he nearly hit himself in the face with it. "I understand a lot more than you seem to think I do."

Chapter Sixteen

Fire and Water

For the rest of the day, Pen refused to speak to his uncle any more than he had to, preferring to stand staring out the window at Percy whenever Napier spoke. He relied on being able to talk to his deputy about anything at all and, for the first time since Marley had joined them last May, Napier had made that impossible. To make matters worse, his uncle was behaving as though it would be Pen's fault if anything was said to remind Marley of the ordeal, which Napier had put him through in the first place.

Pen didn't stay downstairs late and went to his study, locking the door with the heavy bolt and willing it to stay closed until he opened it, hoping he had learnt enough Rite to ensure no one would be able to come in. His books couldn't distract him as much as he had hoped, but they did provide some focus.

He noticed for the first time that his uncle had gone into the room during the Christmas holidays and updated the bookshelves, so the texts were now more concerned with different aspects of being Rendelf. Instead of *An Introduction to the Rite*, there were things like *Diplomacy between Those with the Rite and Those Without,* and various autobiographies by Rendelfs throughout the years.

Although he wasn't interested, he desperately needed something to take his mind off how trapped they were and how much he hated Napier, so he took one of the books down from the shelf and carried it to his room. He was certain he was too angry to sleep but, as he turned the yellowing pages of the book, he found that his eyelids were growing heavy and causing his eyes to water and sting with the effort of staying open. At last, he drifted off to sleep and hoped everything would be back to normal once morning came.

He dreamt he was in Orkney, standing in the cove and listening to the sounds of the sea around him. The crashing and roaring of the waves as they beat against the cliffs made him certain there was a terrible storm going on, but there was no other sign of it. Pen looked up at the staircase hewn into the side of the cliff and felt the same fear he had experienced last year when he had reached the top only for his terror to make him physically sick. He tried to tell himself there was a barrier and began to climb and then, when he felt safer, run up the steps. He had nearly reached the top when a gust of wind caught him, and he lost his footing. For a moment, Pen thought he was fine, that the invisible barrier would protect him, but then he found himself falling from the cliff and into the swirling emptiness below, all the time cursing Napier, despite the fact his uncle hadn't even featured in his dream.

Pen awoke and looked around. The book he had taken to bed was lying on the floor, having just slipped from his hands. He glanced out the window and imagined he could see where he had just been in his dream, embracing the situation so completely that he could even smell the salty air. It seemed chilling to think that, just outside his window in the pitch darkness, there was a man who was waiting to enter the house and kill those inside. The Dapplegrim skin had suggested Pen's death was required to make Napier suffer before his own demise. The thought made Pen laugh as he tried to suspend disbelief and imagine a world where his uncle would even notice if anything happened to him. It seemed impossible that Napier could care about keeping Pen happy, safe, or even alive for anything other than to secure his own succession.

It took a long time for him to fall back to sleep again, as he was convinced he would find himself still falling from the sheer cliff which had caused him so much terror. But Pen was shattered and, as the darkness and stillness persisted, he drifted off. His dreams didn't take him back to Orkney, but he was certain he must have dreamt about Isolde, as the Knave's Thaumaturge was the first person he thought of when he awoke. Pen glanced outside and saw that the snow was beginning to fall again, swirling around Honour's Rest, and covering his small window even as he sat and watched.

He wasn't inclined to get out of the warm bed so sat thumbing his way through one of the books with no real intention of reading it, just looking for an excuse to stay away from his uncle and the colder rooms of the house. However, Pen couldn't ignore the gong which rang to get him up – he had learnt early enough that Napier would not tolerate that – so he eventually had to swing his legs round and begin the cold, uninviting process of getting up.

By the time he arrived downstairs, Napier and Marley had already eaten breakfast and the only thing left on the table was a piece of lukewarm toast, which Pen stared at without enthusiasm.

"I expected you up earlier, Pendragon," his uncle said, and Pen shrugged his shoulders. Out the corner of his eye he could see Marley shuffling, so he wondered if his friend had already argued with Napier about the Rendelf's treatment of his apprentice. The irony was, he thought as he chewed the toast so fiercely that he bit the side of his mouth, Marley couldn't know why Pen was so angry with his uncle.

"Do not ignore me, Pendragon," Napier snapped, and Pen spun around.

Unable to contain himself, he sent an angry blast of the Rite in his uncle's direction and watched with a combination of guilt and pleasure as Napier tripped slightly in his attempt to steady himself.

"That was not what I meant," the Rendelf muttered, before marching out the room without saying anything further. Marley made a slight move as though he was torn between following Napier and going to sit with Pen but, in the end, he just stayed standing at the window, looking out at the snow. Even from where he was sitting, Pen could see a scorched area of grass on the lawn, in the middle of which was standing the tall, hooded figure of Percy Fields.

But Percy wasn't his concern right now. In fact, a part of him would rather face the Knave's Thaumaturge alone than spend another moment locked in the house with Napier. It seemed much worse that he was relying on his uncle to be a support and guide but was only receiving snide remarks and torturous punishment for some offence which he genuinely couldn't identify. His anger was so engulfing he could barely swallow the food, which was sticking to the back of his tongue and choking him.

"Napier says we have to think of a way to defeat Percy," Marley said at last, and Pen jumped at the sound of a voice, unsure whether he was glad his friend had spoken or if he just wished the silence had been left undamaged.

"Well, we should, shouldn't we?" Pen snapped, sounding a lot like his uncle had done a few minutes earlier. "I mean, it's not like he's the Rendelf, is it?"

"I think he wants to help us," Marley said. "But he wants us to try and come up with some ideas about how to get rid of him."

"I think I'm going to go, Marley," Pen muttered.

"I'd just leave him to it, if I were you."

"No, I don't mean go after *him*. I'm just going to go. Home. You know, I think that the Christmas holidays made me realise this is just some bizarre world I don't belong in, and Napier's hardly done anything to make me think otherwise. I'm sorry, Marley." He bowed his head in acknowledgment of the defeat.

"Don't be stupid, Pen," Marley whispered. "You can't run away. You've made your Choice, haven't you?"

"I'm sure I don't have to keep it. You've had almost as

much training as me. And you'd do a better job because you've already mastered how to keep the Knave's Rite under control."

"You know that's not true," Marley replied, sounding almost as firm as Napier. "I've chosen the Just Rite and so the Knave's Rite is hidden from me. It's got nothing to do with any ability to control it."

Pen didn't need to feel any more trapped than he already was, so Marley's words just made him feel as though the ground had opened up in front of him and the only way out was to dive into the abyss and hope for the best. He got to his feet and walked away, feeling slightly numb.

The halls and rooms seemed to close in around him, so Honour's Rest felt even more like a prison than it had when he had voiced his concerns to Marley. Eventually, he found himself sitting on the steps in the entrance hall, staring at the sword he had once used in an attempt to kill his uncle.

"Thinking of happier times?"

Pen turned around and saw Napier walking towards him. He forced a laugh.

"Pendragon, you will make a great Rendelf one day. But you have so much to learn between this day and that. I hope it will be a long time in the future and that you will have weeks or months to prepare for the day when it arrives. But that may not be the case. I am as mortal as anyone and could drop dead at any second. I need to make sure you are ready to take over. Remember, as soon as you are sixteen, you will be the Deputy Rendelf. That will no longer be Erlend's responsibility."

"But it isn't what I want!" Pen shouted, causing

tapestries and swords to shiver in an echo of his anger. "I haven't got the ability to control it. You saw what happened yesterday! You saw how much I listened to those voices in the darkness."

"We all listen to the voices in the darkness, Pendragon," Napier whispered. "That is how we know we're travelling in the light." He turned to walk away but then seemed to think better of it and moved closer to Pen. Without saying another word, he sat down beside his nephew on the step.

Pen felt his temper waning with the silent company and began to believe that perhaps there was a future for him in this place. He looked around and was reminded how he loved Honour's Rest and just how much he had missed it while surrounded by his school friends, who had understood nothing about the world he lived in. He found some peace in the beautiful glow which was filling the rooms, as though the sunset was penetrating every window in the house.

Pen leapt to his feet. He had only just had breakfast and, as short as the winter days were in this part of the country, it was definitely not time for the sun to set.

"Fire!" he hissed. He had meant to shout but his voice seemed to have abandoned him. Napier leapt up and rushed to the window, looking down. Clearly Percy, tired by being denied entry into the house he was claiming as his own, had started a fire with the intention of smoking the three inhabitants out. *Or perhaps*, Pen thought with a shudder, *he simply wants us to die in here.*

After all, what good was Honour's Rest to Percy for as long as they were alive?

As the thoughts occurred to Pen, he felt the panic

welling up inside him, until he just wanted to open the door and run out. Surely it was better to die through any means other than fire? As he turned to run towards the door, he felt Napier grip his arm.

"I can keep the flames at bay," he said, his free hand already contorted with the effort of stopping the fire from burning the house, "but that is all. I think our uninvited guest has overstayed his welcome though, so it will be down to you and Marley to sort that out."

Pen nodded and was about to ask where Marley was, when his friend ran into the room, pointing at the windows.

"Have you seen?"

"Yes," Napier replied. "Now, if you would excuse me, I think I may be able to concentrate better in my study, so perhaps I can leave it to Pendragon to explain what is going on." He left without another word, so Marley could only stare after him.

"He wants us to get rid of him," Pen said, turning to his friend.

"You mean kill him?"

"I suppose so," he shrugged. "Percy hasn't got any intention of going anywhere without a fight to the death."

"I don't think I can kill someone."

"Oh, I'm sure you could if you really needed to."

"No, Pen," Marley said pointedly. "I *can't*. I made the Choice, remember? So that Rite's denied me. It's going to have to be you who actually kills him."

Pen stood still for a moment. Suddenly, the flames and smoke and the threat from Percy Fields didn't bother him. It hadn't occurred to him that he would need to single-handedly kill the human being who was standing just outside. He thought of his mother and her hatred of any violence. He would never be able to look at her again after doing such a terrible thing, but he knew the safety of his uncle and his best friend depended on him.

As Pen was trying to steel himself to make the sickening decision, his attention was diverted by a sudden crash as the glass in the large window exploded in the heat and scattered across the floor. He stared down at his reflection, broken in the fragments, and nodded his head.

"Well, that's what's going to have to happen then," he said at last. "Not that I have command of any kind of Rite which would allow me to kill someone. I haven't been reading those books well enough, I know, but I didn't think I'd need to know it so soon."

"There's got to be something."

"Well, there's a whole lot of swords here, but Napier managed to get rid of the one I sent after him. *Fortunately.* I suppose I could push him in the loch, but I couldn't be sure he wouldn't just swim, or be able to breathe underwater, and I'm not sure I like the idea of him living in the loch."

"That's it!" Marley said, jumping with excitement. "The kelpie. Call the kelpie. I can't do it, for reasons discussed."

"I don't think I can do that," Pen muttered. "I wouldn't know how to start."

"Just really will it to come to you, to do your bidding. I'll come with you."

Together, the two boys pulled the door open and walked outside. It was bitterly cold, despite the flames which tried to reach them as they walked past. Percy made a move towards them and, for the first time, Pen was able to get a good look at the man.

His face was contorted either with concentration or anger, but there was a terrifying hatred in his eyes as he stared across at them. He had a brand across his forehead which looked like a pair of lips, as though he had been kissed by a woman whose breath burned with hellfire. Pen tried not to think about the Percy who his uncle had said 'kept himself to himself' and focussed instead on how the man was so determined to hurt and kill the occupants of Honour's Rest.

Every time Pen glanced across at Marley, it was to see that he had almost disappeared in a cloud of spray from the loch, as though it was protecting him from the Knave's Thaumaturge. On the other hand, although Percy seemed to be spending as much concentration as he could on ensuring the flames never stopped stretching towards Honour's Rest, he kept sparing dark glances across at the two boys who had appeared, apparently trying to assess the danger they posed.

"Come to me," Pen called, staring into the loch. The floating panels of ice stirred, but nothing else happened. Percy began to laugh.

"You've got to believe it, Pen!" Marley cried from behind the cloud of spray, which he had begun to direct towards the flames surrounding the castle. "Believe it will come, and it will."

"I, who have ridden you into the depths to which you belong. I, who have caught hold of your mane to bend you to my bidding. I call on you to come to me." It did not feel to Pen as though he could have spoken the words, even to his own ears it didn't seem like something he would say, but he was relieved and terrified as the ice broke apart and a great head rose from the water: a horse so huge that

Pen would never have believed it possible until that day when he had been struck dumb by the sight of it. Now he needed to make it respect him enough to do his bidding.

You have called me, Rider.

Pen glanced across to his friend as the water-horse spoke, but Marley didn't seem to have heard or understood the words as he ducked to successfully avoid one of Percy's bursts of white fire.

"Yes," Pen replied at last.

I do not readily come upon the land, Rider. The kelpie tilted its massive head as its voice surged straight into Pen's mind, but he was relieved as it bent its knees and allowed him to place his shaking hand on its wet face. It was so terrifyingly beautiful, so magnificent that, for a moment, Pen could do nothing but watch it, and listen to its voice in his head repeatedly saying *command me!*

It was a pause he should have done without. As he relished in its beauty, he felt himself being thrown backwards through the air, hurtling towards the thick walls of Honour's Rest at a speed which would leave him as little more than a mess of blood and broken bones against the grey stone. He caught Marley's eye as the world seemed to slow down around him, then saw the triumphant look on Percy's face. Frantically, he told himself that the walls of the house were soft, that there was a barrier to stop him from being killed.

He still hit the wall, but it felt more like falling hard and headfirst against a gym mat, rather than solid stone. Still, his vision swam, and he fell in a heap on the ground some ten feet below. He could see Marley running towards him, but the kelpie needed only a single bound to be at his side.

Command me, Rider! it demanded, nudging his bleeding head with its soft, watery nose.

"Kill him," Pen murmured.

The water-horse turned around and charged at the Knave's Thaumaturge. Pen could feel Marley's shaking hand sliding under his head, but his eyes were fixed on Percy Fields as the kelpie caught him with its teeth and threw him into the air. The Knave's Thaumaturge struggled, throwing out blasts of white fire which came to a hissing death as they struck the creature's watery body. Pen's vision was blurring, and Marley's voice sounded further and further away, but he fought to keep his focus on the kelpie as it finally flung the man down onto the ground and trampled him to a watery death beneath its massive forefeet.

As Percy lay a short distance away, his cold eyes staring blankly towards the house he had laid siege to, the water-horse turned to Pen, who found that his voice had left him.

Thank you, he thought as the world around him went dark. *You can go home.*

Take care, Rider, the kelpie said, plunging back into the water as Pen gave in to unconsciousness.

Chapter Seventeen

Away from Home

There was something around his head, something blocking his vision and making it impossible for him to open his eyes, but Pen was very aware of his surroundings. The Rite was coursing through his body as though his blood was carrying that instead of oxygen to his vital organs, and he felt dizzy and terrifyingly breathless. He was certain he was on the chaise longue in his uncle's study again but was unsure what had passed between the moment the kelpie had dived back into the water and now.

"Good evening," he heard Napier say. "Don't bother trying to get up."

"He's dead," Pen whispered. "I killed him." His voice sounded painfully loud, each syllable hitting against the sides of his skull and reverberating until another one took its place.

"Yes, he's dead. I'm dealing with that. But you are my primary concern right now."

Pen felt the thing being moved away from his eyes and he blinked them open to see two of his uncle staring at him, one in focus and the other blurry and a short distance away.

"Are you using the Rite?" Pen asked, putting his hand up to shield his eyes.

"No."

"Oh. Then there's something not right with what I'm seeing." He felt himself drifting off into unconsciousness again and the double vision of Napier seemed to multiply and swim around him as he heard his uncle saying words he couldn't follow or understand. The world was collapsing into his mind, as though he would wake up and discover that it was still the Christmas holidays, or perhaps that Justin Murchison had never fallen into the school pond.

Something was very different the next time he woke up. The Rite was no longer suffocating him, and he was lying on a strange bed, staring up at a white ceiling. He could hear voices which didn't belong to either Napier or Marley and yet were oddly familiar, so he felt guilty for not recognising them.

"Pendragon." Now it was undoubtedly his mother's voice, and he tilted his head to look at her. The effort made him dizzy. "Pendragon, sweetheart."

She got to her feet and leant over him so he could see her without having to move. Her eyes were red. Did she already know what he had done?

"I'm sorry," he whispered. "He would have killed us."

"Shh," his mother said, running her slender hand down his face.

He glanced past her. He could see his father in the doorway, staring intently at a screen and raging in silence at his older brother.

"It wasn't Uncle Napier's fault," Pen said as clearly as he could, and the two brothers turned around to look at him.

"Hello, Pen," Jarvis said, moving over and kissing his son on the forehead. "Who said I thought it was your Uncle Napier's fault?"

"You didn't send me to live with him because you thought he would teach me maths," Pen replied with a smile, raising his hand and tapping his head lightly with his forefinger. Even that was an effort.

It was true that, as he became more aware of his surroundings (which, apparently, was a hospital ward), the Rite was giving him glimpses into people's minds. He could hear his mother's tearful relief that he was awake after a day of unconsciousness, and his father's anger that Napier hadn't called an ambulance sooner. The Rendelf seemed to be deliberately attempting to connect with his nephew, despite what was going on around them.

Don't worry, Pendragon, he was thinking. *You'll be fine. It's nothing a good rest won't fix. And your father is absolutely right: I really ought to have called an ambulance as soon as you didn't wake up when I brought you inside.*

"No harm done," Pen said aloud, so his parents both smiled at him, and Napier, the intended recipient of his words, nodded appreciatively. It felt strange to have his parents there, stranger almost than being in hospital. Despite the fact he had only parted from them days before, everything which had happened had made them seem more distant than ever. What made things more confusing was how he kept getting flashes of the guilt Napier was feeling, compared to his parents' anger. All through Christmas, he had made sure he never once entered his mother's or father's minds, but now he couldn't stop himself.

"Did you do something about Percy?" he asked eventually to break the uncomfortable non-silence.

"Yes," Napier replied, his voice as clipped and emotionless as ever. "He has been cremated, and I will scatter the ashes around the old farm."

Pen nodded. He could see the look of horror on his parents' faces and knew they would never understand just why the man needed to die. Perhaps in forgiving him, they had pinned all the blame on Napier, as his mother glared at her brother-in-law, whilst still stroking her son's hair. It made Pen feel almost painfully guilty. They would all have died had things not worked out as they had done, burned to death, or suffocated by the smoke which Napier had skilfully kept at bay. But there was no point in telling them, and he could hear his uncle having the same thoughts, combined with a willingness to accept that his younger brother was furious with him.

Pen stayed in hospital for another two days but, before he was discharged, his mother and father had to go south for the funeral of a friend, so it was Napier who picked him up in the vintage car. During the time that he had been lying in the uncomfortable bed and watching inane television programmes with the other boys on the ward, Pen had been trying desperately to get the Rite under control. He didn't want to know that Callum (two beds down) kept having fantasies about his girlfriend in a nurse's uniform, or that Nick (two beds down from Callum) was enduring painful flashbacks to the car accident which had landed him here and his little sister in the Intensive Care Unit. He had been so buffeted by other people's thoughts that he had hardly managed any time for his own. His uncle didn't speak in the car though, and Pen was relieved to find he wasn't being bombarded by Napier's thoughts. There was, however, one thing he was desperate to talk to the Rendelf about, feeling certain there was only his uncle who could share the conversation.

"I killed him."

"He would have killed you," Napier said, sliding his hand down the steering wheel as he spoke. "It was self-defence."

"No," Pen whispered. "It wasn't self-defence."

"No, I know. It was in defence of others. And that is why you will make an excellent Rendelf." There was silence for a while as Pen realised what a compliment his uncle had just paid him. "And you used the Rite masterfully. Not only in summoning the kelpie, but also in acting quickly enough to stop yourself from getting killed. Your parents needed to blame someone for what happened. I'm happy to bear the brunt of their anger. I could not bear to watch them grieve though."

"Didn't you have anything to do with my dad when you were growing up?" Pen asked, looking out at the snowy hills.

"Not really. He was so much younger. But you've got his temper, Pendragon," Napier said with a fond smile. "I was reminded of that during the last couple of days."

Pen smiled back. He liked to think that he had something in common with his father, who had always been one of his heroes. The rest of the journey was conducted in silence until they reached Honour's Rest. Pen got out and stood looking at the loch for a while.

"Is it unusual to have ridden a kelpie?" he asked as his uncle returned from the garage.

"Very," Napier said, staring at the water. "It is rare enough to be able to command a water-horse and it can only be done with a strong use of the Rite. That's how I knew you had chosen your deputy well. But to *ride* a kelpie? You will have its allegiance for life, I think."

"That was how I killed Percy," Pen whispered. "The kelpie–"

"I know."

"It called me *Rider*."

"Because that is how it will always define you. Just remember, Pendragon, it is cruel to summon a kelpie to spend too long on the ground. They belong in the water and cannot survive for long outside of it." He put his hand on his nephew's shoulder and led him inside, perhaps noticing how Pen's eyes had slid towards the place where Percy had been trampled to death.

As they walked into the house, Pen had an overwhelming feeling of being home, as though Honour's Rest would always be the place to which he would return. He spared a thought for his parents' bungalow but, although he loved them, the house couldn't rival the affection he felt for the enigmatic castle in the middle of the loch.

"Hello, Pen," Marley said, walking out of the drawing room. "Sorry I couldn't come and see you." He made no other reference to his hospitalisation, and Pen was grateful for this. "Napier, there's someone to see you. About Percy."

"From Edinburgh?"

"No, London."

"Right." Napier walked into the drawing room and closed the door behind him.

"You were amazing, Pen!" Marley blurted out as soon as Napier was gone. "Honestly, the kelpie seemed to be connecting with you!"

Pen laughed, and the pair of them wandered into the living room, where they sat for a while, discussing what had happened and what they wished had been different. Pen's annoyance at Marley for being protected by Napier seemed to have died along with Percy Fields, so it was as though they were talking for the first time since he had gone south for Christmas.

It turned out that the man from London had summoned Napier and the two boys to a hearing which, Napier assured them, was common practice whenever a Rendelf had to kill in order to fulfil his duties.

"They aren't like trials," he said as they sat down to dinner. "But they're serious enough. We'll take the train down first thing tomorrow and have a full day in London before the actual inquiry. Pendragon, if you wish to go home for a while then that would be fine."

"No," Pen said. "I've just seen Mum and Dad. Have you been to London before, Marley?"

"No. But I have a list of about a hundred things to do there."

"If there is anywhere in the world where you can do one hundred things in three days, Marley," Napier said with a smile, "it is London."

The journey down was uncomfortable for Pen, who found the motion of the train left him feeling sick. Instead of joining his uncle and friend at dinner, he crept away to bed and lay there alone, thinking about how he had become a murderer. It was the thought which most occupied his mind whenever he was alone, and he kept replaying the moment over in his head and wondering if there had been any way he could have defeated the Knave's Thaumaturge without killing him.

The next day, he was feeling less sick, and he enjoyed taking Marley to see all the sights. Napier had given them his credit card, which had an absurdly high limit and, as a result, they went into all the museums and attractions they could reach in the day. Despite his fear of heights, the London Eye was Pen's personal favourite, although Marley seemed to enjoy Madame Tussauds. Pen didn't have the heart to tell him that it was his least favourite place in London, as he found the blank stares of the waxworks slightly creepy.

Napier joined them at the Tower of London and pointed out veiled references to the Rite which had been carved patiently into the walls hundreds of years earlier. Afterwards, he took them out to dinner at a place of their choosing. Napier was dressed for something upmarket, so he sat in the fast-food restaurant in a suit while Pen and Marley both shovelled sushi and noodles into their mouths. It was only when they sat down for dinner that Pen realised they had been walking around London the entire day with only crisps to sustain them.

When the morning of the hearing came, they breakfasted early and then took a black cab to the office where it was going to be held. As soon as they entered, Pen knew they had nothing to worry about. The office staff greeted Napier warmly and with a kind of hero-worship which extended to his two apprentices. Pen and

Marley politely grinned their way through a number of introductions to people they knew they would never remember, before being guided to the room where the hearing was going to be held.

The table was set out in a circle, and Napier indicated for the boys to sit at either side of him and wait for the rest of the board to come in. When they did, they were as excited to see Napier and meet Marley and Pen as the others had been.

"So," Mr Usman, who was chairing the session, said after everyone had been introduced and was sitting around the table. "You know the drill, Napier. But for the sake of Pendragon and Marley, perhaps I ought to explain?"

"Be my guest, Aban," Napier said, with a smile and a polite wave of his hand.

"This isn't a trial," Aban Usman said. "We need to know what happened so we can be confident that no one is taking the law into their own hands. However, it's also to make sure the Rendelf has the support he needs from us." Pen and Marley both nodded and Mr Usman grinned. "You really don't need to look so nervous. Napier, perhaps you'd show them how it's done." Pen watched his uncle nod politely and lean forward on his chair.

"From my written report dated the eighth of January, the board is aware of the events up to and including the seventh. On the eighth, the Knave's Thaumaturge, Percy Fields, took up a hostile position outside Honour's Rest. One day later, he attempted to set the house on fire. While I used the Rite to stop the fire from reaching the building, I instructed Pendragon and Marley to deal with him."

"And," said an elderly woman opposite them, "when you say, 'deal with', you mean?"

"Neutralise the threat," Napier replied coldly. "In reality, kill."

"And then?"

"I believe Marley distracted Percy while Pendragon summoned a kelpie – or water-horse. During this time, Percy Fields became aware of what was happening and attacked Pendragon to stop him from commanding the kelpie. I believe Pendragon then instructed the kelpie to kill the Knave's Thaumaturge, at which point I was able to stop the fire and Marley went to Pendragon's aid."

"Very succinct, Napier," Aban said, his eyes twinkling across the table at the Rendelf, who bowed his head politely. "So, boys, I will ask you to give your own report of what happened. As Apprentice Rendelf, Pendragon, you ought to be first."

"You can call me Pen."

"No," Napier interjected, "you can't. Unless you wish to be known as Abi for the rest of your life."

The chairman chuckled. "Sorry then, my boy, but Pendragon it is. Tell us what happened."

"Beyond what my uncle has already told you?"

"How did you summon the kelpie, Pendragon?" Napier asked.

"I had ridden it last year when, ah, when the occasion presented itself. It seemed almost keen to do what I asked. It wasn't difficult."

"Excellent," Aban said. "But you were hurt?"

"A bit." He didn't want to go into details and was relieved when no one pressed the matter further. Marley gave a brief report and Pen thought his deputy was much better at it. It seemed like a long time later that Mr Usman got steadily to his feet.

"I think we can all agree that the correct procedure has been followed here. Pendragon, your uncle told me you are feeling guilty about what happened."

"Wouldn't you?" Pen found himself asking, and Aban smiled.

"No," he replied, as though it was the most obvious answer in the world. "Through your actions, you saved the lives of your uncle and your deputy, as well as countless others who would have suffered if Percy had not been stopped. I hope we can draw a line under this now." There was no arguing, and Pen felt a smile flicker across his face as the other members of the board joined in with a chorus of 'hear, hear'.

Afterwards, they were invited into Aban Usman's office for refreshments, which was a relief as it had been so long since breakfast. While they were eating, Aban Usman moved over and put his chubby arm around Pen's thin shoulders, so he had to quickly shuffle his feet to withstand the weight.

"Pen, you're just what is needed around here. And what a change in Napier since he selected an apprentice! I don't have the Rite, but I can see just what a positive difference you've made to him. Did you know I knew your father when he was younger than you are now?"

"Oh right," Pen said awkwardly, not knowing whether to try and look at the man or to keep looking away. If he did try to look at him, they would be almost alarmingly close to each other.

"Yes. My mother had the Rite, you know? She knew the previous Rendelf, so we visited Honour's Rest. Napier had just turned twenty-one and his parents and little brother had come for his birthday. Jarvis – I mean, your father – and I are only a year apart in age, so we got on like a house on fire and explored the whole place. We even found the Guardians' Room. But we soon got chased out of there."

"The Guardians' Room?"

"Yes, you'll have to see if you can find it. Please send my best wishes to your father, Pen. By God, I'd give anything for an excuse to go back to Honour's Rest." With that, he patted Pen hard on the back and walked away to talk to Napier, leaving Pen wondering what on earth the Guardians' Room could be.

Chapter Eighteen

The Vow of the Dying

Despite the fact Pen's interest had been piqued by the man at the office in London, there was no time to discuss the challenge which had been set before them by the extremely likable Aban Usman. Although Pen tried to talk to Marley about it on the way back, they had to take brief opportunities which hardly presented themselves, as Napier was determined they would maintain the challenging level of study which had started their year. He did not seem to realise that, with no lunatic outside wanting them dead, Pen couldn't focus, and his thoughts kept straying back to the Guardians' Room.

As January became February, and then March appeared on the calendar, he despaired of the idea. Napier seemed determined to have them shadow him in everything he did, until the promise of a trip to London, Cardiff or

Belfast started to hold little interest, and Pen found he could recite the stops between Aviemore and Edinburgh. The most exciting days were the rare occasions when the trains were delayed and the boys were able to explore the hills around Aviemore and mess around on the ski slopes, much to Napier's annoyance.

Pen had expressed his wish to go home over Easter, so Napier and Marley made plans to go to Orkney and spend the holiday in Deerness with the Shipperbottoms. Pen would be sorry to miss Erlend and Bernadette, but he was excited to see his parents again. He hadn't seen them since they had left him at the hospital in the middle of January, which felt like a lifetime ago. Still, Easter was particularly late – almost the middle of April – so Pen still had plenty of trips and reading to do to satisfy his uncle.

He had always enjoyed hard work, but now Pen found himself wishing he had some energy left at the end of the day so he could play his guitar, which he was missing as though a part of himself had gone on holiday and forgotten to return. But, at the end of each day, he was so tired that all he could do was haul himself up the stairs to his room and collapse, exhausted, on the bed and hope he had remembered to change into his pyjamas.

It came as a relief when Napier announced he was going to leave the pair of them at the house while he went out, but the amount of work he left them prohibited anything else. Still, not having to rush around the country allowed them to catch their breath after everything they had been through since the trip to London. However, Napier's return brought with it a kind of sadness, which they would willingly have endured another month of dashing around the country to avoid.

"Ishbel Mackenzie died this afternoon," he said, as Pen passed him a cup of tea.

"Ishbel?" Marley asked, but the name was imprinted on Pen's mind from the only time that they met. He glanced across and, as soon as their eyes met, Marley looked down at his feet. "Oh, her. Well, at least she isn't suffering anymore."

Napier gave Marley a long, challenging look, which was made even more frightening by the fact that Marley couldn't meet his gaze.

"I think it's important that you both attend the funeral next week. We'll go shopping for some clothes tomorrow in Inverness. Neither of you have anything suitable."

It wasn't a lot of fun shopping for funeral clothes, Pen thought as they wandered through the cold, wet streets. The sombre nature of the occasion meant that neither of them felt like making jokes or sneaking into shops which would otherwise have been very appealing. Napier chose their clothes and insisted they had them fitted properly so, once they were finished, the pair of them looked very dapper and much older than their fifteen years. Napier paid on his credit card and the boys stood to one side, discussing how expensive it was to buy clothes for the funeral of a woman they had only met once.

"I can hear you," Napier said, putting his pin number into the machine. "I'm afraid this will not be the last funeral you attend before you outgrow these clothes."

Pen and Marley fell silent, and the cashier looked across at them sympathetically. What made it worse was that Pen knew his uncle was probably right.

As they left the shop, Napier continued to explain. "I'm

afraid it is part of being Rendelf. Whenever anyone dies who has had the Rite, they ought to have a representative at their funeral. As Rendelf, you must strive to be that representative whenever possible. Out of respect for the life they have lived."

He didn't say anything else apart from pleasantries for the rest of the trip and, when they got back to Honour's Rest, went straight to his study and did not emerge again for the rest of the evening, even when Pen tried to fetch him down for dinner. Although it was the opportunity both he and Marley had been waiting for, neither of them felt like exploring and they both disappeared to their rooms early, pretending they were tired.

As Pen sat on the side of his bed thinking about what could have made Napier so unhappy, he remembered the request David Mackenzie had made of the Rendelf, pleading with him to end the struggle Ishbel was enduring. Had Napier finally taken matters – and lives – into his own hands? At first the idea was terrifying, as though his uncle believed that he could be judge, jury and executioner but, as the night went on, Pen began to dwell on the memory of how lost Ishbel had become without the sons who had been taken from her. He wondered if he would ever be able to make the kind of decisions that the Rendelf had to accept as part of their daily lives. Somehow, he doubted it. He wasn't as educated as his uncle, nor as confident in his decisions.

As he drifted off to sleep, Pen found himself thinking about Niamh again, and he wondered what she was doing at that moment. It had been a long time since the girl had occupied his thoughts but, for some reason, she was there at that moment. He thought he saw her offering the candle to someone, before turning around and leading a shadowy figure into a place which Pen could only assume was an inner-city park, filled with laughing children, and lovers leaning against old trees to share whispers and kisses. Then Niamh turned around, encouraging the figure to go on without her, as it was bright and sunny in the park and there was no longer any need for candlelight. Turning back to the darkness, Niamh lifted her free hand and waved to Pen, who instinctively waved back, a strange feeling churning through his body, as though he had just witnessed something which wasn't his to see.

Pen didn't tell anyone about the dream. After the events with Isolde last year, he knew better than to share those secrets with his uncle, preferring to keep them to himself and think about them at any moment when he wasn't reading, or being quizzed or tested on his ability to control the Rite.

Ishbel's funeral was in a small village church, and her coffin was already in front of the altar by the time they went in. On it were framed pictures of six little boys with round faces and blonde hair, who smiled out to the congregation. Pen thought there was something strangely familiar about them but, just as he was beginning to panic about where he might have seen them before, he guessed that the photographs must have been displayed in the Mackenzies' living room.

The service focussed on the importance for Ishbel to be back with the sons she loved so much and who had been cruelly taken from her. The priest leading the service clearly had no idea they had been killed by their own grandfather, but it didn't matter, as the message was one of hope and not anger. As the coffin was carried out of church, Napier walked over to David and Charlotte, and whispered a few words to them. David stopped part way down the church aisle to give Napier a warm and tearful embrace, thanking him for everything he had done, which Pen took to be proof that his uncle had played a role in Ishbel's death. It just made him feel more conflicted than he had before. There was not a doubt in his mind that David Mackenzie had adored his wife, and yet he had begged Napier to finish her life.

Marley pushed Pen out of the pew and the two boys stood at the church door as the rest of the attendees walked to the graveside and watched the coffin being lowered into the earth.

"I know what you're thinking, Pen," Marley said. "You're not the only person who remembers."

Pen smiled across at him and then pointed to the small gathering of people. "We should go down there."

"I don't know. It doesn't really seem right."

The two boys moved slightly further down and stood so silently and respectfully that, when the vicar walked back up to the church, he assumed they worked for the undertakers and had to rein in a laugh when they explained his mistake. They didn't feel like laughing though and, in the car on the way back, Pen made it clear to Napier that they wanted some time off. His uncle didn't challenge his request but joined them for dinner for the first time in a week and things seemed to go back to a kind of normal, although Pen was certain he would never be able to look at Napier in the same way again.

When the Rendelf left the following day, explaining that he had to go down to Newcastle and would be away overnight, the two boys felt some excitement at the prospect of finally being able to rise to the challenge Aban had set them two months earlier.

They split up and wandered through the corridors and into every room they could find, apart from Napier's bedroom. They discovered several exciting things, including almost a whole battalion's worth of armour, but they couldn't find anything which seemed to be a Guardians' Room. Pen wondered if it was a joke. Aban Usman did seem like the sort of person who would have enjoyed playing a harmless practical joke on the two boys, even if he wasn't able to see the resulting confusion.

"There's nowhere else," Marley sighed as they closed the door to a small room which harboured only a flag and an old desk, piled high with forgotten and cobweb-strewn papers. "I think he was either having a laugh or else mistaking this place for somewhere else."

"I know," Pen said. "Because there are so many places like this that someone could wind up in." He stared hard at Marley, who gave a nervous chuckle. "There is one place we haven't looked: Napier's room."

They hurried to the Rendelf's bedroom, but the door was locked.

"He's probably protected it with the Rite," Marley muttered, but Pen wasn't going to let that put him off. The curiosity bubbling up inside him would overflow at any moment and he couldn't let that happen. He had to find the room his father had seen decades earlier.

The door isn't locked, he told himself. *Napier forgot to lock it this morning. It isn't locked. The handle's just stiff.*

He tried the handle again and the door opened. Marley grinned across at Pen, but he was too busy rushing into the room. Napier's bedroom, including the many packed bookshelves, was as neat as anything else his uncle did or owned. It was spotlessly clean and tidy, as though he never spent any time there. A photograph on the bedside table showed a young Napier alongside his three deputies, his arms around Erlend and Ramin. Isolde, looking very young and beautiful, was resting her head between Ramin and Napier.

"I've seen that picture before," Marley said, when Pen picked it up. "My dad has a copy, but it's not on display."

Pen just nodded and moved over to the wardrobe, wondering if he would find any other interesting souvenirs which might give him an insight into who Napier had been when he was young. Instead, he found himself walking into a room, with the door slamming shut behind him. He could hear Marley fumbling with the handle, but his interest was drawn to a candle in the middle of the room. It was one of the tall pillar candles he had seen in church, and there was a box of matches beside it. The curiosity he had experienced in his hunt for the room seemed to force Pen's hand towards the box of matches, and he struck one with a flourish which sent sparks flying across the room. Then, very carefully so the match did not go out, he leant forward and lit the wick of the candle.

The light shot out in all directions and Pen stumbled back as he was suddenly aware that he was surrounded by about forty people, each one made only out of the candlelight and the thin threads of smoke which still rose from the match he clutched in his frozen hand. Their clothing suggested they spanned centuries. Some looked as though they could have been alive today, but others wore ruffs or powder wigs, which would have been amusing if Pen hadn't been so horrified.

"You should not have summoned us, boy," one of them said, his voice thin and reedy.

Pen shook his head.

"The knowledge we hold is not yours yet," said another.

"Perhaps you wish it was?"

Pen shook his head again, more desperately this time. He wanted to ask who, or what, they were, but he was too afraid of the answer. How had two eight-year-old boys felt about the terror of finding what he could see now? One of the spectres looked at him quizzically, and he could feel it penetrating his mind as though it took no effort at all.

"But they never struck the match and lit the candle," it said, pointing to the table and the flickering orange flame.

With absolute terror spurring him on, Pen flung himself forward and slammed his hand down on the candle flame, his desperation dulling the pain it caused. He remembered his uncle telling him there were no ghosts in the house, and his father commenting on how old it was and how there must have been some kind of supernatural activity. As the room grew quiet and still again, and he became certain he was the only person there, Pen let out a sigh and stumbled over to the door.

"That's it," he murmured to Marley, who looked at him with an expression of sheer disbelief.

"Well? What's it like?"

"Uh." Pen couldn't think of what to say. "Weird."

"Weird how?"

"Let's just leave it at weird," Pen replied. He pulled the door closed, trying to ensure it locked, but he couldn't seem to lock it with the Rite and eventually had to just give up because Marley was becoming suspicious.

They sat downstairs for the rest of the day before going to bed early, but Pen couldn't sleep after what he had seen in the room. He remembered his uncle telling him about how the Knave's Rite could be used to disturb the dead, and he wondered if that was what he had done. It was only as the sun was beginning to rise that he was able to get to sleep so, by the time he got up, it was closer to lunchtime than breakfast. Marley didn't comment on it, apart from to say he was grateful to have had the opportunity to write to his parents.

Napier was still not back by midnight so, after agreeing with Marley that they ought to just go to bed and greet Napier in the morning, Pen located a hammer and a box of nails, crept into his uncle's room, and began hammering the nails into the door frame. He wasn't really sure what he was hoping to achieve, but even the knowledge of how angry Napier would be wasn't enough to stop him. He was quite certain he wouldn't get any sleep until he knew he had done everything within his power to block off the strange room.

As he was hammering the final nail into the wood, the handle of the bedroom door turned and his uncle walked in, unwinding his long scarf and throwing it onto the bed. He seemed to already know that Pen was there as he didn't look at all surprised when the boy leapt to his feet, sending nails scattering across the floor and apologising profusely.

"The Guardians' Room," Napier said, bending down to help his nephew. "Why on earth did you go looking for that, Pendragon? Do you not remember what I told you? If you go looking for trouble in this house, you will find it."

"It was something Mr Usman mentioned," Pen muttered, getting to his feet as Napier dropped the last of the nails back into the box. Then, in an even quieter voice, he whispered, "Who *are* they?"

"So, not only did you go in, but you lit the candle? You fool."

"Have I done something really wrong?"

"For your own sanity, maybe. The Guardians' Room is also called the Room of Knowledge. It contains the knowledge gleaned from each Rendelf throughout the ages."

"You said there weren't any ghosts."

"They are not ghosts though, Pendragon. You do not see all of who they were, only the knowledge they gained of the Rite. Perhaps some of them were good, others cruel. But it is the last act of any Rendelf to bequeath his knowledge to Honour's Rest to help those who come afterwards. The Vow of the Dying, it is called. Although I am certain it cannot be vocalised, as my own predecessor said nothing at the point of death. Yet his spirit is there too."

"So, you talk to them?"

"They are centuries of knowledge, Pendragon," Napier replied. "I would be a fool not to pay them any attention. But they only share their secrets with the Rendelf. You are lucky they did not do you any harm." He paused for a second and, when he continued, he sounded angry for the first time. "I would like to think I can trust you, Pendragon Devon. Do not let me down again. Now, get out of my sight."

Pen didn't need a second invitation to leave and almost ran from the room, his heart pounding and his legs feeling as though they would give way at any moment.

Chapter Nineteen

The Last Summer

Pen wished he would never have to think about the Guardians' Room again, but it wouldn't leave his thoughts until he left Honour's Rest and returned down to England to spend Easter with his parents, who were both relieved and overjoyed to see him again. However, he was irritated when he discovered that Napier had been in touch with Jarvis to make a demand which Pen guessed was punishment for what had happened. It was his mother who told him of Napier's insistence that Pen went into the school to take full responsibility for what had happened to Justin Murchison a year earlier.

"That hardly seems fair," Pen had snapped, as he sat on his bed plucking the guitar strings. "Am I supposed to tell him *exactly* what happened?"

"Your uncle thinks it will do you good to accept

responsibility, however you choose to do so," his mother replied. "You know, Pendragon, I think he's right. You know it was you, so the only lie you'll be telling will be that you told a lie in the first place."

"But that's just it, isn't it? I haven't told any lies so far."

However, the last day of term found him sitting outside Mr Carling's office again, this time in casual clothes and with the knowledge that he was working for a greater good which his old headteacher couldn't even begin to comprehend.

"Pendragon Devon." Mr Carling beamed as he opened his office door and saw the boy, who got to his feet and smiled. "Well, look at you. You're a young gentleman now. Your parents must be proud."

"Thank you, sir," Pen said with a slight bow of his head. The old-fashioned mannerisms he had picked up from Napier seemed to jar with the surroundings, but his ideas of etiquette had changed while he had been at Honour's Rest. "Perhaps we could discuss things in your office." He indicated to the door, and Mr Carling looked at him strangely for a moment. Pen could hear his thoughts, wondering what could have happened to the boy he had known to make him so altered. There was surprise there, amusement and, much to Pen's annoyance, an element of pride. Unaware that the boy before him knew exactly what he was thinking, Mr Carling opened the door and led Pen into the office where, a year ago, he had sat crying at the thought of being excluded.

"Your parents tell me you've been living in Scotland? With your uncle?"

"Yes, sir."

"And have you enjoyed that? Is he a good teacher? Do

you miss people your own age?"

For a moment, Pen wasn't sure whether the headteacher had spoken or whether he had just heard the questions as they had passed through Mr Carling's mind. Still, he knew they all needed answering to maintain politeness, so Pen attempted to do so with the fewest possible manipulations of the truth.

"I love it," he said. "The house is like something out of a novel, and I've been fortunate enough to have the company of a great friend who is my age. My Uncle Napier isn't a bad teacher, but he believes in the importance of self-directed study. I've also had the opportunity to travel and, well, have adventures." He felt his thumb rub absent-mindedly along the thin scar on his hand and wondered what the man in front of him would think if he told him exactly what had happened.

"Good, good," Mr Carling said. "It was a shame about what happened, Pen. You were an excellent student and you're missed by all the teachers. And most of the pupils as well."

"That's kind of you to say," Pen said with a smile, bowing his head again and this time enjoying the puzzlement on the headteacher's face and the sheer confusion in his mind. "But there's one thing in particular that I came here to say."

"And what's that?"

"I should apologise for what happened. It was me who pushed Justin."

"Don't be silly, Pen," Mr Carling said, with a nervous laugh. "Haven't your parents told you? A couple of girls were taking pictures outside the library that day, and you were in the background. You couldn't possibly have done it."

"All the same," Pen said, trying to hide his annoyance at his mother for not telling him the truth, "I was responsible."

It was a great pleasure to know that the tables had been turned so, at the end of the conversation, it was Mr Carling who was nearly reduced to nervous tears, which wasn't made any better when Pen accidentally answered a question which had not yet been spoken. It was only when he left the school with a smug sense of achievement and satisfaction that it occurred to him why Napier may have made the demand, and it had more to do with affection than punishment.

The rest of the Easter holiday passed as quickly as Christmas, and Pen enjoyed spending time with his parents. His father had to work most of the weekdays, so Pen stayed with his mother during the day. For as long as he could remember, she had volunteered as a reader in local nursing homes, and he took the opportunity to accompany her. He used the Rite to make the residents feel calm and settled and, before the end of the two weeks, the managers and carers were begging him to stay, and his mother couldn't contain the pride she always felt in her son.

However, the Easter holidays couldn't last any longer than the three weeks Napier had allocated. As April began its decline, Pen flew from Manchester up to Inverness, where his uncle and Marley met him at the airport. Napier insisted on hearing the story about Mr Carling and Marley laughed hysterically as Pen described how, whilst he had initially read the headteacher's mind on purpose, he had started to accidentally anticipate the next questions and Mr Carling had encouraged him out of the room. Napier didn't mention the Guardians' Room again, and Pen was hopeful he had heard the last of it.

It felt right to be back at Honour's Rest, and he and Marley were able to make the most of the longer days by fitting in as much study as Napier demanded of them and then going into the garden or going fishing on the loch. They continued to accompany Napier on his visits and were both sorry to hear that David Mackenzie had died during the Easter break.

"So soon after his wife," Pen sighed. "They must have really loved each other."

"They did," his uncle replied. "But you do not need to be told that by me."

They had missed David's funeral, but Napier laid flowers at the graveside one evening and took the boys with him. Pen hadn't known many people who had died and perhaps that was why his mind drifted back to the story his uncle had told him about Ramin, who had died when he was younger than Pen.

"Where is Ramin buried?"

Napier looked across at him, one eyebrow raised above a wide eye.

"He isn't," he said at last. "Ramin was a Zoroastrian. They practise excarnation."

"Ex– what?" Marley asked, joining the conversation and making Pen think that perhaps he shouldn't have brought up the subject.

"Excarnation. After he died, the old Rendelf built a tower to hold the body, which was left to be – ah – recycled."

"Recycled?"

"When a person is buried, Pendragon, their body is given to the earth. When a person is excarnated, their body is given to birds of prey, and other scavengers."

"That's a bit horrible," Marley said, walking away, but Pen stayed there for a moment, looking across at his uncle.

"Where is the tower?"

"What a strange question, Pendragon," Napier said, suddenly interested in rearranging the flowers on the graveside and positioning the accompanying card carefully. "Why would you ask that above anything else?"

"I just wondered," he shrugged, trying to make it sound like he didn't desperately need the answer.

"I believe the tower was built somewhere in the south of Caithness. Quite near to Dunbeath Strath."

Although it was the answer Pen had been expecting, he still felt a nervous shiver run down his neck and freeze the warmth from the spring sunshine. So that was why Isolde had been so desperate to claim the land there. To be near the boy she worshipped and adored.

The visit to the cemetery left Pendragon with yet more things to think about and, as the weeks wore on and summer returned, he kept trying to imagine the desperation Isolde must have experienced.

Perhaps the surest sign of the summer was the reappearance of tourists, who would stop their cars at the end of the causeway and take pictures of Honour's Rest. The two boys attempted to photobomb as many people as they could, either fishing or messing around on the causeway. On one occasion, Napier had to come out and stop them when a particularly keen American tourist crossed the causeway and began talking to Pen and Marley, who found it hilarious to regale him with completely fictional and rather gruesome stories about the house.

In some ways, it felt as though their whole lives had been building up to that summer, and Pen was certain he would never feel as unbound as he did in those months. After his birthday in October, he would need to be ready to take on the role he had been training for, and Napier was bound to increase the amount of work he expected them both to do. For now, though, his uncle left the two boys to their own devices and spent an increasing amount of time away from Honour's Rest, so the house was often left in their care.

Pen did not venture into his uncle's room again but, on the rare wet days or the more common humid days, when the midges would swarm around the loch-side and attach themselves to anything or anybody, he and Marley filled their time by using the Rite to clean the house. Once they had finished, the books were sorted in the library and all the ornaments around the house, from the claymores to the small china money boxes in the Stuart Room, were as clean as they had ever been. It seemed, at that point in time, the best way to thank Napier for giving them the time and space they were enjoying so much.

Whenever he was alone in his room, Pen took up more self-directed study, reading his way through the various biographies and memoirs which his uncle had put there at the start of the year. He also began playing the guitar more often, making up soundtracks to the stories and trying to record them using his mobile which, although it had no signal anywhere near Honour's Rest, was still one of the last links with the world he had left behind.

At the end of August, Napier went away on an

international trip to meet with other Rendelfs, which he explained was common practice. Pen, however, couldn't help but notice that he came back seeming slightly distracted, as though something had happened which meant he had been forced to leave some of his attention overseas. Between them, he and Marley tried to decide whether it was possible for Napier to have found a girlfriend, but the thought caused them both to choke with hysterical laughter.

It was September by the time Napier had returned, so it was time to prepare for the darker nights which would envelope Honour's Rest in that familiar darkness that never quite descended in summer. The first evening the Northern Lights made a reappearance, Pen laughed at the memory of how his excitement last year had reached the front page of the news. He felt like he could never lose control of the Rite again: as though all the hard work and practice he had endured at Napier's insistence had left him fully aware of how the Rite needed to be handled.

Marley, on the other hand, had chosen to explore the healing Rite so Napier sent him to stay with a healer who worked at the hospital, leaving Pen alone with his uncle for the first time since last year. They had more in common now, but it was still a challenge for Pen to find a topic of conversation which Napier would approve of and engage in.

"Are you pleased with your progress, Pendragon?" Napier asked one evening as they sat down in the living room together. Pen paused whilst closing the curtains.

"Yes. Yes, I suppose so."

"There's a very unpleasant task I need to do next month," Napier said slowly. "I would appreciate your support, but I need to know you are prepared for the darker parts of the role."

"What do you mean?"

"What has upset you most, in the seventeen months since you moved in here?"

Pen couldn't think of the answer. Had it been letting Marley be tortured by Isolde because Pen had been sure he could take on an experienced Knave's Thaumaturge? Or had it been abandoning Niamh to a fate he still didn't know? Or killing Percy? Or finding the Guardians' Room? Too many terrible things had happened and, for a moment, he stayed silent at the thought of them.

"I don't know," he whispered. "I suppose becoming a killer was pretty bad."

"But not a murderer," Napier said, holding up his hand. "Whatever your mother may say, Pendragon, there is a difference. Can you imagine how different everything would be if you had not killed Percy? Everybody would be at the mercy of Isolde."

"So, what did you expect me to say?"

"Whatever was the truth," Napier replied. "I need to know which aspects of the job will distress you the most, and then we can work on them. I cannot send you out to kill – as you know, that happens extremely rarely – but it is useful to know that you are concerned by that. Have your parents ever mentioned it to you, by the way?"

"Never."

"What I expected. They still hold me responsible. And they will hold me in even lower regard if they hear what I have to ask you to do now."

"That sounds ominous. Worse than killing someone, you think?"

"Do you remember what happened to Amanda Shipperbottom?"

"She fell off a cliff."

"And why was that?"

"Because Bernadette wanted to leave the Knave's Rite."

"Next month, I need you to come down to Edinburgh with me. A young man wishes to go through that process."

"Does he understand what will happen?"

"I hope I have made it clear to him," Napier snapped. "If you believe you can talk him out of his decision then perhaps you ought to try."

Pen just shook his head before trying to change the subject, but it occurred to him this was the beginning of the life his summer had been building towards. This was clearly the part of the job which Napier hated the most, which had led the Rendelf to assume that his nephew would feel the same way. As soon as Pen realised that Napier was no longer in the mood to talk and his answers were becoming shorter and sharper, he excused himself and went to bed.

Somehow, the change in atmosphere seemed worse because he had known all along that the summer was to be his last period of freedom. As he looked ahead to the autumn in which he would legally become able to hold the title of Rendelf, Pen felt as though a cage was being set up around him. Witnessing this man's oath to change his life at the expense of another was just the beginning.

While sitting alone on his bed, watching the darkness which swirled around the house and the starlight reflecting in the loch, Pen thought for a second he saw a gleam of silver, like a curved blade. He knew he had seen this before, but it took him a moment before he realised it looked like the same thing he had cut himself on at the bottom of the loch. But who was wielding it down there, where it reflected the stars as though the light was drawn to its shining silver surface? He got up from the bed and moved to the window but, in the darkness, he couldn't make out anyone, and the silver blade seemed to have disappeared.

Chapter Twenty

Self-Sacrifice

Marley returned from studying two days before they were due to go to Edinburgh, but he told Pen and Napier that his tutor had secured him a work experience placement at the local hospital, and he was keen to put his newly-found talents into practice. Although Pen encouraged him to accept the opportunity, he was painfully disappointed that Marley would be unable to go south with him and Napier, as he felt he would need the company. However, perhaps because of his family history, Napier was almost as relieved as Marley at the prospect that he wouldn't be there.

"You don't mind, do you, Pen?" Marley asked, as they sat down to dinner on the evening before they were due to leave. "Apparently I'm quite good at healing, which will make my dad happy."

"No," Pen lied through his teeth as he moved his food around the plate without eating. "I'm really happy for you too. Just don't get drawn into reading any minds at the hospital. Trust me, it's better not to."

Marley smiled and then went back to eating, unaware of just how uncomfortable Pen was with the revelation. He didn't have much opportunity to notice however, as Napier began to talk to him about the placement and how he expected it to differ from the work he had already been doing.

Pen hardly heard them. He was too worried about what to expect from his trip to Edinburgh and, the next day, he took the opportunity to talk to Marley about it, despite knowing it would make his uncle furious.

"That sounds like a terrible way to spend a Friday morning," Marley said. "I'm guessing that's why Napier was so keen for me to do the placement, because he thinks it will bring up thoughts of Amanda. But I'll go with you if you want?"

"That's why I like having you as my deputy, Marley," Pen said with a smile. "Because I knew you'd say that. But honestly, I think I'm overreacting. I mean, this man has made his own decision, hasn't he? Are there any rules to say that a Just Thaumaturge can't be married to a Knave's Thaumaturge, or vice versa?"

"I haven't ever come across any. It's more of a safety thing. It makes others safer around them. I don't think it would have bothered my dad, but if Napier had died and he'd become Rendelf then he couldn't have my mum being some kind of liability. As it is, the Rite she can use is limited, but at least she can't do any harm."

It made Pen feel better about the whole situation to

hear Marley, whose family had suffered so much at the hands of the Commitment, talking about it so frankly. Marley's attention, however, diverted to his concerns for the role he was taking on at the hospital, and Pen was happy to encourage the change in topic. They managed to laugh about some of the things which might happen, discussing the difference between the role of a healing thaumaturge and that of a standard doctor or nurse.

"Could you fix your finger then?" Pen asked, gesturing to Marley's hand. His friend shook his head.

"No. You can't just magic things back. I could have made a better job of your hand. Or your head, for that matter."

"You make it sound like I'm falling apart," Pen laughed, although he wasn't sure it was funny.

Marley was so excited about his placement that, when the morning came and Pen shuffled his way into the breakfast room, his deputy was already prepared to go. Napier was taking them both to Inverness, from where he and Pen would get the train down to Edinburgh, and Marley would stay with his mentor. Pen tried to keep buoyant so he didn't dampen Marley's spirits but, as soon as he and his uncle were on the train, he sat staring out of the window and refused to be drawn into conversation.

Edinburgh had never looked so uninviting, despite the autumn sunshine lighting Princes Street and guiding them towards the Royal Mile. Ever since his first visit to the city, Pen had loved it, but now he could feel nothing but disgust as he turned his head to look at the castle which dominated the skyline to his right. Napier seemed not to notice but took his arm firmly.

"Did you know," his uncle said, pulling him across the

road, "that this is where they used to burn witches?"

"Were they?" Pen asked.

"Were they what?"

"Witches?"

"In the sixteenth century, three occupants of Honour's Rest were burnt at the stake here. And it's a common misconception that it was always women."

"Why are you telling me this?" Pen asked, pulling away from his uncle's grasp but already feeling annoyed with himself at his sullen outburst.

"Because there is always a price to pay, Pendragon," Napier said. "And you will not get through the next two days if you do not accept that."

Pen didn't like the way that his uncle spoke to him, but he knew him well enough to accept the advice and follow him to the hotel, where they were greeted warmly by the manager, who assured them that their 'usual rooms' were prepared and ready. Pen, who knew his uncle would want him to keep studying, had brought two books with him. As the night went on, he read *History of Murder within the Rite*, which seemed appropriate given the entire chapter on Witch Burning.

Pen didn't think he would sleep that night, so he was surprised to find that he was woken up by the alarm call from Reception, reminding him that Napier had booked breakfast for seven o'clock and it was now nearly half past six. They ate in silence and the Rendelf didn't mention what was going to happen, which made Pen feel even more nervous. After they had finished, they wandered down to Holyrood, where the formalities of the day would take place.

There was a small gathering of people already waiting

for them, and Pen soon realised that the man who was the subject of the Commitment was surrounded by his family: a wife and four little children, none of whom seemed to recognise the struggle which Pen could see so clearly in their parents' eyes.

"I don't mind," the wife was saying as Pen passed. "It's going to happen either way, and at least now something good can come of it."

Pen tried to distract himself from his surroundings but, however hard he attempted to remember lyrics from ancient pop songs, he couldn't avoid the ceremony unfolding before him. As the Rendelf took a seat at the front of the room and the other people present sat in the audience (*or*, Pen thought, *was it a congregation?*), the man entered alone.

"Are you Richard Gander?" Napier asked, waving him to a small podium.

"Yes, sir."

"And you are here to take the Commitment to leave behind the Knave's Rite, which you selected of your own volition when you were fifteen?"

"Yes, sir."

"And no one is tricking you or forcing you into undertaking this Commitment?"

"No, sir."

"And you understand the full cost of what you are about to do?"

The man looked down at his hands but did not speak and, for a blissful moment, Pen thought he was about to change his mind. Napier, however, looked even more firmly at the man before him.

"Do you understand the full cost of the vow you are

about to take?"

"Yes, sir."

Napier nodded his head. "Richard Gander, when you were fifteen years old, you chose the path of the Knave's Rite and committed to be a Knave's Thaumaturge. What made you change your mind?"

"I'm worried my kids aren't safe around me," the man replied, sounding certain.

"The price of changing the Choice you made when you were fifteen is the life of someone you love."

"I know," Richard Gander said, his voice breaking slightly.

"And who is that?"

"My wife." Now his voice was shaking so much that Pen was surprised there were no tears in the man's eyes. Perhaps he was beyond that kind of sadness.

For the first time, Napier's tone became softer. "If your wife is willing to sacrifice herself for your freedom from the Knave's Rite then you have been very lucky in marriage. Do you know the oath that you must take now, or should I speak it first?"

"I know it," Mr Gander said, and Pen noticed that the man was clutching the lectern behind which he was standing, his knuckles white and purple with the tightness of his grip. "I vow to leave behind the Knave's Rite, which I selected as my path. For freedom from its bounds, I will give a person who is willing to make that sacrifice for me and for my children. I swear the oath upon her life. Upon the lives of our children, may I keep it."

There was silence in the room, and Pen felt a hot tear roll down his cheek. No one said anything further, but Napier walked across to Richard Gander, shook his hand, and then embraced him, apparently trying to assure him he had done the right thing. Pen was unsure what he believed and was so deeply lost in thought that he allowed himself to be swept out of the building along with the rest of the small crowd and, realising Napier was still inside, he sat down at the edge of a pond and watched the ripples.

At last, Napier emerged, his hand upon Richard Gander's shoulder in what seemed to be a reassuring manner. As soon as Mrs Gander saw her husband, she hurried towards him, leaving the children on the opposite side of the road, perhaps to stop them from hearing the conversation they needed to share.

For as long as he lived, Pen knew he would never forget what he saw unfolding before him, although even a second later he couldn't have explained where the car had come from. As she was about to reach the pavement, Richard's wife was hit and thrown over the bonnet of the speeding car, eventually falling in a still heap just metres away from where Pen was sitting.

Pen thought he wouldn't be able to move ever again. He could see the woman's eyes, open wide in shock and terror but seeing nothing. There was blood around her face and on the ground, but it was still the eyes that, for a moment, seemed to freeze Pen's soul. Then, he hurried towards her, even as he saw the children running across to their mother, and Richard, screaming, racing to his dead wife.

Napier, who had apparently been far closer than Pen realised, pulled the children away and led them back into the building, having to restrain them as they fought to get back to their parents. It all seemed to Pen as though he was watching it unfold on a film.

"No," Richard was saying, one hand on his wife's head and the other clutching Pen's sleeve. "We were supposed to have longer than this. We were supposed to have time to sort things out. We were supposed to have six months."

"I'm so sorry," Pen murmured, hoping that he sounded as painfully sympathetic as he felt, but knowing he couldn't express it in words. "Is there anything I can do?"

"No. No, I don't think so. Where are the kids?"

"My uncle took them."

"Your uncle?" Richard Gander leapt to his feet. "And who, in the name of hell, is your uncle?"

"Napier," Pen whispered. "Napier Devon."

He had never been punched by a grown man before and so, as Richard's fist swung around onto his jaw, Pen had a moment to realise how different it was from being hit in the playground by the school bully. Every bit of pain that Richard Gander was feeling was put into that punch, and Pen felt another blow hit him in the stomach, doubling him up in agony. Bystanders came in and pulled Richard away from the boy who, from their point of view, had done absolutely nothing wrong. Someone pressed a tissue against his mouth to stem the bleeding, but Pen hardly noticed.

When the police arrived, he refused to give any statement apart from that he was certain the driver of the car had been speeding. He wouldn't compound the man's suffering because he had needed to take his anger out on the nearest thing to Napier he could find. The Rendelf himself gave no statement at all but led his nephew through the gathered crowd of police officers, ambulance crew and onlookers, as though none of them could see him. Pen allowed himself one glance back at Richard Gander who, by that point, had gathered his children around him and was watching as his wife's body was wheeled silently into the ambulance.

Pen didn't speak to his uncle again that day and, when they walked to Waverley Station together, it was in absolute silence which Napier did not challenge. After the police had taken statements, the Rendelf had met briefly with a delegation whose role it was to ensure the matter was handled correctly. Pen couldn't stand how clinical everything was and, when he closed his eyes, all he could see were the faces of the children who had just lost their mother.

He chose not to speak to Marley about it when they were back at Honour's Rest, but he didn't know whether Napier mentioned it, as he avoided his uncle at every possible opportunity. Each night he dreamt about what he had seen and, every time, he saw Napier there at the wheel of the car. Even though the young driver had been arrested and charged, there was no doubt in Pen's mind that his uncle was responsible for the timing and manner of the woman's death.

The October that year brought an Indian Summer and, with it, hordes of midges which laid siege to Honour's Rest and made it impossible for Pen and Marley to make the most of the good weather. However, when the wind picked up, they were able to go fishing on the loch or sit on the dry lawn and admire the autumnal colours which surrounded them amidst the summery heat. The last of that weather was just one day before Pen's birthday and, as he and Marley were rowing their way across the loch in search of brown trout or perhaps a glimpse of the kelpie, a taxi came speeding across the causeway. As soon as the door opened, Pen gave a quiet cry of surprise and happiness at the sight of his mother, who stepped out of the car and stood for a moment, looking around at the house and its surroundings. His father followed, immediately spotting the boys on the loch and, waving to them, he alerted his wife to their presence.

Pen and Marley called across and began rowing as quickly as they could back to the jetty, but it was still not quick enough for Pen, who was desperate to speak to them about everything he had kept to himself during the last few weeks. When they reached the tiny jetty, he let Marley fasten the boat while he hurried over to his parents, catching them both in a tight embrace. His mother laughed softly.

"That's quite a welcome, Pendragon," she said with a smile. "Your father and I thought we'd surprise you again this year."

He couldn't tell them just how pleased he was to be with them again, to be a family, but they seemed to understand without any words. As Napier came out and expressed polite surprise at the appearance of his brother and sister-in-law, Pen felt his mother take his wrist to lead him away from his uncle.

"What's happened, sweetheart?" she asked, her voice as calm and gentle as ever. "Tell me."

"I saw someone get killed in a road accident a couple of weeks ago," he whispered. "A young mum. Her kids were there, and her husband too. It was horrible."

His mother squeezed his arm gently, but Pen couldn't find the comfort he had hoped for. He had believed he would be able to tell her everything, but there was no way she would understand how or why this woman's life had been claimed by the Rite. He had enough trouble coming to terms with it himself. Pen glanced across at his father, who was speaking awkwardly to his older brother, and was reminded that the last time they had met they had shared a blazing row at the hospital.

This awkwardness went on throughout his parents' visit. Both his mother and father wanted him to know just how proud they were, but Pen knew he was keeping the truth of his role from them by not saying what had happened. His birthday was spent in a confusion of presents, food, and alcohol, and both he and Marley got so drunk that they ended the evening lying outside on the rain-soaked lawn.

By the time his parents left, Pen felt as though he had wasted the opportunity to spend time with them and they said nothing about another visit, although they made sure he promised to go home for Christmas. He and Napier were still barely sharing even a glance in each other's direction, let alone a conversation, so his only companion was Marley. As he stood waving his parents off as Napier drove them to Inverness, Pen got a horrible feeling he hadn't just wasted his sixteenth birthday, but the last chance they would get to be a family together.

Chapter Twenty One

Running Away

After his birthday, Pen found that Napier was less willing to let him do whatever he wanted so he was forced to accept his uncle's company once his parents left. Napier was furious that Marley and Pen had become so drunk, and wanted them to pay a kind of penance for having made such fools of themselves. It was Napier who had provided the wine, but his argument was that Pen ought to have understood the importance of the celebration, rather than take the opportunity to experience inebriation for the first time.

As a result, one week after his birthday found Pendragon Devon sitting in his study poring over books, his uncle leaning against the door to ensure the work was completed. Marley was continuing his training as a healer, and so it was just the two of them at Honour's

Rest that morning. Every so often, Napier would throw something at his nephew and expect it to be deflected by means of the Rite, which Pen found increasingly annoying, as it distracted him from the reading his uncle also expected him to do. He had better control of the Rite now though, as he had accepted the importance of not knowing everything but rather embracing the unknown and moulding it into whatever he wished it to be.

Pen looked up for a moment and gazed out the window. For some reason he couldn't understand, that familiar face from his dreams reappeared to him. Niamh seemed to be standing there, which was impossible given that they were some fifteen feet above the ground, and she was holding out her hand to him, trying to draw him towards her. He got to his feet and moved over to the window but, as he did, he felt a dull pain in his back and realised Napier had thrown a heavy book in his direction while he had been distracted. He spun around angrily and, by the time he had turned back to the window, it seemed obvious that Niamh couldn't possibly have been in front of him. He wondered why he had allowed himself to make such a mistake.

"What are you looking at?" Napier asked, moving over to the window so Pen had to step aside to avoid contact with him. "There is no one out there."

"I thought I saw something over the loch," Pen muttered, going back to his books.

The rest of the morning was spent in the silence they had become used to but, when it was time to go down to dinner, Napier stopped his nephew before he descended the steps.

"You are not a child anymore, Pendragon," he said. "I

expect that you will begin acting like an adult imminently but, in the meantime, kindly attempt to make some pretence of understanding just how important your role is now. Do you understand, Pendragon?"

"What?" Pen snapped. "Do I understand what?"

"Erlend Shipperbottom is free. He is no longer the Deputy Rendelf. You have to rise to the challenge which you have repeatedly accepted."

"Perhaps I didn't know what I was letting myself in for when I accepted. After all, you waited until a month ago to show me one of the most horrific things I've ever seen. How was I supposed to know whether or not I could do that?"

"You mean accept someone's sacrifice?"

"Sacrifice?" Pen spat, racing down the spiral stairs ahead of his uncle. "Let's call it what it was. Murder."

"If you believe that then you are even more childish than your behaviour would suggest." Napier sounded no less angry than his nephew, and the whole building seemed to be shaking with the force of his annoyance and pent-up rage. "Would you say that she was unwilling to sacrifice herself then?"

"Well, who is?" Pen scoffed.

"Someone who loves their family more than themselves? She knew that when he took that vow, he had two choices. Either for her to die, or for their eldest child. She willingly undertook the role of sacrifice. Perhaps it is harder for you to comprehend because of your age, but thaumaturges who have wished to make those changes have been doing so for centuries."

Pen spun around to stare at his uncle and then turned away again almost as quickly. He was unsure whether he could even believe what Napier was saying. As they sat down to an angry dinner, Pen asked the question which was most preying on his mind.

"Did you know what was going to happen?"

"Yes," Napier replied, helping himself to vegetables.

"But did you know that it would happen straight away?"

Napier paused. "Yes," he said at last. "I knew it would happen straight away. It is the law of the Rite that the sacrifice must be given, but it is down to the presiding Rendelf to select a suitable moment. Within a given timeframe."

Pen looked hard at his uncle, desperate to see some sign of remorse but, although Napier's face was set, he could see nothing which suggested guilt. Pen felt anger welling up inside him again and the food he was eating started to choke him.

"Then why didn't you give them time? The Shipperbottoms had Amanda for three years, didn't they?"

"And do you imagine they enjoyed those years, knowing she would be taken from them? Perhaps that is why you do not understand, Pendragon, because you have never been forced to wait for something terrible to happen, knowing it will be both unavoidable and devastating at the same time."

"So, when you invited me, you knew I would see her die?"

"I knew that you would be present when she died, yes. But I did not know that you would be the first person to reach her, and I am more sorry for that than you can know."

"More sorry because I had to watch three children lose

their mother? Or a husband lose his wife? Or because said husband took it out on me because I happen to be your nephew?"

Pen was feeling increasingly hysterical. He realised he had risen from his chair and was leaning over the table towards his uncle. He didn't care if Napier's rage exploded now, he just wanted to make the man before him understand what it had meant for him to have witnessed that terrible thing in Edinburgh.

"None of those things," Napier said quietly. "Sit back down. I am most sorry that I was not there to make sure you understood the necessity and importance of what you were witnessing."

There was now nothing angry about Napier's voice, which only made Pen more furious. He was winding the invisible thread around his forefinger, and Pen wondered what his uncle was doing with the Rite, and whether it had anything to do with how calm he had just become. For a moment, he wished he could use the Rite to control his anger, something he had never learnt to do, but then it occurred to him that masking his anger would only lead to being as cold and unfeeling as the man in front of him.

"So, who gives the Rendelf power over life and death then?" he asked at last, sitting back down but ensuring his voice didn't waver.

"It is an accepted part of the role," Napier replied.

"Well, what if I wanted to change that?"

"You cannot change it. You should know from all the reading you do that the role of Rendelf is not one which can be altered to suit individual whims. Think about it for a moment. If, when someone is fifteen, they take a vow to become a Just Thaumaturge but then change their mind because they want to seek revenge upon someone and, ultimately, end a life, they must pay for that decision. It may not seem nice – I don't think it *is* nice – but it is right. Should someone who wishes to make a Commitment from Just Thaumaturge to Knave's Thaumaturge be forced to lose someone, but not the other way around? You will have to grow used to it and recognise its importance, or else you will never understand your role."

"I think you just enjoy playing God, Napier," Pen snapped. "I mean, you started young, didn't you?" As soon as he had spoken, he wished he hadn't chosen this topic of conversation. Napier rose to his feet, his fingers almost white as he continued to thread the invisible skein around them, and his voice now dangerously quiet.

"Perhaps you would like to explain that comment, Pendragon?"

Pen paused and wondered if he had the courage to continue, but then his anger returned and he leapt to his feet. "I think you know I'm talking about Ramin." The tapestries fluttered in the breeze which stirred up around their anger.

"Then I think you are nothing more than an immature child, who will say anything to cause hurt or upset. And I think I am a fool to have selected you."

Pen's teeth clenched for a second. "Well, perhaps you just don't want to be reminded that you dragged your friends off on a wild goose chase, which resulted in one of them being killed? Yet your only mistake is that you selected me? How penitent of you." As he stormed out of the room, his uncle began to talk, but Pen was filled with a childish determination to have the last word. "I swear to you, Napier Devon, that I will never, ever preside over someone's life in the way that you did."

"I think," Napier said calmly, sitting back down at the table, "that you will not have a choice."

Pen marched out, feeling his heart pounding in his chest. He didn't want to go anywhere his uncle would think to look, so he left the house and charged across the causeway, not caring that he had nothing other than his indoor clothes to protect him from the rain and fog which swirled around him. When he reached the road, he turned towards Aviemore and began walking, ignoring the cars and lorries which hurtled past, honking horns to let the solitary young man know that he was risking his life by walking down the road in such poor visibility.

He had hoped the bad weather would serve to awaken him from the anger he was feeling towards his uncle, but it only made what was already a very miserable day even worse. When he turned around to glance back at Honour's Rest, he could no longer see it, and he realised with a sinking feeling that he must have been walking much quicker than he had thought. There was too much anger welling up inside him to turn around and go back, but it made him feel uncomfortable to think he was walking without any idea of where he was going. Another car passed him, this time only missing him by a few inches and, for a second, he wasn't sure if it had actually hit him.

He began to think about how Mrs Gander must have felt as she was struck by the car. Certainly, the look on her face suggested she had understood what was happening, and he wondered if she had realised the impact would cause her death. Had she really been as willing to sacrifice herself as Napier had argued? He couldn't imagine it.

The fog continued to swirl around him, and the rain

was becoming heavier, so now he couldn't see anything in front of him. Anger gave way to fear, and Pen became terrified of being hit by one of the passing vehicles. He clambered down from the road and sat on the grassy verge, beside a bag of putrid rubbish which looked as though it had been left there after a summer picnic. The rain was making him feel tired and he closed his eyes as he sat there, feeling lucky that in such inclement weather he couldn't be seen.

It was a couple of hours later that a car stopped beside him, and Marley clambered out the passenger seat, shaking his friend to wake him up.

"What on earth are you doing, Pen?" he asked, pulling him to his feet. "Trying to catch hypothermia?"

Pen shrugged and managed to force a smile. "I'm soaked. Can you give me a lift back?"

"That's why we stopped." He led Pen back to the car. "Pen, this is Liz Farrell, who I've been working with. Liz, this is Pendragon Devon." Pen clambered into the back of the car, shivering and feeling like an embarrassed nuisance.

"Why are you out in this weather?" Liz asked. "There's nowhere you can walk to from Honour's Rest."

"I just wanted some fresh air," Pen replied. "Thanks for the lift."

He hoped it was clear he didn't want to talk, but the manners his parents had instilled in him meant he was careful not to appear ungrateful for the fact that Liz and Marley had picked him up from the side of the road and saved him from death by exposure.

"Did you fall out with Napier?" Marley whispered, as the car pulled up outside the house almost ten minutes later. "I'm guessing that's the only reason why you would just head out here on your own."

"Yep," Pen said. "He's doing his usual trying to manage everyone's lives. He *killed* that woman in Edinburgh, Marley."

"I thought—"

"Shut up," Pen snapped, although being angry with Marley just made him feel worse.

They wandered in and Napier invited Liz into the house, making her a cup of tea to thank her for returning Pen safely. After she had left, he turned to his nephew.

"Go and have a bath to warm up, Pendragon," he said.

Marley glanced from one of them to the other and Pen deliberately avoided his gaze but did as he was instructed and immersed himself in a bath which warmed his body but failed to make him feel better about the events of the day. In fact, it just gave him time on his own to consider everything which had happened, and to feel guilty about the cruel things he had said to his uncle. He wondered if he would have become so harsh if the Rite had never been introduced into his life, but it seemed almost impossible to imagine. It made Pen wish that he had taken the opportunity to speak to his parents more during their visit, but he had been too busy feeling sorry for himself.

As he walked out of the bathroom, he once again thought that he could see Niamh just a short distance in front of him, and he hurried to follow her, but she dissolved into shadows just past the door which led to Napier's bedroom and the Guardians' Room. Pen stood for a moment with his hand resting on the door handle but, after remembering the occasion when he had lit the candle and found himself surrounded by dead Rendelfs, he quickly withdrew and walked the distance back to his room. He climbed the spiral staircase and curled up on the bed, watching as the fog began to clear and unveil the shining stars.

The following morning, he awoke feeling more embarrassed than he had the day before. He was also very hungry, having gone to bed before having any tea after his dinner had been disturbed by his fight with Napier. Pen hurried down the stairs and threw himself onto one of the chairs at the breakfast table, forcing himself to grin at his uncle, whose mouth merely twitched into a polite smile.

"You'll be pleased to hear that I am leaving you in charge of Honour's Rest," Napier said as he sat down and began dishing up eggs, bacon, and mushrooms for himself and the two boys. "I have been invited to give a presentation at a conference in New York."

"Oh," Pen muttered, suddenly feeling very guilty, as though he was chasing Napier away from his own house. "What kind of conference?"

"The Conference is for the American Guild of Rendelfs. Because of the size and political makeup of the country, they run it as a Guild rather than having one individual."

"What's the presentation about?" Marley asked.

"Ironically, given the past couple of days, it is about training someone to take over the role. I'll be leaving today and getting the train down to Glasgow to fly across to New York. There are some friends I'm quite keen to spend time with over there as well, so I won't be back before the end of November."

"That's over a month away!" Pen exclaimed, and Napier

just nodded.

Pen's feeling of guilt only intensified as the boys stood outside and waved Napier off as the taxi took him to the train station. He was leaving the car, as he didn't want anything to happen to it during his long time away, and he had told Pen that, in case of absolute emergency, he should find himself capable of driving it through the Rite. Napier waved from the taxi once before it disappeared down the causeway, and Marley and Pen wandered sadly back into the house, feeling responsible for the dark cloud which had descended over the residents of Honour's Rest.

Chapter Twenty Two

What Niamh Could See

That night, it seemed to Pendragon that sleep would never come to him. He repeatedly played over the conversations which had led to Napier's departure, until he was convinced it was all his fault the Rendelf had left. He couldn't regret how angry he had been about his uncle's decision to take him down to Edinburgh to witness the death of an innocent woman, but he had been wrong to bring up the subject of Ramin, who had given his life willingly to save his friends. Napier had been right when he condemned Pen as immature and, as he turned around in bed to view the stars and the low crescent moon, he wondered if his uncle knew just how sorry he was.

However hard he tried, he couldn't fall asleep so he got dressed and attempted to persuade himself into tiredness. But even playing the guitar didn't bring him any comfort so, in a moment of rage, Pen threw it down on the floor, snapping the high E string so he had to leap backwards to avoid it cutting his hand. He stormed out the room and began to pace through the building, reminding himself that Napier had left him in charge so it was an acceptable thing to do.

He saw nothing surprising – Marley had been in bed for some time – but something kept him walking through the halls, and in and out of the rooms. He even walked down to the State Room, and sat for a while on the floor, imagining the different events which had taken place within those walls. Honour's Rest had seen so much over the centuries, but it didn't make him feel any better about how selfish he had been to chase the Rendelf out of his own home.

As he was sitting alone and watching the pinpricks of starlight coming through the stained-glass windows, he heard a quiet movement behind him and turned around to see Niamh standing there. She was translucent, as the spirits of the Rendelfs had been, but at the same time she seemed alive and almost breathless as she leant against the doorframe.

"Niamh?" he whispered, moving over to her. "What are you doing here?"

Her mouth didn't move but, in his head, he heard her whisper, *I am not here, Pendragon Devon. I have sent this shadow of myself to ask you for help.*

"Help?"

Follow me.

She led him through the corridors of Honour's Rest, and he struggled to keep up with her. She was gliding rather than walking, so he had to run to match her pace. There was still no sign of Marley, for which Pen was grateful as he didn't know how he would explain the appearance of the strange girl. Niamh led him out the front door and into the darkness. The starlight shone in her eyes and, for the first time, Pen noticed there was something else different about her.

"You can see!" he exclaimed.

This is my soul you are seeing now. The soul can't be blinded by anyone but its owner.

Hearing the profound comments in her soft Irish lilt brought a smile to Pen's face, despite how nervous he felt.

"So, you can see me?"

I can see your soul, Pendragon Devon, she whispered, leaning towards him so he could feel the warmth from the candle she carried. *I can't see your face.*

"You can call me Pen, you know?"

Pendragon is a name of kings, isn't it? Niamh whispered. *Why would you want to be called anything different? The king and the hunter are both in your soul, I can see it. Pendragon Orion Devon.*

Pen didn't want to ask how she had come to know his full name, but the way she said it brought another smile to his face.

"What do you want to show me?"

She led him into the boat, and he rowed across the loch. Honour's Rest fell away, and he found himself looking at the green of Dunbeath Strath. As the light became brighter, he saw two people on their knees in front of a third person, who was standing over them, laughing almost hysterically.

"Who are they?" Pen whispered, but Niamh raised a finger to her pale lips and then pointed at the figures. It seemed so bright now that it could almost be daylight, and Pen recognised the kneeling people as Erlend and Bernadette Shipperbottom.

"You can't do this, Isolde," Erlend was shouting above the woman's laughter. "You don't frighten me. I remember you when you were nothing more than a scared child. A little girl, who enjoyed spending time with her three friends because they would protect her from all the bad things in the world. But you had to come along too, didn't you? Napier didn't want you to. And Ramin didn't either."

"Shut up!" Isolde screamed, swinging for Erlend, and striking him around the face with the back of her pale hand. "If Napier hadn't wanted to be everybody's hero, then Ramin would still be alive. And I could have had the man I always wanted."

"Ramin wasn't a man, Isolde," Erlend laughed, although Pen got the distinct impression he was only trying to distract the Knave's Thaumaturge. "He was a boy. Anyway, it didn't stop you, did it? You still got what you wanted from him. You animal!"

Isolde struck him again, this time with her fist clenched but, in a fit of rage which saw her break free from Isolde's control, Bernadette caught her arm and pulled it back. Pen had suspected for some time that Marley's mother was the stronger of the two Shipperbottoms. He realised he had been correct. Bernadette leapt to her feet, twisting Isolde's arm backwards with a set look of anger on her face. Pen heard the crack as the bone snapped, but it didn't stop Bernadette, who just stared at Isolde. Although she had shrieked when the bone was broken, Isolde raised her other hand and Bernadette was thrown backwards, landing awkwardly three metres away. Pen cried out, but

Niamh put her cold finger against his lips to silence him.

"I will kill you, Erlend," Isolde said, clutching her broken arm. "And your wife can do nothing to stop it. Both you and your son are dead if she attempts to use the Knave's Rite. You idiots! Why would anyone leave such power behind? Apart from the fear of being something greater?" She bent down beside Erlend and pulled his head back by his hair. "Tell me, where is your friend? The person who must be held answerable."

"Oh, you choose your moments, Isolde," Erlend hissed. "Napier is not even in the country."

"What?" For the first time, Isolde sounded surprised and upset. "But the boy?"

"The boy is the reason he left. Perhaps if you didn't blind and lock up your own daughter then you would understand something about the difficulties of dealing with young people."

"Where is he?"

"Napier or Pendragon?"

"Napier!"

"Gone," Erlend replied. "Gone so far that I can't summon him back."

Isolde let out a roar of anger and frustration and threw Erlend backwards. "Call him!"

"You're still the stupid little child you always were, Isolde," Erlend replied, and Pen was filled with admiration at the way he remained undaunted. "I can't call him. I told you, he is gone further than my Rite can reach."

"If I can't persuade you, then perhaps she can." Isolde pointed a short distance away. From the cry which Bernadette and Erlend gave as one, Pen had no doubt that the child who had just appeared was their dead daughter. She looked alive, apart from the fact that her skin was grey, and her small head was matted with dried blood. She toddled up to her mother, who gave a heart-breaking scream as she tried to reach out to her, only for the child to vanish and reappear just in front of her father.

Pen looked across at Niamh pleadingly, but he knew that the girl couldn't do anything. He could see silvery tears in her eyes though, which he thought must be reflected in his own.

"Call him!"

"Don't you understand?" Erlend sobbed, running his hand across his face to avoid looking at the child who tugged at his sleeve. "We can't!"

"Then I'll take his nephew," Isolde snapped. She turned around and walked away, ignoring the desperate cries of the couple being tortured by the vision of their dead daughter.

"Pen!" The voice seemed to be calling him from some distance away, but Pen couldn't stop looking across at the Shipperbottoms. "Pen!" It sounded a little like Erlend's voice, but he knew it couldn't be, for the man in front of him didn't even move his lips as he crawled towards his wife, trying to shield them both from the vision which was haunting them.

Go back, Niamh whispered. *You are being called.*

Pen tried to catch her hand, but she disappeared before he could touch her. He looked around to find the early morning sun reflecting in the windows of Honour's Rest, and Marley was standing on the end of the jetty, calling out to him.

"Pen! What the hell are you doing? Have you been out here all night?"

Pen looked around him, confused. He desperately wanted to believe he had been dreaming, that he hadn't just witnessed what he knew he had seen, but if he allowed himself to believe that then he would be betraying Niamh and leaving Marley's parents to be tortured.

He lifted the oars and rowed back to Marley, trying to work out how he would explain what he had seen whilst not coming across as being totally insane. He no longer felt guilt about Napier's departure, but anger that he had gone so far and had left the two boys and, as it turned out, his closest friends, to suffer at the hands of Isolde.

"Were you sleepwalking?" Marley asked, helping Pen out of the boat. "You're not even cold! It's four degrees out here!"

"I don't think I was sleepwalking," Pen replied. He launched into an explanation of everything which had happened since he had been trying to get to sleep: how he had wandered through the halls of Honour's Rest and finally ended up in the State Room, where he had been found by Niamh, who had given him a vision of what had happened. As he spoke, Marley grew paler, and Pen noticed his friend's fists were clenched.

"She'll kill them," he whispered. "My mum's not even able to think about Amanda without getting hysterical, and my dad is just, well, my dad."

"She wants to find Napier," Pen explained. "That's why she's torturing them. She's trying to get Erlend, I mean your dad, to summon him from New York."

"Isn't that a bit far?"

"Exactly. That's why she started losing it with them." Pen paused. "Napier said we could use the car in an emergency. I think this qualifies, don't you?"

Marley nodded and they rushed back into the house. In his hurry to pack something for them to eat, Pen accidentally spilt raisins all over the kitchen, but he didn't want to waste a moment tidying it up, so just promised himself he would clean it when he got back. For a second, it occurred to him that he might not come back, and he heard Isolde's voice in his head saying, 'then I'll take his nephew'.

He shook his head, reminding himself he had to do this, if for no other reason then for Marley, his constant friend for the last year and a half, closer than he could ever imagine a brother to be.

They met each other in the garage and stood for a while staring at the car, as if that would let them learn to drive. Although Napier had assured him he would be able to drive, nothing in the car looked like Pen remembered, and Marley's pestering only made him more nervous that something would go wrong. However, he put the key in the ignition and turned it as far as it would go, glad that the car seemed to have been brought to life and grateful that, for the time being, Marley had stopped commenting on how they would never get to his parents in time.

The drive along the causeway was one of the most terrifying things Pen had ever done. The water stretched out around him on both sides and, each time a gust of wind blew up around them, he felt as though the car would be swept into the loch. However, he tried to keep his head, telling himself repeatedly that he was perfectly capable of driving a car. He could hear Marley humming snatches of Moonlight Sonata, the first time he had thought of the piece in ages, and he wondered how his friend was using the Rite at that moment. Was he attempting to reach his parents and tell them that help was on its way? Or maybe he didn't trust him fully and wanted to do everything he could to help? As they pulled gingerly onto the main road, Pen tried to convince himself he wasn't afraid, but it didn't seem to work.

Lorries and cars whizzed past them, and he felt as vulnerable as he had when he had walked the road alone, except now there was pressure and responsibility. Terrified that his sweating hands would slide off the steering wheel, Pen pulled into a layby.

"What are you doing?" Marley demanded. "We've got to get there."

"I don't think I can drive."

You can.

As soon as he heard the words, he knew Marley hadn't spoken them. Niamh's voice in his head was as clear as it had been when the vision of her had been standing in front of him. Pen felt again the touch of her hardly-present hand against his lips and sighed at the imagined closeness. Then, without another word, he pulled back into the road, allowing the Rite to direct his driving until he knew how the car wanted to be driven.

As if Pen's crisis of confidence about his driving wasn't enough, they couldn't remember the direction to Dunbeath, although they both agreed it was north. Pen was concerned when they reached Inverness and had to attempt to remember how to reach the Strath.

"Was it Ullapool?" he asked as they sat together in front of a signpost. "Or Thurso?"

"Thurso's where the boat comes in. Well, Scrabster anyway. That's almost Thurso."

Pen looked across at his friend, unimpressed. "But

what does that have to do with anything? Do you mean we're supposed to be heading towards Thurso? And which one is Wick?" He could feel hysterical laughter bubbling up inside him but didn't want to let it out in case Marley thought he wasn't taking the situation seriously. Instead, he pulled back out again and followed the road for Thurso.

After they had been driving for a while, he began to recognise the road, especially the hill with the hairpin bends. Absolutely petrified he would make some mistake, he closed his eyes and just made himself believe he would be taken safely around the bend. At the top of the hill, they found themselves in a layby once again, but this time Marley kept silent and didn't suggest they keep driving until Pen was ready to go.

The Strath wasn't far from where they had stopped and, when they reached it, they looked at one another. There was no sound: not even birds singing or the noise from the river visibly pulsing its way through the valley. Pen could feel his heart beating but couldn't hear that either. It felt as though someone had put their hands over his ears in an attempt to make him feel cut off from the world around him, and it was working. He got out the car and stood in that silence, knowing it was the Rite which kept the land around them hushed.

"Well," Marley said, making Pen jump back to his senses, "we should go and find them. Shouldn't we?"

Pen just nodded his head, and they began to walk down the Strath, following the river through the autumn colours until they reached the bridge. He crossed it first, keeping his arms outstretched so Marley couldn't get past him, and then shouted out for the Knave's Thaumaturge. A kind of reckless abandon swept over him, as though he didn't care what Isolde might do. Pen was still feeling that way as he felt himself plummeting through the earth again and into that prison where darkness had surrounded him for the only time in his life, but where he had met the person who had brought such unexpected light. He didn't know if Marley was behind him but, as he hit the floor, he felt strong hands helping him gently but firmly to his feet and he gave a sigh of relief at the knowledge he wasn't friendless in the pitch black.

Chapter Twenty Three

The Cambion and the Rope

For a while, Pen only looked around, seeing nothing, but desperate to identify the helping hands which had lifted him up. He could hear noises in the darkness and, for a moment, he remembered the Kashkaan which had terrorised him last year, but then realised that the noise was someone attempting to keep their sobs quiet. He had landed awkwardly on his ankle as he plummeted through the earth, but whoever was holding his arm did not let him fall as he attempted to put weight on it.

"It's fine, Pen," he heard Erlend whisper in his ear. "Nothing broken. Just a sprain. How did you know we were here?"

"I told him," said a quiet Irish voice in the darkness and, as it came closer, so too did the light. Niamh's candle illuminated the rag over her blind eyes, and she looked older than she had done in Pen's vision. Still, she spared him the same warm smile and, even in the prison, he couldn't help but return the gesture.

Pen saw Erlend's eyes shining in the darkness as he looked at the girl and was about to ask what inspired his sad smile but, at that moment, the ground above them opened and Marley crashed through, giving a cry of surprise as he set eyes on his father.

"You're alright!" he gasped, and Erlend smiled at him.

"Yes. Your mother will be very pleased to see you," he said, before adding quickly, "as I am. But don't you both understand how dangerous it is for you to be here? Isolde wants to get her revenge on Napier for something which happened years ago. Pen, it's especially dangerous for you, the closest thing Napier has ever come to having a child of his own. Once she realises your value, I don't doubt she'll make you pay for your connection to the man she hates so much."

Marley, who had moved over to comfort his weeping mother, looked across at Erlend. "But we couldn't just leave you. Could we, Pen?"

"Your lives are more important, Marley," his father said, but he didn't comment on it again. In the darkness, lit only by the flickering light of the candle which Niamh clutched in her hand, there was no use in falling out over who should be there and who should have stayed out of danger. There was just no point in pursuing something which could only lead people into arguments.

"We should get some sort of an idea of what we can do," Pen said. "Something must be done about her and I get the feeling that, with Napier away, we're the only people who can sort Isolde out." It sounded like a badly thought-out line from a film and Pen couldn't help but expect sniggers or comments from the others, but he was relieved when they didn't come. At last, he saw Erlend nodding in the shadows.

"Even when she was a child, there was only one person who could speak sense to her, and he died years ago. Any connection she has made with Ramin since is not genuine. She only reanimated him into what she wanted him to be."

"What do you mean?"

"He means that there's no reasoning with her." Although Bernadette's eyes were swollen with tears, her voice was as steady as ever. "She must be killed."

"That's harsh," Marley muttered, but there was no denying his mother was right. "None of us can kill her though. Right? We're all Just Thaumaturges or, at any rate, can't use the Knave's Rite."

"No, you're wrong," Pen said. "I can use the Knave's Rite to kill. Remember, I made the Choice to be what I had to be. But we have to make sure we can get out of here before I actually finish her off. I just wish there was some other ending than me killing her."

"Killing her won't be a punishment," Niamh said. The room fell silent to hear what she was going to say. "She is already dying."

"Dying?" Pen gasped. "How do you know?"

"I can feel it," Niamh replied, almost dreamily. "She's ill and she's got no means of recovery. She's become an enemy to anyone who would help her. I am sure I don't need to tell you that a Knave's Thaumaturge has no skill to heal."

Pen felt his fingers move over to Niamh, almost of

their own accord, but she allowed them to rest on her own small hand without comment or response.

"What do you mean, you can feel it?"

"I don't know," Niamh said. "Only that–"

"Shh," Erlend put his finger to his lips dramatically. They all sat in absolute silence for a while but heard nothing and, by the time Erlend had apologised for being so jumpy, they had forgotten what Niamh had been saying.

"But I don't want to kill her as a punishment anyway," Pen explained. "I don't ever want to do that. To play God." He shuddered as he remembered what he had said to Napier on that topic. He couldn't believe it had been only a few days earlier. "I just want to make sure that she can't continue the damage she's started. If the only way to stop it is to kill her then that's what we'll have to do. But how can she be killed?"

"The same as anyone," Bernadette replied. "But she's better versed in avoiding death than most. She has a grasp of the Rite darker than anything I ever explored. And the determination to see it through."

"I have to do something," Pen said, hoping his tone would silence the others, none of whom seemed to think he had much chance of succeeding. "With the Rendelf away, these responsibilities fall to me. Not you anymore, Erlend."

"You're right," Mr Shipperbottom said. "I don't think I'd realised until now, but I should be celebrating my freedom, shouldn't I? What did she hope to achieve by kidnapping us?"

"I think she overestimated Napier," Pen said under his breath, but gasped as Bernadette slapped his cheek.

"You may be sixteen, Pendragon Devon," she snapped, "but you are behaving like a child. Don't take it into your head that you can understand why Napier behaves in the way he does. He wouldn't have gone to New York had he not believed it was the best thing for you."

Pen sat still, thinking on what Marley's mum had just said to him and not daring, or wanting, to contradict her. He kept swinging from hating Napier for leading him into everything which was going wrong, to wishing that his uncle was nearby for advice or help.

Even as the others began talking again, Pen stayed lost in his own world of confusion, his only connection with the others being the small fingers which tapped his own every time he threatened to move away from Niamh's reach.

At last, Erlend insisted they all get some sleep and Bernadette led Marley away into the corner of the room, where they spoke in hushed voices until Pen heard Marley telling his mother he was shattered and just wanted to sleep. Niamh, apparently grateful of the closeness, rested her head against Pen's legs and fell asleep, putting the candle down on the ground as she slept so that it continued to give a flickering light to the surroundings. No matter how long it kept burning, there was never any change in the candle. When it became clear that there was only Erlend and Pen left awake, Mr Shipperbottom shuffled over and sat down beside him.

"How do you know her?" he asked, gesturing to the girl who was asleep at Pen's side.

"I don't," Pen replied. "Not really. We met when we were last here."

"What do you know about her parents?"

"I know Isolde's her mother. It isn't her fault."

"No, no, I know that. Niamh's a sweet girl. I know her adoptive parents. They miss her. So much. Napier took no pleasure in leaving her here, you know?"

"I don't think he's a monster," Pen replied and Erlend nodded his head, his smile shining in the candlelight.

"I knew her birth father too."

"I don't know who he is."

"Oh, Pen, I think you do. What does everything you know about Isolde tell you? Who could be the only father for this strange creature?"

"I don't understand."

Erlend clicked his tongue, and Pen wondered if he was annoyed by the fact that he was deliberately avoiding guessing, or whether he just knew the answer was dawning on him, even as they were speaking.

"I think you do," Mr Shipperbottom repeated.

"So, her father is Ramin? But he died ages before she was born."

"Have you heard of a cambion?"

"It rings a bell. Honestly, I've read more than I ever thought possible during the last two years. It's probably come up at some point."

"A cambion is the child of a woman and an Incubus," Erlend explained. "Folklore states that the Incubus is a demon, with origins in the Bible. But it's actually the soul of a dead man, lured back to the world by a woman and tricked into giving her a child."

"I don't understand," Pen whispered.

"Niamh is a cambion. Her candle should have given it away. And, just in case you weren't sure, she could sense Isolde was dying, because she will always dwell on either side of the proverbial veil."

"So, is she alive?"

"Can you feel her breath? Her heartbeat? Her warmth? Yes, she's alive. But your uncle and I both agreed she mustn't be made aware of her true nature until she is old enough to understand. At the moment, she believes that what she can sense and experience is just another way in which she can access the Rite and, with her blinded, that's very logical."

"Do you think Napier killed Ramin?"

"How can you ask that, Pen? Surely you know the answer already."

"I know what I think, but you were there."

"I was," Erlend replied slowly. "And the day is burnt into my memory. It was Isolde who wanted to go after the Knave's Thaumaturge, Obadiah Crick. The child he had killed was her cousin and, although they weren't close, she understandably wanted justice. We all did. The little girl was only six and had been tortured before Obadiah killed her. I suppose now he was totally insane but the Knave's Rite had taken a hold of him. From our point of view, he was just someone we could cut our teeth on and the old Rendelf didn't do anything to discourage us, although I'm certain he knew what we were doing. Anyway, we found Obadiah and killed him. It was simple enough and we should have realised there was something not quite right about it all. I think he wanted to die. But he'd left poison and one of us had to drink it to open the door. Napier was about to, when Ramin used the Rite to distract him into talking to us about it. Then he snatched the cup and drank it all. There's no way Napier could have known what Ramin had done, but that just made Isolde more bitter. She was sure Napier had tricked Ramin in some way. In fact, it was completely the other way round."

Erlend stopped talking and gave a long sigh, which led into a kind of silence Pen had never experienced before, and during which he was haunted by how he had used Ramin's death against his uncle.

"I didn't mean for him to go to New York," Pen whispered. "I really didn't."

"Well," Erlend said, with an attempt at brightness, "perhaps it's for the best. Isolde is so desperate for revenge that his life would be in danger if he weren't thousands of miles away. As it is, we just need to make sure you have the protection you need."

As Erlend spoke, Pen found his eyes closing. The promise of protection was all he needed to find enough peace to fall asleep. His head dropped down so his chin was resting on his chest and, as his eyes flickered open and closed, he kept them fixed on the girl just inches from his face. The child of a dead man and an evil woman. How was it that she could be so pure and untouched by her disturbing parentage? He ran his hand over her face, feeling the softness of her skin before catching his hand against the rag which covered her eyes. For a moment he wondered what it was, but then sleep overtook his train of thought.

He awoke to find there was natural light pouring into the dungeon, and he could feel Niamh's thin hand gripping his wrist. There was other movement around him but, in the sudden brightness, Pen's eyes took a while to acclimatise.

At last, he realised that Isolde was standing above them, looking down at where they were all cowering from her. Filled with a kind of rage he had never experienced, Pen leapt to his feet.

"So, boy," Isolde said, with a smile which curled up around her teeth, so she looked like an angry dog. "You decided to come back, did you? I can't say I'm disappointed. You've saved me a journey. I would have gone to find you." She lifted her hand and Pen was pulled towards her, feeling panicked as Niamh's grip fell away. He could hear all three Shipperbottoms crying out as he disappeared.

He found himself in a small room in what seemed to be a big house, but the only thing furnishing the room was a large wooden structure, from which hung a noose. As Pen looked at it in horror, he heard Isolde laughing behind him.

"I would offer you a seat," she said through her laughter, "but I'm afraid I can only stretch as far as a rope. Try it on then, don't waste time! Let's see if it fits."

Pen felt her pushing him backwards and, as she clicked her fingers, the noose leapt out and tightened around his neck. His feet were still firmly on the ground and he tried to stay as calm as he could, but a terrified sickness rose up within him as he considered the helplessness of the situation.

"So, you're going to kill me?" Pen asked, trying not to let his fear become apparent through his voice. Isolde laughed again.

"No, you're going to kill yourself, little boy. But I might let you swing for a while." She shoved him and he lost his footing, causing the rope to tighten around his neck. As he scrambled around to regain his balance, Isolde clapped her unbroken hand against her shoulder. "I really thought killing Napier would make everything feel right. But how can I condemn him to what I have experienced if he is dead?" She pushed Pen again, in a different direction, and he fell and began to choke. This time though, Isolde pulled him back to his feet by his hair and wrenched his head back, placing her lips against his own so he had to choose between the rope and her kiss. He opted for the rope, letting himself fall backwards and stop with such a violent jolt that he was sure for a second his neck must have broken.

"You mad witch!" he hissed, unable to muster anything louder but determined she should know exactly how he felt about her.

"A mad witch? Is that how you see me? But, you see, Ramin was younger than you when we consummated our love."

"You never consummated anything," Pen whispered, clutching desperately at the rope which was scratching into the swollen skin of his neck. "He was dead long before then. You just mutilated his soul and created a beautiful child you don't deserve."

"One second, please, little boy," Isolde said with another laugh. "Are you talking about Tahmina?"

"No," Pen replied, although he knew that they were indeed talking about the same girl. "I'm talking about Niamh O'Hare."

"The little Irish girl in the dungeon? She will be Tahmina again."

"You mad witch!" Pen repeated, but Isolde simply pushed him again and, as his feet skidded out from under him, she caught one of them in her hand so the noose pulled tighter around his neck. "Mad witch," he hissed.

For a few seconds, Pen was certain he was going to die, that the pain and suffocation could only lead to one thing. It seemed he needed to reach that level of desperation to remember he had the Rite, and it appeared in his mind, providing a rail on the wall which he could snatch. He wasted no time in grabbing it and pulling himself away from Isolde.

"Ah, little boy!" she laughed. "You finally decided to make this a fair fight."

Pen felt himself drop to the floor as the rope was cut and, letting go of the rail he had created, he moved towards the woman in front of him, suddenly confident in how to end a life. He didn't need the kelpie this time: every fibre of his body was telling him exactly how to strike.

"Bring them up," he demanded, his voice so quiet that he could hardly hear it himself.

"Very well," Isolde said, with a faint smile. She raised her hands and suddenly Marley, Bernadette, Erlend and Niamh were brought into the room through the same powerful Rite she had used to bring him there a few minutes earlier.

"Goodbye, Isolde," Erlend said, and the Knave's Thaumaturge glanced across at him in surprise. Pen, on the other hand, kept advancing on her as slowly and menacingly as he could whilst unable to breathe properly.

"Then my time has come," she snapped. "Perhaps I should thank you. But I wish you good luck in your escape, Pendragon Devon. Fire and water like my poor brother? Fire and water hemlock, gathered with a silver sickle wet with your own blood! I couldn't have planned it better."

Pen didn't understand what she was saying but, just as Erlend cried out for him to control himself, he brought his hands crashing together. With all the Rite he could muster, he threw Isolde backwards, and watched as her skull crushed against the wall and, for a second, the smile flickered around her mouth. She held her hand out to her daughter as she died, but Niamh turned away, covering the candle which Pen assumed Isolde had hoped would light her way to Ramin.

Chapter Twenty Four

The Unexpected Saviour

Pen stood absolutely still, his heart racing as though it would leave his chest at any moment. The bloodied body of Isolde lay before him and, from the horrified looks on the faces of those around him, his decision to kill her at that moment had caused more problems than it solved. Niamh was still turned away, shielding the light of the candle from the woman who had reached for it in her dying moments. Marley was clutching his mother's wrist, and Bernadette had her arm stretched out in front of him, shielding her son from an attack which would never come. They stood like statues and Pen could only stare at them, wondering why they were showing no signs of relief that Isolde had been defeated. Finally, Erlend moved towards him and, taking his arm firmly, led him out into the corridor.

"Have you ever seen a silver sickle?" he asked. Pen raised his hand to his throat as he tried to speak but no words came out. "Have you?"

He nodded.

"And did you come in contact with it? Did you ever cut yourself on it? Even just a scratch?"

Knowing that, even if he tried to speak, no words would come out, Pen nodded again and held up his left hand, where the scar from the blade still showed. Erlend started to breathe heavily and paced the corridor, hardly sparing a glance for Pen, who began to realise there was some reason he should have kept Isolde alive. In his panicked and exhausted state, he had no idea what that reason was. He watched as Erlend hurried to the window and beckoned him over.

"Do you see that?"

"Yes," Pen whispered. Below them, in the chasm from which they had been brought just minutes earlier, was a raging fire. Its long yellow and orange tongues weren't yet close to reaching the house, but Pen suddenly understood the comparison Isolde had made to her half-brother, Percy, who had attempted to burn down Honour's Rest. "We need to get out."

"I think that's going to be a problem," Erlend replied and then, once again taking Pen by the arm, led him back into the room where the three others were now standing together, the dead Knave's Thaumaturge at the far side of the room. He looked from one to the other of them, and each attempted to raise a smile, although there was only Niamh who looked as though she was happy he was there. She moved over to him and took his hand, placing her fingers in between his own so it felt like they were clasped together in a prayer.

"The house will be on fire soon," Erlend said, giving his wife a look which Pen knew was part of an unspoken message. "We need to get out."

Bernadette nodded and left the room, dragging Marley behind her like a child. Erlend gestured for Pen and Niamh to follow, which they did, and together they walked through the house until they came to a door which promised to lead them outside. Erlend put his hand against the door handle but jumped back.

"What is it?" Marley asked, reaching out towards the handle. His father slapped his hand down and Marley glared at him.

"I think there is only one of us who can open this door," Erlend said, and turned to Pen, who shrugged his shoulders and put his hand on the door handle. He felt a sharp pain and realised a tiny blade had cut into his hand, drawing just enough blood to follow Erlend's into the strange pattern on the door handle. He pushed open the door to reveal another room, furnished with a table, upon which was a tall phial and a silver sickle. Pen moved over to it.

"Don't drink it!" he heard Marley cry out, and he felt his hand being pulled back from where he had leant forward to pick up the bottle. "What do you think you're doing? It's poison!"

"He's right, Pen," Erlend said quietly. "Not fire and water, but fire and water hemlock? I think Isolde has left that there for you, and specifically you. I don't doubt that the only way we will get out is for you to drink it."

"No," Marley snapped, pulling away from his mother and father, and hurrying over to the bottle. "I'll drink it."

As he reached out for the phial, Pen jumped onto him, pushing him to the ground so Marley let out a cry of surprise.

"Don't be such an idiot," Pen said, as loudly as he could. "If anyone is going to drink it then it's me. But surely there's a way around it?"

Erlend tilted his head and stared at the phial. All the time that he did this, the others looked from one to the other, apart from Niamh, who just gripped Pen's arm to hold him back from rushing forward and drinking the poison. He didn't understand how she knew what he was thinking, but it made him feel both happy and sad to believe she was on his wavelength.

"I should drink it," Erlend said at last. "Don't complain or tell me not to be stupid. I've had a good life. And I have my daughter I would be returning to. If you give me a minute then I think I can trick the Rite into believing it's you who will drink it, Pen."

"How selfish," Marley snapped. "You aren't Pen's deputy. You aren't even Deputy Rendelf anymore. How is Mum supposed to live without you? It's my job to drink it, isn't it? That's the whole point of the role I've been learning: to help Pen when something like this happens."

"That's what happened to Ramin," Pen whispered. "But it's not what I want. I don't want either of you to drink it. I don't even believe you could, even if you tried. It wants my blood to make sure that it is me who drinks it."

He took hold of Niamh, for a moment wishing with all his heart that he had longer to spend with the strange, beautiful cambion, whom he had grown to love even with all the distance that existed between them. She raised her free hand up to his head and pulled it down to her own, finding his lips and laying a soft kiss on them.

"You are too precious, Pendragon Orion Devon," she said. "And I can't lose you now you've come back to me."

"I'm the only one who can drink from the phial. I'm sure of that. This whole exercise is Isolde's way of making us experience what happened to Ramin. Mr Shipperbottom, I'm sorry this is happening for a second time. I think that was all part of her plan. Perhaps there's a way I can be healed afterwards?"

Erlend bowed his head. "You're a brave boy, Pen, but that's all you are. Just like Ramin. You're only a year older than he was and your arguments are the same. To protect your friends, you would give your life."

"I don't think there's anyone more deserving," Pen said, shrugging his shoulders. "I suppose there's no way the Rite can be cheated anyway. If there's one thing Napier has taught me then it's that."

"Oh, I think Napier has taught you a great deal," Bernadette said, in an uncharacteristically quiet voice. "But you're right. The Knave's Rite cannot be cheated in this way, although I can't tell you how I know this. Isolde has ensured she will have revenge for the loss of Ramin, and that revenge is to take the person who matters most to Napier, her enemy. No, Pen," she continued, "you were never her enemy, not even a target. You're simply a weapon, designed to inflict as much pain on your uncle as Isolde could possibly hope."

"I thought she wanted to kill him," Marley said.

"Napier? Yes, she wanted to kill him. But then it occurred to her that there are more effective ways of making someone suffer. Pendragon is correct in all but one of the things he's said. Yes, he must be the one to drink from the phial. I doubt it will even open for anyone else. Yes, Isolde has recreated the day that Ramin died, even down to the choice of poison, I believe. But no, there's no way that a person can be healed after drinking a poison of natural power, harvested with a silver sickle wet with the blood of the intended victim."

"So Pen has to die?" Marley stammered. "No! No, I refuse to believe it. It doesn't even make any sense. I've learnt loads about healing. I'll be able to do something."

Pen shook his head and moved over to his friend, pulling him into an embrace so, for that moment, they were as close as if they had grown together since the womb. But now, after everything they had been through during the past seventeen months, Pen had the opportunity to repay everyone for their kindness. After he and Marley had broken apart, he moved over to Erlend, who shook his hand, and then turned to Bernadette, who took hold of him and hugged him so tightly he couldn't breathe.

Finally, he wanted to kiss Niamh goodbye, but it felt like torture, so all he could do was put his hand on her cheek and bend his head down in front of her. She placed her lips gently against his hair. After a moment, he turned back to the phial and lifted it above his head. He had no idea how to get it open, let alone whether he would even be able to drink it so, for a moment, he just stood and looked at it.

As he stared, the whole room froze, apart from something which seemed to be moving within the bottle. A distorted hand reached out and took it from him. Pen turned around and found himself looking straight into the familiar dark eyes of his uncle. A rush of excitement burst through him, as he remembered how the same person had come to his rescue after his last encounter with Isolde, and he felt a smile twitch across his face.

Napier returned the gesture and then smashed the bottle down against the side of the table so the glass at the rim shattered. Still looking straight at his nephew, he slowly scratched his lower lip with the glass and, without flinching, let his blood trickle into the phial.

"Here's to you, Pendragon Devon," Napier said. "May you make a wonderful Rendelf. I, personally, have no doubt of it." He threw his head back and drank the contents of the bottle. Pen could not have acted quickly enough to stop him and, even as he watched his uncle swallow the bloodied mixture, he knew he would be haunted by the sight for as long as he lived. "I think we should awaken the others now," Napier said, smacking his lips as though he had just drunk something delicious.

"Napier!" Erlend said, clearly overjoyed. "What on earth are you doing here? How did you know where to find us? Aren't you supposed to be in New York?"

"Three questions at once," Napier laughed. "I am here to right some wrongs. Some recent, and others which have been my burden for decades. I knew where to find you because I made sure I would know exactly where my car was at all times. I could not trust it to two teenage boys."

"And why aren't you in New York?"

"I went to New York," Napier replied, "and gave the presentation. But something made me think I was needed here, so the reception had to wait." He put the broken phial back on the table, and Erlend and Bernadette exchanged horrified glances.

"Do you know what you have done, Napier?" Marley's

mother asked.

"I always do, my dear," Napier replied. "Only Pen's blood could be used to open the poison bottle and then the door. But, between genes and the Rite, Pen and I share much the same blood, don't we? In that way it would appear that things can be cheated after all." He pointed to a door which had appeared just in front of them and was slightly ajar. "Ladies first."

Bernadette, still staring at Napier as though he was insane, took Niamh's wrist in one hand and Marley's in the other, pulling them out into the daylight. Erlend followed them, but Napier grabbed hold of Pen's sleeve for support and, for the first time, Pen realised his uncle's mortality.

"Why did you do that?" Pen asked, his voice cracking. "I would have drunk it, you know? It was my duty to drink it."

"Just as it was my duty to drink the concoction Obadiah Crick left for us? No, that was Ramin's destiny. Yours is to live. To become a man. To become a Rendelf." Napier was clearly trying to steady his voice, but he seemed to be in an almost overwhelming pain, which was one of the worst things Pen had ever seen.

"You shouldn't even be here," he wheezed, tears and pain of his own making it impossible to talk. "I got us into this mess, and I should be the person who gets us out. Why did you take the bottle from me? I would have drunk it!"

"That is why I took it from you and made it impossible for any of the others to stop me. You will know one day when your time comes. When Niamh's candle burns a little more brightly. I saw that. You know what she is, don't you?"

"A cambion," Pen replied. He felt as though he could keep his uncle alive for as long as he kept up the conversation. "But is there anything I can do for her?"

"Do for her?" Napier repeated. "You cannot change what she is: the daughter of a dead man. But I am sure if anyone can find a way to help her embrace her blindness and grant her back the Rite then it is you."

Pen nodded. "Is that appropriate for a Rendelf?"

"You know the answer to that," Napier said with a smile. "Stop trying to delay things. We should get out of here before the whole place burns to the ground." With visibly clenched teeth, he pulled Pen out of the building and, seconds later, they were standing in the blinding sunlight of the Strath, watching in silence as the flames leapt out of the ground and devoured the house, leaving nothing but a pillar of black smoke.

"Goodbye, Isolde," Napier whispered. "You may not believe it, Pendragon, but there was a time when she was a beautiful creature in body and soul. If you had told me then that this day would come, I would either have laughed, or else struck you down."

As he finished speaking, Napier fell violently to the ground, his whole body convulsing as the poison began to take hold. Pen tried to calm him, tried to sit him up so breathing would come more easily, but he couldn't. Erlend hurried over and put his hand on Napier's chest, whispering words which Pen didn't hear, but the seizure ended, and Napier began to breathe normally again. He held his hand out to Pen and, as he was apparently too exhausted to get to his feet, his nephew crouched down and took it. It was strange to have such close physical contact with Napier, who had always avoided anything like that. It added finality to the situation.

"You will be fine, I promise," his uncle said. "Don't change a thing. You'll be fine. Stay angry. Stay young. Stay open to being wrong and just as open to being right." He rested his head against his nephew's chest and Pen noticed that, for the first time since he had known his uncle, he could see the silvery skein Napier had wrapped tightly around his fingers. "You're hurt," he whispered, and Pen shook his head.

"Not much."

"Make sure your father doesn't hate me for that too," Napier laughed weakly. "But perhaps he'll forgive me this time."

As Pen opened his mouth to assure Napier that Jarvis would forgive him anything, his uncle once again disappeared into a seizure, and Pen felt himself being pulled backwards as Erlend and Marley both tried to make the dying Rendelf comfortable. Pen fought to break free from Bernadette's grip, but she was as strong as he had ever believed her to be, and all he could do was exhaust himself by trying desperately to get away. At last, Erlend walked over to him, his eyes shining with tears.

"Time to say goodbye, I think, Pen," he whispered, and Bernadette's grip loosened. Pen walked back over to his uncle, who was lying very still on the ground, his eyes, dark as his nephew's, staring up at the sky. Pen put a hand on his shoulder and shook it gently.

"Erlend says it's time to say goodbye," he whispered. "Isn't there anything I can do?"

"Nothing," Napier murmured back, taking Pen's hand and holding it against his chest. "But there is something

Niamh can do."

Pen called the cambion over and Niamh bent down beside the Rendelf, who gestured to the candle.

"Of course," she said to Napier, and then turned to the boy at his side, who knew he couldn't disguise his confusion that she had seen Napier's gesture. "Don't worry, I won't let him leave alone, Pen."

"Pendragon," Napier whispered, with a slight smile as he corrected her.

Pen watched as the cambion held the candle up in front of Napier's face and its light seemed to reflect in his eyes, as though it was welling up from within him. Niamh placed her other hand gently on his still chest, and Pen knelt in absolute silence, watching in an agony he had believed he would never experience.

Chapter Twenty Five

Back Home

Pen couldn't speak, or even move. He could only kneel there, looking down at the Rendelf's body. Napier's hand was heavy in his own, but Pen let it rest in his grip, squeezing it gently to try to generate a response which could never come. The sunlight around him seemed to mock the darkness in his soul, and even the light from Niamh's candle was dull, as though Napier had taken some of it with him. Pen couldn't bring himself to stop looking at his uncle, willing some sign of life to return, even with it the kind of comment he had grown to hate so much from the man who had always known best on every subject. Even in death, Napier had known exactly what to do, requesting guidance from the girl who could take him to the place she had experienced before she was even born.

He could hear sobbing behind him, but somehow that only made him feel more alone. Erlend, Bernadette and Marley had each other. Pen felt as though he had no one, as though his uncle's death had plunged him into a kind of aloneness, the threat of which always haunted him.

Niamh's hand slid over his shoulder as she got to her feet. She wasn't looking for reassurance, but rather volunteering the comfort he needed. Pen got up and pulled her towards him and she buried her head in his chest, letting him cry into her hair and, as each tear fell into the silver strands, she seemed to become more and more alive.

Out of the corner of his eye, Pen saw Erlend walking up to him, but he didn't want to speak to anyone or be near anyone apart from Niamh and his uncle. He wanted to get down onto his knees and beg that mysterious Someone to give him another chance to drink from the bottle, to know exactly what was required of him, to have not hesitated and let Napier pull the phial from his grasp. Instead, he shakily pushed Erlend away, but Niamh caught his hand and squeezed it.

"He's grieving too," she whispered.

Pen nodded and looked at Erlend, whose face was already red and swollen with tearstains. It felt as though they had all been crying since time began and as though they would continue to cry until someone or something brought the world to a close.

"I'm sorry," Pen said to Erlend. "I'm sorry. Oh, God, I'm sorry!" His final exclamation made Niamh squeeze his hand more tightly and bring it to her lips to kiss over and over again. "I shouldn't have stopped. I should have just drunk it."

"No," Erlend said, shaking his head. "He made the decision. Clearly Ramin's sacrifice haunted him. We all think about how loss affects us individually, Pen. I didn't realise just how much Napier must have struggled to come to terms with the fact another person died for him. Now you carry that burden. I hope it will make you the kind of man he was."

Pen bowed his head but said nothing. He couldn't think of anything he could say to make Erlend realise just how much he wished it was him lying dead on the ground, rather than standing there already carrying the burden which had dictated Napier's life and, in the end, his death.

"We'll stay with you and get everything sorted," Pen heard Bernadette say, in a voice strained through tears.

Pen just shook his head. He didn't want them to stay. He didn't want to be surrounded by people who would try to make him any less sorrowful.

"No," he whispered. "You go home. All of you. You too, Marley," he said, as his best friend opened his mouth to protest. "Please, let this be the first thing I ask you to obey. Niamh and I will call an ambulance, or police, or whoever we need to call. There'll be someone who'll pick up on what's going on, won't there?"

Erlend handed him a mobile phone and for a moment Pen was filled with anger that there had been a connection with the outside world. Surely then, they could have found help for Napier. But the older man shook his head.

"There was nothing we could do, Pen," he said, placing his hand on Pen's shoulder and looking at him, eye to eye so Pen did not even dare to blink. "It would only have meant that Napier would have been removed from us for the last minutes of his life and, knowing him, do you really believe he would have wanted that?"

Pen shook his head, although accepting there was nothing he could have done for his uncle only made him feel more guilty, as though he was looking for a way that this wasn't his fault. There was no escaping the fact that it was his responsibility. Erlend shook him gently, perhaps hearing what was going through his mind.

"Call the police," he said, pointing to the phone. "Then call Aban Usman and tell him what's happened and that you've been in touch with the police. I've got no doubt at all that he'll be able to sort things out. You've met him, haven't you?"

Pen nodded and felt a smile flicker across his face. Although it felt so alien, he couldn't help but smile at the memory of the man whose larger-than-life personality had made a nervous situation into something so bearable it was almost enjoyable.

"Aban is a good man," Erlend said. "A great man. And he has a lot of power which he won't hesitate to put to good use." He paused and looked at Pen again, before placing his hands carefully around the boy's swollen neck and whispering something under his breath. Almost immediately, the physical pain subsided, but that only made the emotional agony more acute. "Are you sure you don't want us to stay?"

"I'm sure," Pen replied, in a quiet voice. "You all need each other. And Niamh and I will handle things. Won't we, Niamh?" Niamh nodded and then allowed herself to be embraced by both Mr and Mrs Shipperbottom at the same time. "You're not hurt, are you, Marley?" Pen asked. "I just think you need to be with your parents."

"No," Marley said slowly, as though he was thinking out every word before he allowed himself to speak, "because I agree. But I'm concerned about what *you* need, Pen."

"Don't worry about that. Just make sure that you come back to Honour's Rest in time for–" Pen stopped. He couldn't bring himself to say 'in time for the funeral': it sounded too formal and final. "Anyway, just don't stay away too long."

He watched as the small family gathered and, within a second, disappeared. Niamh reached out, confused, as they vanished, and her blindness suddenly seemed to unsettle her. Pen took her free hand and, with his other one, dialled 999 for the first time in his life.

It was one of the most surreal conversations he had ever endured. The woman on the other end of the phone wanted to know everything. Did his uncle still have a pulse? How long since he had consumed the poison? Pen tried repeatedly to explain to her that she didn't have to send an emergency ambulance, that he knew Napier was dead, but she kept trying to persuade him to perform first aid. Finally, he described where they were and then hung up. He realised he hadn't asked Erlend for Aban Usman's number but, as he thumbed his way through the contacts list, he found his name and pressed the call button.

"Good afternoon," said a cheery female voice. "Aban Usman's office. How can I help you?"

"Hello," Pen murmured into the phone. "Is Mr Usman available at all?"

"I'm afraid he's in meetings all day," the woman said.

"It's really urgent."

"I'll see if I can get a message to him. Can I ask who's calling, please?"

"Pendragon Devon."

"Please hold the line for a moment, Mr Devon." Pen put the phone away from his ear as the hold music began to blare obtrusively into his quiet mourning. Niamh smiled up at him and, a few moments later, the female voice came back on the line. "I'm just putting you through," she announced, and Pen heard Mr Usman's voice greeting him.

"Pendragon, what on earth can I help you with, my boy?" he asked. "Something urgent, Yvette tells me."

"Mr Usman," Pen said, successfully swallowing back his tears, "my uncle is dead." He didn't allow any time for a response. "I've called the police, but I need to make sure that everything's handled as Napier would have wanted."

"Napier's dead?" Aban whispered down the phone, his voice changing instantly. "Oh, God."

For a moment, Pen didn't know what to say and the phone line went quiet, apart from Aban Usman's strained breathing at the other end, and the strange background noise of a busy office. At last, Pen tried to break the silence.

"Erlend Shipperbottom told me to call you. He said you'd be able to help with the police. We're at Dunbeath Strath in Caithness."

"Yes, yes," Aban said, springing back to life. "Don't worry about a thing with them, Pendragon. I'll make sure the message gets across clearly. You go back to Honour's Rest. Is there anyone you can call?"

"My parents."

"Yes, yes," Mr Usman said again. "Call your parents. The best people in the world at these times. Goodbye then, Pen. Oh, and please pass on my very best wishes and most sincere condolences to your father."

The phone went dead, and Pen let it drop from his hand, before falling onto his knees beside the body of his uncle, and beginning to cry, clutching Niamh as tightly as he could for comfort.

He was still crying when the police arrived twenty minutes later. Two uniformed officers in a Land Rover drove them to the end of the Strath before turning back to where they had been forced to leave Napier. A pair of detectives were waiting for them in the car park, but they asked no questions at all, and didn't even begin to challenge them for details about what had happened. Pen took a moment through his tears to wonder what on earth Aban Usman actually did, which meant he could control the police through a single phone call from hundreds of miles away.

Pen was never exactly sure how he and Niamh managed to get back to Honour's Rest but, that evening, he found himself pushing the heavy door open and looking around him with a sad satisfaction. Everything was just as he had left it, even down to the scattered raisins on the kitchen floor, dropped by someone who had considered the possibility he might not make it back, but not that someone else would be lost. He led Niamh to one of the spare rooms and apologised there were only boys' clothes so, after she bathed, she would need to wear something from his wardrobe. While Niamh was in the bathroom, Pen walked to Napier's study and stood at the desk, imagining for a second that his uncle was sitting in front of him. Then, with a shaking hand, he picked up the phone and dialled his parents' number.

It was his mother who answered.

"Pendragon, sweetheart," she said, when he began to cry as he explained what had happened. "There was nothing you could have done. You must give Napier the credit he deserves for making that sacrifice." She was crying too and, a moment later, his father picked up the other receiver.

"We'll be up on the next flight," Jarvis said. "Just stay where you are. I'll handle everything."

There was no flight until the following day so his father called back and told Pen that they would drive up immediately to try and sort things out. Pen was grateful: he had no understanding at all of what Napier would want or, in fact, whether his uncle had left a will to dictate what should happen in the event of his death.

As he put the phone down, Niamh walked steadily into the room, running her free hand along the wall so she could find her way, until Pen took it lightly and guided her to the desk. Although he couldn't bring himself to sit in his uncle's chair, he felt certain Napier would have invited Niamh to do so, and he held it still while she sat down. Then, telling himself he knew the telephone number for Patrick O'Hare, he punched the numbers into the phone and left Niamh to talk to her parents.

Pen and Niamh stayed in the living room that night, neither wanting to be alone. Both naturally slender, they were able to lie side-by-side on the deep sofa, and Pen had never been so grateful of closeness with anyone. Whatever her heritage, it was Niamh who managed to get him through that night, and he knew, as he wrapped his arm around her, he would never forget it.

It was about half past three in the morning when his parents arrived, and Pen gently moved past Niamh so he could go and meet them. She was unsurprisingly exhausted, and it didn't seem like the moment to be introducing her to his parents. He wandered outside and stood in the doorway as his mother and father came out of the car and hurried towards him.

"Oh, Pendragon, sweetheart," said his mother, just as she had on the phone. He put his arms around her but felt as though he had no more tears to give, so watched jealously as tears poured down her face. "Have you been all alone all day?"

"No," Pen replied, leaning his head against hers. "I've got company, but she's asleep." He turned to his father. "I'm sorry, Dad. I really don't think there's anything anyone could have done."

"No, I know," Jarvis replied, putting his hand on Pen's arm. "I've made an appointment to see the solicitor tomorrow. We'll get things sorted for the funeral."

After his parents had declined a drink, Pen led them to another spare room. He switched the light on and stared at the unmade bed, noticing his parents jump as he waved his hand towards it and it made itself.

"I'm sorry," he whispered. "I'm just too tired to do it normally. There's a bathroom down the hall and I'll make sure there's breakfast in the morning. I'm sleeping in the living room." With that, he wandered out and went back to where Niamh was sleeping alone.

When Pen woke up the following morning, it felt as though he was living someone else's life. He walked almost aimlessly into the kitchen to find his mother was already up and making breakfast. It was odd that there was no food set out on the breakfast table by means of the Rite, but there was something comforting about the homeliness of being with his mother.

"Your father left first thing this morning," she said, passing him a plate of pancakes. There was something very un-Napier about having pancakes for breakfast and, for a moment, Pen just looked at them uncertainly. "Who's your friend?"

"Her name's Niamh," he replied, with a slight smile. "She's like me, you know? A thaumaturge. But she's blind so she can't easily access the Rite."

"Will she be joining us for breakfast?"

Pen shook his head. "No, let her sleep. It's her first proper night's sleep in ages. Her parents are coming this afternoon." He paused and glanced in the direction of the living room. "I suppose she can see in her dreams."

"Will Marley be coming back at all, Pen?"

"Yes. Just as soon as things are sorted for, you know, Uncle Napier's—" He stopped. Something kept choking him every time he tried to talk about his uncle's funeral. Only dead people had funerals.

Pen spent most of the morning tidying the house, including mending the guitar which he had thrown down heavily just a couple of days before. He tried to remember how angry he had been with Napier in the hope it would dull the sense of loss, but it didn't work. Instead, he just cut his fingers painfully and often as they slipped whilst he was attempting to restring the guitar, but somehow even the pain felt as though he was just witnessing it through someone else.

Later that day, just after Niamh had woken up and been introduced awkwardly to Pen's mother, Jarvis returned from his meeting with the solicitor. His wife made him a cup of tea and the four of them sat down together in the drawing room, watching the heavy October mist swirling across the loch and into the hills and mountains beyond.

"You'll be unsurprised to know that Napier was in no doubt whatsoever about what should happen in the event of his death," Pen's father said with a faint smile. "I've arranged for his body to be brought back here as he requested, where he'll stay in the State Room. It's been a long time since I've looked around here, Pen, so I'm hoping you know where that is?"

Pen nodded.

"He also made it abundantly clear that you are in charge. It seems his will was rewritten just before he went to New York, to account for the fact that you're now sixteen and, as he considers it, an adult. I don't know what I think about this. You know there are a lot of things you can't do until you're eighteen?"

"I think things are different for Pendragon," Niamh said, the first time Jarvis had heard her speak beyond a quiet welcome.

"Well, there's time to discuss that," Pen's father replied.

Niamh's parents arrived at lunchtime and, after spending a few minutes in Honour's Rest, they took their daughter in their little car to the Bed & Breakfast they had checked into in Aviemore. Pen had offered them a room at the castle, but they had declined quickly. Without her in the house, Pen felt as though he had no one to speak to, despite his mother's and father's attempts to engage him in conversation.

When the hearse appeared on the causeway, Pen went outside and met the undertakers, who respectfully carried the magnificent coffin through the house and into the State Room. There, they lifted the wooden lid and Pen stood in silence, staring at his uncle.

Napier looked for all the world as though he wasn't asleep but thinking. His forehead was slightly creased in contemplation and, below his closed eyes, a faint smile was on his lips. Pen's dry eyes prickled as he realised it was the smile with which Napier had whispered his nephew's name as he died. The Rendelf's gloved hands were clasped across his chest, as though at any moment he would begin to twist the invisible skein through his fingers.

It's almost eerie, Pen thought as he stood there alone, *how Napier looks so ready to go, so alive.* Yet, even in his confusion about spirituality and religion, Pen was quite certain there was nothing else this strange shell of his uncle would ever do again.

He would have slept in the State Room beside his uncle's body, had Niamh not returned and wandered down to find him, her candle stretched out in front of her as though she was able to find her way by its light.

"Don't stay here, Pen. It's dark down here."

"I think I deserve the darkness," Pen replied.

"It's only through the darkness that we can see we're walking in the light," Niamh said and, as they walked away from the room and its eternally-silent occupant, Pen couldn't quite remember when he had heard words like those before.

Chapter Twenty Six

A Time to Weep

In the days which followed, Pen spent a lot of time in the State Room, sitting alone and practising the Rite repeatedly, demonstrating to his uncle that he was willing and able to take everything seriously. Niamh would sit with him sometimes, her candle flickering in the chill breeze which surrounded them. She rarely spoke and any words she did say were limited to commenting on the weather or informing him of what she had been doing with her mum and dad, who weren't particularly pleased with her decision to stay at the castle. She didn't mention Napier, or Pen's parents, or anything about what had happened during the past week or what was about to happen.

The Shipperbottoms came down to Honour's Rest in the middle of the week, and Pen was relieved to be reunited with Marley, as well as being pleased that there were now other adults in the house to distract his parents, who had started to become anxious about Pen's self-imposed solitary confinement. Erlend and Bernadette had similar interests to Pen's mother and father, so the time which passed between Napier's death and his funeral wasn't without its lighter moments.

The day after Marley arrived back at the house found the three teenagers sitting on the edge of the loch, the first time Pen had been outside since he had walked into the building alongside Napier's coffin. The fresh air simultaneously made him feel better and worse, and he was reminded of stories he had read about survivor's guilt. This, he knew, was what had moulded Napier's life since the moment Ramin had tricked him and drunk the poison. Now his uncle's death would spur Pen on to the same sense of duty.

"What do you think it's all about?" he asked, dropping stones into the loch absentmindedly with one hand, whilst curling Niamh's fair hair around his fingers on the other.

"What?" Marley glanced up at him as he spoke.

"The Rite. What makes some people have it and others not? I never asked, but now I want to know. Why is it usually the eldest child? Why does my dad have it, but not in the same way as Napier?"

"So many questions," Niamh whispered. "But, you know, the answers don't lie at the bottom of the lake."

Pen looked down. "I know, but I need to understand. I know there's the Knave's Rite and the Just Rite; and that a thaumaturge must choose their path at fifteen or else face the consequences. But I don't understand why some people don't have it at all, and others experience it in a different way. Napier told me once that my father had the Rite, which is what made him so clever. So, does the Rite make people good? Or bad? Does it make us into the people we're always going to be, so we don't actually have any choice?"

Neither Marley nor Niamh attempted to answer his questions, but Niamh didn't comment again about Pen dropping stones into the water. They sat for a while longer in silence, wondering whether their natural ability to wield the Rite had already dictated the paths they would have to take. At last, it was Marley's voice which broke the silence.

"I have a question too," he murmured, and Pen looked across at him with a faint smile. "When did Napier drink the poison? He appeared, and suddenly he had drunk it all."

"He used the Rite," Pen replied. "Just like Ramin. That's just it, the whole thing: it's cheating. The Rite is just a way of manipulating nature to cheat."

"Yes," Marley agreed. "Otherwise, one of us would have stopped him."

Pen couldn't answer, apart from a non-committal grunt. He just didn't have the heart to tell Marley that he hadn't fallen under the power of the Rite which had made the others so distanced from their surroundings: he had watched as Napier had cut his own lip on the bottle and mixed water hemlock with the blood which had sealed his fate, even as he had offered it in a toast to his nephew. It had all been done with the kind of old-fashioned style Pen would have expected from Napier, yet that only made it harder to bear. He tried to remind himself there was nothing anyone could have done but, for as long as he knew he could have stopped his uncle, he couldn't bring himself to believe it.

That evening, Pen hosted a dinner for the people who were staying at Honour's Rest: his parents, the Shipperbottoms and Niamh, who had been accepted by his mother and father as 'Pendragon's girlfriend'.

The meal was a success, which came as a great relief to Pen, who had created it all by means of the Rite, something he was not in the slightest bit familiar with. His mother and Bernadette congratulated him as they returned for second helpings, while Marley and Niamh managed to find enough humour in Erlend and Jarvis' conversation to laugh along with them. Pen enjoyed sitting and watching them but, as he did, he began to feel the sensation of the Rite creeping through his body and pulsing from his heart as though it had replaced his lifeblood. For a second, he didn't think he would be able to contain it and he pushed his chair back suddenly. His father's eyes flashed over to him.

"Are you alright, Pen?" he asked, as his son leapt up.

Pen stood for a moment, feeling as though the whole room was pulsating along with his experience of the Rite. He nodded his head.

"Just tired," he forced himself to say. "I'm going for a breath of fresh air."

Pen stumbled out of the building and into the darkness of the October night. For the first time, it occurred to him that it was the 31st of October. As a child, he had loved Halloween: his father and mother had taken him trick-or-treating every year until he was old enough to go unattended with friends. Last year, Halloween had been swallowed by the continuing newness of life at Honour's Rest but, with everything preying on his mind now, the night gave Pen an opportunity to experience that closeness with the world beyond. Standing alone on the gravel, he could hear the kelpie's hooves beating beneath the water: deep and constant, like the pounding of a waterfall. He had never heard it above ground before. Further away, he could hear children's laughter, as though some neighbouring youngsters were enjoying the clear, still evening. But he had never heard any other soul from Honour's Rest. Around him, the world seemed to come alive: people were pleading, others laughing, others crying, others he could see in his mind's eye were silently staring straight at him, featureless yet full of expression.

Pen jumped as he felt a slender hand on his shoulder, and he turned around to see his mother.

"Did you know," she said, as though she could understand his thoughts, "that the Celtic name for Halloween was Samhain?"

Pen said nothing. The aftereffects of the Rite were too powerful for him to give way to any words.

"It was the time when people killed their animals for the winter, to make sure they would have enough to eat over the long months to come." His mother's voice sounded dreamy, and Pen felt himself leaning his head against her, wanting her to keep talking just because he found comfort in her voice. "Do you think that's how your uncle saw things, Pendragon? He knew he was getting older. Sometimes we must make sacrifices for the young. I'm not saying we should all die for others," she laughed as she noticed Pen looking at her, unimpressed. "But perhaps there comes a point when we need to accept that the next season is coming. We have to look ahead to the winter and spring, instead of remembering the summer."

Pen nodded but remained silent.

"It is also the time when the veil between the spirit world and the mortal world is at its thinnest. Do you know, Halloween's the only time I'm sure I've seen a ghost? It's true, you know? We're particularly susceptible to these things as the days shorten and the nights get darker." She patted her son's arm and then reached up to kiss him firmly on the cheek. "Come on inside, Pen. You've done a wonderful job this evening, but you still need to make sure that your guests are comfortable for the night."

It was as though the Rite had retreated with the appearance of his mother, but Pen wasn't sorry to have lost the connection with the people who had swamped his thoughts and vision. He could no longer hear children playing and yet he knew in his heart they were still there, just as surely as they had been three minutes earlier. He turned his back on the loch, where the kelpie still galloped, unheard, through the water.

Two days later, he had a different kind of guest to worry about, when Aban Usman arrived with another man, who looked sternly at Pen through a pair of thick-lensed glasses. Mr Usman took Pen's hand.

"I'm so sorry," he said. "I know I said I would give anything to be back here, but I realise now I didn't mean it. How are you holding up?"

"I'm surviving, thanks," Pen replied. "Are you looking for somewhere to stay ahead of tomorrow? There are still spare rooms."

"No, no. We're staying in Inverness. Pendragon Devon,

may I introduce you to François Leclerc. François is the French Rendelf. I'll feel happier knowing he has gone through a few of the finer points of the role. Anything Napier may not have had chance to mention."

"Come in then," Pen said, directing them both to the drawing room.

"Is your uncle still here?" Aban asked. "I would like to pay my respects."

"Yes," Pen replied, his voice as emotionless as he could make it. "He's in the State Room. Marley will show you the way."

As Marley appeared to lead their guest down to the State Room, Pen and François walked into the drawing room together and sat down opposite one another. François was a much older man, older than Napier, and he looked slightly condescending as he stared across at the boy in front of him.

"You are young," he observed. "Much younger than I had been expecting."

"I'm sixteen. And a couple of weeks."

"That is young. Too young."

"Not according to international law," Pen pointed out, in what he hoped was a politely firm voice, but his stomach was jolting. Did this man have the power to deny him the path Napier had set him on? To deny his uncle's dying wish?

"No, you are right. You are of age according to the conventions which have been laid down regarding this matter. But they are mistaken. I think only of you when I say you are too young. You have heard them, I think?"

"Who?"

"The voices. Those calling out to the Rendelf to answer

questions and solve problems. You must learn to hear each voice and to answer each query, with only as much energy and time as the next man. Your ability is now theirs. Your time is theirs. Your life is theirs. Do you comprehend?"

"Yes, sir."

"Had I met you prior to discussing the matter with Mr Usman, I would have recommended that Erlend Shipperbottom took on the role of Rendelf and you continue your training under him. However–" François paused to hold up his hand and silence Pen's imminent complaints. "Aban tells me you are qualified. So, I will act as your mentor for the foreseeable future and, the day after tomorrow, you will become the Rendelf for the United Kingdom."

"Thank you," Pen said with a forced smile, relieved the short and painful interview seemed to be ending.

"Do not thank me, Pendragon Devon," François said. "I am not sure that I am doing you the service you deserve. But Napier was a good man and often an ally to me." He rose to his feet and held out his hand to Pen, who shook it. "Tomorrow must be the last day you mourn, Pendragon. After that, there will be no time, and I am thinking you must learn to tell the difference between guilt and gratitude."

Pen hated to hear the Rendelf's words, particularly because he knew they were right. The following day, as he rode with his parents and the Shipperbottoms in the limousine which followed the hearse from Honour's Rest to the church, Pen looked down at the funeral clothes Napier had bought him a few months earlier. To remind himself to breathe, he repeated the words 'a time to weep, and a time to laugh; a time to mourn, and a time to dance' over and over to himself in his head. His mother had found them in Napier's old Bible and had copied them down on a postcard for him. He kept this clutched in his hand as he walked past the camera crews which were parked outside the church gates, and through a congregation made up of people he had only ever seen on television.

The Prime Minister was there, speaking in hushed tones with the Leader of the Opposition, who stared across at Pen as the boy followed the coffin up to the top of the church and sat down in the front pew. He glanced in the other direction and saw the First Ministers of Scotland, Wales and Northern Ireland sitting a short distance away. It was evidently these people who had drawn such interest from the media, as Pen was quite sure no one in the press could have identified Napier.

It rained at the graveside, but Pen hardly noticed as he became soaked to the skin. He couldn't help the jolt he gave as Napier's coffin was lowered carefully into the ground, fuelled by an almost overpowering compulsion to scream out that his uncle wasn't dead: this must all be another test which had been set for him. But he kept François' advice in mind and told himself he was now not only an adult, but an adult responsible for hundreds or even thousands of others.

So, Napier was laid to rest with cautious tears and no hysterics from his nephew and heir, but Pen took comfort from the knowledge that this was exactly how his uncle would have wanted it.

Later that day, the mourners sat in a small pub in the village, sharing stories about Napier and trying, but failing, to do him justice. The service had been moving, powerful even, but it didn't seem to matter how many stories were shared now, Pen couldn't get rid of that horrible feeling of finality which the funeral had brought. The major dignitaries had left immediately, and it was a local councillor who pointed to the television screen as they were talking.

"Look!" she cried, making Pen jump. "We've made the news." Jarvis leant over to the television and turned up the volume. They all strained their ears to hear what was said.

"Security was tight at the small village of Kinkeerie in the Highlands today as dignitaries from around the country gathered at the church to pay their respects at the funeral of noted diplomat, Napier Devon. The Prime Minister and First Ministers from all three devolved parliaments were in attendance, as were United Nations officials from around the globe. Napier Devon died suddenly whilst hiking in northern Scotland and a post-mortem revealed a heart attack. He was forty-nine years old. In other news, Inverness Caledonian Thistle—"

Jarvis leant over again and switched off the television. For a while, those gathered sat in silence, looking from one to another to find someone who could say anything which might numb the pain of hearing their friend's, brother's, uncle's, and mentor's life condensed into a few words, focussed more on the people who had attended his funeral than the man he had been.

At last, it was Aban Usman who broke the silence with a flippant remark to Pen about the number of post-mortems for which he had written the results.

"Of course," he said, with an attempt at joviality, "you know that no one touched Napier's body. I wouldn't have had it. But a heart attack at his age and in his position is something which nobody would question. I hope you don't mind?"

"No," Pen replied. "I don't mind at all."

That evening, he returned to Honour's Rest with his parents and the Shipperbottoms, Niamh having gone to Aviemore with her parents after the funeral. He turned to walk up to his room, but he opened the door to discover his books had been tidied away and, in the top room, the bedding had been folded. For a moment, Pen wondered what could have happened, but then remembered what François had said about becoming the Rendelf. Slowly, he made his way back down the spiral staircase and walked along to what had been Napier's room, where he almost jumped in surprise to find the door was unlocked.

Inside were all his things. The photograph of Napier, Erlend, Ramin and Isolde was gone and, in its place, was a picture of Pen with his uncle and Marley. It had been taken last Christmas when they had decorated Honour's Rest. Napier was standing behind the boys, his right hand resting on Pen's shoulder and his left on Marley's. He looked formal and yet, Pen realised as he picked up the photograph and looked at it more closely, his expression suggested he was laughing at the two boys or at the person who held the camera, who Pen thought had been Erlend.

He put the picture down and, getting into his pyjamas, slipped into the large four-poster bed and drew the curtains around him so he didn't have to look at the door which, months earlier, he had attempted to nail shut. Pen knew he wasn't ready yet to strike the match, light the candle, and watch Napier's form materialise out of the smoke, but knowing he had the option made him feel a kind of nervous closeness to the person he had lost.

Chapter Twenty Seven

Ash and Ice

When Pen awoke the day after Napier's funeral, it took him a moment to work out where he was and why he was in his uncle's room. But, as he had done each day since Dunbeath, he remembered what had happened and felt that familiar sensation of loss.

But, that morning, it was tempered with something else, something which Pen simultaneously resented and appreciated: determination. He greeted the day determined to achieve everything he could, finally starting to come to terms with the sacrifice his uncle had made as something he should be thankful for and not guilty, just as François had said.

Later that day, in the presence of his parents, Marley, the Shipperbottoms, and with Niamh holding his hand tightly, he took his oath as Rendelf before François and

Aban Usman, who solemnly reminded him of the duties which lay ahead and the importance of being aware that he was dedicating his entire life, long or short, to the service of others.

Afterwards, Aban Usman cracked open a bottle of champagne and, although he did not drink any, took great pleasure in watching the others. It was, he said, important to celebrate the new Rendelf. The mourning had to be behind them, and it was time to look to the future.

When Aban and François left a short time later, Pen hurried to his room to begin writing down a list of the different names and faces which suddenly began to appear to him. The Rite overtook him, and he witnessed what every Rendelf had to learn to live with.

As soon as he had made notes about each person, they disappeared from his mind and he was left with a kind of ringing quietness until it all began again.

Uncertain how to manage these new challenges, he asked Erlend if Napier had ever shared these finer details of the role with him. Marley's father could only assure him he would grow used to it and would work out the best way to reach everyone without spreading himself too thinly. He also suggested consulting the Guardians, which Pen point-blank refused to do.

Pen's parents left later that day. The compassionate leave available to Jarvis had already been stretched as far as possible and they needed to take a day for travelling down from Aviemore, although they were timing it with a conference in Newcastle. As they gathered outside the castle, Pen's mother took him aside from the others and put her hands firmly on his arms.

"You can come home with us, you know? There is no

reason at all why you should stay here."

"No, Mum," Pen replied, putting his arms around her. "There is. Honour's Rest is my home. I didn't want it to happen like this, but you know better than I do that there are some things we can't control."

It was a difficult goodbye, and there were tears from both Pen and his mother. Niamh and Jarvis stood back and talked with one another, and the Shipperbottoms hung back as well, not wishing to intrude.

At last, Pen waved them off as they drove down the causeway and, as they turned the corner onto the main road with arms waving frantically out of the window, he got the impression that his childhood was now concluded. He spared a thought for his school friends who would be about to enjoy the last Christmas holiday before their GCSEs and, for a moment, he couldn't believe he had ever been part of that world.

A day later, Niamh's parents appeared at the house while Pen and Marley were at a meeting in Edinburgh. From what Bernadette said, they had begged Niamh to return to Antrim with them, but she had refused, stating that she was needed in Honour's Rest but promising to go home before Christmas.

Pen could believe it when Erlend told him the loch freezing over in the second week of November was the earliest he had ever known it. It was to this wintry scene that Pen bade farewell to him and Bernadette as they set off to begin the journey back to Orkney.

As Marley said goodbye to his parents, Pen stood back, his breath steaming in the freezing air and his right arm wrapped tightly around Niamh's waifish shoulders. They had said their goodbyes already, and it didn't feel right to intrude on any of the time Marley had remaining with his parents. Instead, Pen looked down at the girl beside him and smiled warmly, hoping she could sense the gesture.

Marley was staying with Pen until Christmas, when he would return home to spend the holiday with his parents in their little cottage near the cliffs. They were sorry to be leaving, but Erlend had to return to work, and it made sense for the three young people to attempt to get their heads around what needed to be done. Erlend had, as Pen had told him the night before, served his time and no longer needed to worry each day that he would be wrenched away from the life he had built. Pen was certain that Napier had always done everything within his power to protect Erlend from having to take on the responsibility. As the days passed after the funeral, Pen had become more and more aware that Napier had juggled an awful lot of things, with such mastery that no one would ever know their lives had been so moulded by the previous Rendelf.

The Shipperbottoms' car pulled away down the drive and the three teenagers wandered back into the house they had prematurely inherited. As Rendelf, one of the smallest tasks which fell to Pen was to ensure there was always food on the table or a cup of tea whenever anyone needed it, but Marley had taken that burden from him.

As the days passed, however, Pen began to realise he couldn't rely on either Marley or Niamh to help him in any of the biggest challenges of the role. He would wake up crying in the night, sobbing at the death of a child he didn't know, or haunted by the bargaining of a young woman faced with the loss of her wife. The voices wouldn't go away and, in fact, became harder to manage as he wrote more and more of the names down in notebooks which just piled up on the desk in the room Napier had kept so spotlessly tidy.

In the morning, he would go downstairs to find that the postman had delivered letters from around the country, inviting him to conferences and meetings, which would need to be prioritised in notebooks and diaries as well. Marley offered to represent him, but Pen felt that wouldn't work. He had accepted the challenge which lay ahead, and now he had to address each issue as it arose, to the best of his ability.

Even in his first fortnight of being Rendelf, Pen got better at driving Napier's car, and would take Niamh out in the evenings, to beautiful places which he would describe to her until she could imagine what they looked like. Or he would spend the day with Marley, visiting some of the people who had reached out to him, or who Napier had introduced them to during the past eighteen months. Although he was still nearly a year away from being legally able to drive, Pen was constantly grateful he had it as a distraction from the other pressures.

The dawn of the last day of November found Pen standing alone on the white lawn, watching as the snow continued to fall around him, as it had done for the past three weeks. Weather forecasters kept commenting on the unusually cold weather, but it had not occurred to Pen that there was anything strange about it. However, as he turned his back on the loch and looked up at the turret window in his old room, he didn't notice the heavy creature emerging from the loch until he turned around at the sound of ice cracking.

Composed of ice now instead of water, the kelpie looked far more horrific, made up of hundreds of dark, razor-sharp blades. For a moment, Pen could only stand and stare at it in a terror the creature hadn't instilled in him since the first time he had seen it. At last, it bowed its head.

Rider. Its voice echoed in Pen's head, and he held out his hand to gingerly touch its frozen muzzle. *It is time.*

"Time?" Pen asked. "Time for what?"

Time to question, Rider. To question the winter.

"It's winter, isn't it? Scotland gets a lot of snow in winter."

The kelpie looked unimpressed and moved away from Pen in a crackling of icy sinew. *You think you can teach me of my own country? I have known more winters than you ever will. This is a false winter. A knave's winter.*

"I don't understand," Pen admitted, bowing his head. The kelpie moved back over to him and nudged his hand with its freezing lips. Pen couldn't tell whether he felt comforted or threatened by the closeness, but he raised his hand and put it down gently against the ice of the kelpie's curved neck. It felt as sharp and cold as it looked.

You do not need to understand all things, Rider. You only need to be willing to act upon all things.

"You sound like my uncle," Pen whispered, and the kelpie only nudged him more firmly with its enormous head.

It is the duty you have accepted. As Napier Devon would tell you himself, should you consult the knowledge he bequeathed to you.

"I can't do that," Pen said. "Not yet, at any rate."

In that case, the kelpie nudged Pen round so he was

314

facing it and looking into its terrifying face, with the bottomless dark eyes which seemed almost red, *discover the power behind this early winter. It may help you to fulfil a promise you made.* The kelpie turned around and leapt back into the frozen water, sending a spray of icy shards so Pen had to cover his head to protect his face.

For a moment, the world returned to the silence he had been enjoying before the appearance of the kelpie, but it didn't last long as the voices began to return and he ran inside, hurrying to his room to write the messages down.

After he had filled another notebook with the messages he could hear, and the voices had drifted off into the back of his mind, Pen looked through the notes he had made during the past month, trying to find any correlation between them. As he had been writing them, the words had hardly sunk in, lost in his desperation to note down the names, facts and figures. Now he looked at them, they seemed more human, and he began to notice patterns.

In a small village just outside Carlisle, a little girl had drowned in a pond after she had left her parents to feed the ducks with a cloaked stranger, who had promptly vanished. Her parents had hurried after her to find that the pond was frozen over with the child trapped beneath the ice.

In Swansea, a young man had been killed by an icicle which had fallen from a derelict building straight onto his head. His girlfriend, who had made the petition to Pen, had been with him and swore she had seen a cloaked figure clambering over the roof. *No one,* she had said, *could have easily got up there. And it would have been impossible for them to climb back down in the short* space of time it took for the police to arrive. But, sure enough, there was no one on the roof five minutes later.

A car full of teenagers had gone flying off a bridge into the river below, killing all but one of the occupants. The police said a combination of icy road conditions and carelessness by the seventeen-year-old driver were the factors behind the tragedy. The sole survivor, however, told a different story. He had been in the middle of the back seat and was adamant that a cloaked man had leapt out in front of the car, causing his friend to swerve.

Other stories began to string together as Pen thumbed his way through the notebook and, for the first time in days, he felt a genuine stillness, as no further voices reached him. In so many cases, innocent people had been killed in an accident involving ice, but there was always a witness who was certain they had seen the cloaked figure at the scene, even if only for a fleeting moment. Many of them said they had told the police and, although their concerns had been taken seriously at first, the lack of evidence meant their claims were put down either to Post Traumatic Stress Disorder or, in harsher cases, blatant misuse of police time.

Pen wandered over to the bookshelves and picked up *An Encyclopaedia of the Rite: Everything from A to Z for the Inquisitive Thaumaturge*. He flicked through the pages until he came to the short entry about Ice.

Early thaumaturges (see p.58 – Beginnings) erroneously believed that the Rite could be reached through either water or fire, not understanding that it was the senses they employed to experience these things which generated the ability to wield the Rite.

As such, there arose a cult around Ash (see p.25) and

Ice, which Knave's Thaumaturges argued were the sources of their own, darker version of the Rite. Ash from the death of fire, and ice from the death of water.

Despite an increased understanding of the Rite from the mid-fourteenth century, these cults are believed to have enjoyed their heyday during the seventeenth century. In fact, several scholars have argued that the Great Fire of London in 1666 was started deliberately by a Knave's Thaumaturge of Ash. Those who followed the cults were persecuted by the Rendelfs of the time, with many sentenced to death. By 1718, there are no records listed of any persons openly following the Ash or Ice Cult.

However, there have been various small resurgences of their popularity, usually marked by unexplained deaths involving ice or ash. Ice produces less suspicion as it is, by its nature, both common and dangerous.

Ice has other properties relating to the Rite. Whilst most of these are disproved superstitions, it is believed that True Ice, like True Ash, can undo even the most powerful acts of the Rite. However, True Ice is difficult to obtain: it must be the first ice of the year. Other texts cover this in more detail, see Further Reading at the end of this book.

Pen put the book down and a smile stretched across his features. It made sense to think of it as a cult, as though this cloaked figure may not be one person, but many people, covering vast areas in a short space of time. Now he could understand why the kelpie had been so concerned, as ice was being employed as an enemy of water.

Still grateful for the continuing silence in his head, Pen leapt to his feet and ran through the house. Niamh and Marley were sitting together at the breakfast table, and they both stopped eating and looked across at him as he burst in, unable to hide the broad smile which accompanied his discovery of the focus he so desperately needed.

"I know what we need to do," he announced. "I've finally found out what we need to do."

"And what's that?" Marley asked, returning to eating his toast but not taking his eyes from Pen's excited face. "And why are you so happy?"

"Because I've been waiting for this eureka moment for the last month!" Pen exclaimed, hurrying over to Niamh and kissing her silvery head. She waved him away, but even that wasn't enough to undermine his happiness. "It's all about the ice. If we find the source of the ice then we'll find who's been doing all this."

"Doing all what, Pen?" Niamh asked, pulling him down so he almost fell onto the floor. He managed to snatch a chair at the final moment but sitting down seemed too normal.

"There have been reports everywhere about a cloaked man who's going around killing people on the ice. I think it's a Knave's Thaumaturge who is part of the Ice Cult."

"Ice Cult?" Marley repeated, dropping his toast.

"It was apparently huge in the, erm, sixteenth century. No, seventeenth century, because they apparently started the Great Fire of London?"

"With ice?" Niamh asked with a laugh.

"No, that was the ash people. Anyway, this cloaked man is going around killing people. Here. Now. In the twenty-first century. And I'm sure that's what I'm being directed to sort out."

"Oh," Marley said. "Wow. That's not going to be simple, is it? And, I mean, we're on a kind of timeframe in terms of the fact winter doesn't last indefinitely."

"Exactly," Pen said, smiling broadly. "We'll need to get on with it straight away. Niamh, come with me for a minute." He didn't wait for an answer but took her by her free hand and pulled her away from the table and into the entrance hall. "There's something else. I wanted the first thing I did as Rendelf to be helping you see again, and I think there's something about ice which will make that possible."

"But I don't want the first thing you do as Rendelf to be helping me, Pen. Not when there are people being killed. I make my own light, remember?" She reached up and kissed his cheek with her soft, cobwebby lips and walked back into the breakfast room.

For a moment, Pen just watched her, unsure whether to hurry after her or to return to his room and continue reading through the notes he had made.

Outside, there was snow swirling around the windows of Honour's Rest, and he could see the cracked ice of the loch where the kelpie had burst through earlier. There was something both peaceful and promising about the world, and he found himself drifting into a daydream.

In his dream, he was a fourteen-year-old boy sitting in the headmaster's office, watching with tearful confusion as the man before him signed a letter confirming his exclusion from school. A boy who had never, even to that point, done anything wrong. A boy who would go on to wield something terrible and enjoy it; who would kill and would lose people he loved.

"Pendragon?"

Pen spun around, but there was no one there. He could hear Marley and Niamh talking to one another in the breakfast room, so it couldn't be one of them. Slowly, he turned around and began to climb the stairs back to his room and, walking through a doorway covered in nails, he stood for a second in front of the large pillar candle, clutching the box of matches.

At last, he struck the match in the darkness of the room and placed it against the blackened wick of the candle. The figures peeled from the smoke and stood staring at him, and he found himself looking once more at the face of his uncle and mentor.

Taking a deep breath and looking straight at Napier, Pen said firmly, "Tell me about the Ice Cult."

Then he listened as the shades began to explain.

Also by Judith Crow

When Rebecca Williams' mother dies, she is sent from the city to rural Lincolnshire to live with her father. What she finds is a quiet, unassuming man who lives alone on a large country estate. Lonely and nervous, Rebecca makes friends with a boy she meets at the lake. However, as their friendship develops, she discovers that her new friend is haunted by a secret which Rebecca must first unearth before it can be laid to rest.A ghost story inspired by the guidelines used by the great M. R. James, but with the freshness in tone of the twenty-first century. The Backwater weaves together the guilt of the living and the anger of the dead to produce a chilling but tender story of one girl's struggle to find her place in the world.

A finalist in the Wishing Shelf Book Awards

www.judithcrow.co.uk

www.crowwus.com

Printed in Great Britain
by Amazon

80718176R00185